THE DAGGER
X

Also by Brian Eames

The Dagger Quick

THE DAGGER
CHRONICLES

THE DAGGER X

Brian Eames

A PAULA WISEMAN BOOK

SIMON & SCHUSTER BOOKS FOR YOUNG READERS

NEW YORK   LONDON   TORONTO   SYDNEY   NEW DELHI

SIMON & SCHUSTER BOOKS FOR YOUNG READERS
An imprint of Simon & Schuster Children's Publishing Division
1230 Avenue of the Americas, New York, New York 10020

SIMON & SCHUSTER BOOKS FOR YOUNG READERS
is a trademark of Simon & Schuster, Inc.
For information about special discounts for bulk purchases, please contact Simon &
Schuster Special Sales at 1-866-506-1949 or business@simonandschuster.com.
The Simon & Schuster Speakers Bureau can bring authors to your live event. For more
information or to book an event, contact the Simon & Schuster Speakers
Bureau at 1-866-248-3049 or visit our website at www.simonspeakers.com.
Also available in a Simon & Schuster Books for Young Readers paperback edition
Book design by Laurent Linn
Map illustration by Drew Willis
The text for this book is set in Minister Standard.
Manufactured in the United States of America
1013 FFG
First Simon & Schuster Books for Young Readers hardcover edition November 2013
2 4 6 8 10 9 7 5 3 1
Library of Congress Cataloging-in-Publication Data
Eames, Brian.
The dagger X / Brian Eames. — 1st ed.
p. cm.
"A Paula Wiseman Book."
Sequel to: The dagger Quick.
Summary: Twelve-year-old Kitto Quick, stranded with his stepmother,
Van, a Wampanoag girl, and a baby rescued from a slave ship on the very island
where Morris hid valuable spices, learns powerful secrets of his past.
ISBN 978-1-4424-6855-9 (hardcover : alk. paper)
[1. Pirates—Fiction. 2. Survival—Fiction. 3. People with disabilities—Fiction.
4. Identity—Fiction. 5. Adventure and adventurers—Fiction. 6. Islands—Fiction.]
I. Title.
PZ7.E119Dak 2013
[Fic]—dc23
2012040713
ISBN 978-1-4424-6856-6 (pbk)
ISBN 978-1-4424-6857-3 (eBook)

FIRST
EDITION

For
all the lucky teachers
who
chuckle,
champion,
and cheer;
who take such pleasure
in the "work" they do,
that depositing a paycheck
sometimes feels larcenous.

And especially for teachers
Jane Pepperdene
and Steve Sigur;
it is hard to believe what with all they gave
that they still likely got more back.

Atlantic
Ocean

FLORIDA

Havana

CUBA

Kitto's path aboard the Spanish galley

JAMAICA
Port
Royal

Kitto's path to Jamaica

Caribbean Sea

CENTRAL
AMERICA

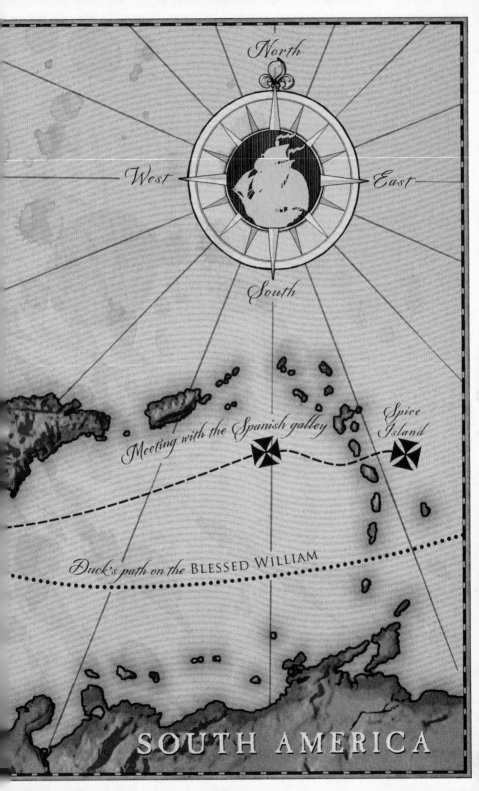

A tale of friends and fiends,
uncharted islands and dim-lit caverns,
glittering gold and ghastly greed,
crocodiles and cunning,
sharks and shipmates,
pirates and pawns,
heroes and hangmen,
slavery and salvation,
and just plain good and evil.

CAST OF CHARACTERS

FAMILY, BY WAY OF FALMOUTH, ENGLAND

Christopher (Kitto)   son of Frederick and Mercy, formerly clubfooted, age twelve years

Elias (Duck)   half brother to Kitto, age six years

Sarah (Mum)   Duck's mother, Kitto's stepmother

William Quick   captain of the *Blessed William*, Kitto's uncle

KITTO'S FRIENDS AND PEERS

Ontoquas   girl from the Wampanoag tribe, escaped slave and resident of Spice Island

Van   member of the *Blessed William*'s crew, age thirteen years

Akin   formerly enslaved boy, age eleven years

Julius   Van's pet monkey

PIRATES

Alexandre Exquemelin (also known as X)   pirate captain, former associate of Henry Morgan

Roger Fowler   Exquemelin's first mate

Quid, Little John, Black Dog, Pelota, Xavier, Pickle, Coop, Robbie   crew members

Pippin   Exquemelin's pet crocodile

FROM JAMAICA

Mercy — Kitto's mother by birth, deceased

Henry Morgan — admiral of the Brethren of the Coast, buccaneer, lieutenant governor of Jamaica

Captain John Morris — privateer, longtime associate of Morgan

Spider — Morris's first mate

Dame Bethany — old friend of William Quick and Kitto's mother, supporter of runaway slaves, owner of rooming house in Port Royal

Nanny — former slave, leader of a maroon colony

Dumaka — escaping slave

Tom Peet — sailor who befriends Duck on journey to Jamaica

Vernon Sims — jailer at Port Royal prison

IN CUBA

The Honorable Ernesto Delgado — judge who condemns Exquemelin and his crew

Padre Alberto — Cardinal Priest of the Roman Catholic Church, Father of the artist Asalto

CONTENTS

England, Early in 1678

The loaded pistol quivers in the boy's hands, his whole body seized with terror. Kitto Quick stands at the top of a long stairwell leading down into the cooper shop below. Traveling up that stairwell comes the cacophony of splintering wood and clanging metal, of grunting men straining to win the upper hand in a deadly battle.

I must go down! I must help Father!

Kitto knows what awaits him down there. Seven years ago—when he was just a small child—Kitto's uncle William Quick and his father had teamed up to steal from the mighty Henry Morgan of Jamaica. It was an act of defense, as Morgan had already planned to rob from William, but the law sees it otherwise. Now Morgan has sent his key man to retrieve what was stolen and to mete out punishments for those foolish enough to have connived against him.

Kitto looks over his shoulder at the shuttered window behind him. *I could open it, jump down into the garden, and escape along the alley. Even with my clubfoot, they would not catch me in time!* A man crying out in pain

1

interrupts his thoughts. Kitto's father is downstairs, and he is in desperate need.

I must not leave Father! I must go down!

Kitto lowers himself slowly down the first few steps, his arms held stiff in front of him, the barrel of the pistol aimed at the clapboard wall where the stairs turn at the bottom, concealing the struggle going on in the shop.

"One shot is all it's good for. . . ." That was what his father had told him moments ago about the pistol.

One shot.

One life.

Kitto descends three more stairs, leading with his bent foot and following with the good one. His heart-beat drums in his ears so loudly he scarcely hears the crash of the workbench being flipped onto its side. But then the sounds lessen, and Kitto can hear the wheezing of a man barely able to draw a breath.

Father!

Kitto thunders down the last several stairs and slams his shoulder into the wall, the pistol held out in front of him. There is Father, half lifted by a giant of a man who has wrapped a thick arm around Father's throat. Father's face is beet red, his eyes gaping.

More chilling still is the other man. He stands apart from the grapplers with a cutlass in one hand and a dagger in the other. A pistol butt protrudes from his belt. This man is Captain John Morris. Seven years ago Kitto's uncle had cut off Morris's nose in a swordfight over the nutmeg that William and Kitto's father had stolen. The ragged holes in his face give him the look of a living skeleton. His appearance is worsened, too, by purpled scars that curve up from each corner of his mouth like some sort of eerie smile. He is Henry Morgan's partner and a cold killer.

Kitto trains the pistol on Morris.

"Easy, lad," Morris says, his voice like the scraping of stones.

"Let my father go!" Kitto screams. The giant man loosens his grip. Father falls to his knees, gasping for air. He lifts his head to Kitto and points at Morris.

"Pull the trigger, Kitto! For God's sake, shoot him!"

Shoot? Kill?

Kitto raises the pistol higher and stares down the barrel. Morris's black eyes sparkle.

"You can never kill me, Christopher Quick!" he sneers. Suddenly Father lets out a cry, tumbles away from the giant man, and leaps onto Morris's back. The two of them spin about wildly, crashing into a pail of fireplace ashes that issue a great billowing gray cloud into the room. Kitto watches, rigid with fear, as the two men contend for the pistol at Morris's belt.

Can I shoot? Should I shoot?

The giant man, now at loose ends, has plucked a hammer from the wreckage of the workroom, a heavy squared hammer used to even up the ends of staves on a barrel. He steps about the shattered ceramics and upturned furniture, trying to get closer to the two struggling men.

The hammer. *What will he do with the hammer?*

"Pull the trigger, Kitto! For God's sake, shoot him!"

There is a flash and an explosion of sound, but it is not Kitto's weapon. Morris and Father both go still. The giant man steps forward with the hammer, raising it high.

"For God's sake, shoot him!" The sound of Father's shout rings again in Kitto's head.

The hammer falls, striking Father a savage and fatal blow to the top of his head.

Father is dead!

Another explosion rips the air, and the pistol bucks in Kitto's hands. Now the giant man is teetering, a stream of blood flowing from his left eye. He falls backward, smashing a chair to pieces behind him.

Kitto drops the spent pistol. He runs toward the back of the shop, the clubfoot swinging forward in a bobbing gait. He reaches the door, opens it, and is running through the garden and into the alley. The chalky voice of Morris chases after him.

"You are dead, boy! Dead! Do you hear me?"

Dead!

On Kitto runs, tears streaming down his cheeks, and before his eyes the alleyway melts. The gate in front of him that separates his neighbor's garden plot from his own is no longer a gate. It is now a ship's rail.

Kitto runs toward it, a cutlass swinging in his right hand. He leaps over it, braces one foot on the rail, and springs out over open space. He hurtles through the air and tumbles onto the deck of another ship. All around

him are the battle cries of men and the ringing of clash-
ing swords.

*Yes. Before Morris left Falmouth to chase my uncle
William and me, he kidnapped my stepmother Sarah, and
he has her now on the ship. I must free her!*

Kitto dodges the fighting men and scoots toward the
bow of the ship where Sarah is tied about the wrists.
She slumps against the rail, her face concealed behind
her long blond tresses. The back of her head is matted
with blood.

"Mum!" Kitto cries, hacking at the ropes with the
cutlass. The severed hemp falls aside.

"Mum, we have to go!" Kitto shrieks. He pulls at her
hand and then recoils from it in surprise. There is a tattoo
on the back of her hand, the tattoo of a skeleton hand.

Henry Morgan's symbol?

Sarah turns to him.

The face that comes into view is not the face of
warmth and love that Kitto has known since he was six
years old. The face that turns to him bears a leering smile
of brown teeth, pale blue eyes, and a frightening tattoo
that covers one eye socket in the uncanny likeness of a
spider, the furry knuckled legs reaching out across the
man's nose and forehead and cheek. It is Spider, one of
Morris's seaman thugs.

"Hello, cripple!" Spider chuckles. He reaches out and
takes hold of Kitto's belt with one hand and a fistful of his
curly black hair with the other. Kitto cries out in pain as
he is lifted into the air. From his belt tumbles a beautiful

dagger with a handle of silver and bone—the one and only token he has of his murdered father. Spider kicks it aside.

"Time to swim with the fishes!" Spider says. He steps toward the rail and heaves. Kitto feels his weightless body twisting through space. He spins in the air and sees the water rushing up at him, and there in the water is a monstrous shark awaiting him. It rolls onto its back, exposing a glimmering white belly and endless rows of razor teeth. . . .

Kitto shot out of his nightmare and into consciousness, eyes wide. He sat up with a jolt on the pallet of palm fronds that was his mattress. Sweat poured down his brow; his hair was wet with it.

Where am I? he thought to himself, and looked about him. He lay in some sort of a structure, open to the elements on one side. Around him splayed three bodies, curled carelessly in sleep. *That is Van,* he told himself. *And Mum.* His eyes drifted to the third figure, a slight one. A child? A girl?

Kitto turned away to look out into the night. A fire ring stood sentinel over the sleepers, wisps of smoke weaving upward from dim coals into a star-filled sky.

The dream. Kitto rubbed at his eyes. *It was both nightmare and memory.*

I am Kitto Quick. I am twelve years old, and I have a clubfoot. My father was a cooper, a barrel maker, and I do have an uncle named William Quick. He showed up in Falmouth to get my father's help in retrieving a treasure—a horde of . . . spice . . . nutmeg!—that they had hidden on an island. The spice they had stolen from Henry Morgan, the mighty buccaneer from Jamaica.

Now the memories came in a rush.

William Quick had been followed by Morgan's men. They did burst into Father's shop, just as in the dream. I could have shot earlier than I did. Perhaps Father would have lived. . . . But I did shoot, and I did kill a man. Then I ran. I made it to my uncle's ship with the help of Van, a boy seaman who sailed with William. And what was it I discovered about Van? Ah, yes. It was Van all along who was giving information to John Morris, information like where and when William would sail, and where the cooper and his boy lived. Why would Van do such a thing? He did it for the money . . . but not for himself. He needed money to care for his sister back in Providence.

They had fled in William's ship, sailing for Cape Verde to take on supplies. There they had freed Kitto's brother, Duck, who Morris had captured and sold into slavery.

I freed Duck, Kitto thought. *But Duck is not safe.*

"Duck is not safe," he whispered. Next to him a sleeping figure stirred, then sat up. It was Sarah, Kitto's stepmother. She reached for him and took his hand.

"Kitto, you have woken!" she said.

"Duck is not safe," Kitto said again.

"Yes, I know." Sarah dabbed a damp cloth at Kitto's forehead. "Elias is not safe," she said, using Duck's real name.

"We tried to get to the spice first, but Morris caught up to us in his ship." Sarah reached out and stroked Kitto's hair, the curls sagging with perspiration.

"I was on that ship," she said. "And you saved me."

Yes, that part the nightmare got wrong, Kitto thought.

"In the fight I cut you loose, and we escaped on a rowboat with Van," Kitto replied.

"He is another one who owes you his life," Sarah said. "Van was thrown into the water during the fight, and it was filled with sharks."

"He could not swim," Kitto said, and now his mind was reeling with the images of great teethed beasts swirling about him. His head felt suddenly light, and Sarah's hands lowered him back to the pallet.

"You must rest," Sarah said. "Van has treated you."

"Treated me. What do you mean, Mum?"

Kitto heard Sarah catch her breath. "Do you not remember?"

Remember. Sharks. Foot.

"My foot," he said.

"Yes. Your foot was taken by the shark when you rescued Van."

"My clubfoot?"

"Yes."

"I want to see." Kitto tried to sit again, but Sarah pressed firmly on his chest.

"Later," she said. "Van has sealed the wound, and you will live."

A silence grew between them for several moments as Kitto contemplated what Sarah had told him. All his life that clubfoot had been his bane. Strangers at the wharf in Falmouth looked on him warily. Children his own age crossed the cobbled street when he came walking. A twisted foot meant a twisted soul. Is it possible that life could go on without it?

From a distance came the gentle sound of waves breaking on a sandy beach. Finally Kitto spoke.

"We do not know where Duck is, or William?" Kitto said.

"We do not. During the battle, we drifted off in a rowboat. We could not make it back to the ship. Duck is on that ship, hidden." Sarah chewed one corner of her lip and drew a deep breath. "But we can pray, and we can keep looking out to the sea every day, hoping it is the right ship that will appear on the horizon, hoping and praying that it will be William's and not Morris's *Port Royal*."

"We are on the island where the nutmeg is hidden," Kitto said. "That is why they will come."

"Yes. So you have told me. About this nutmeg I know almost nothing."

"There is a cave," Kitto said. The figure at the far end of the shelter stirred. Kitto pointed.

"Who is that?"

"Her name is Ontoquas. She was already here. On the island. I do not know how it is possible, but she has been a godsend. Without her we . . ."

Kitto's eyelids sagged.

"We all keep each other alive," Sarah said, knowing it was true. She brushed the back of her hand on Kitto's cheek. "Go to sleep, my son. I will watch over you."

CHAPTER 1:

Bucket

SEPTEMBER, 1678

"Please. Please."

The words woke Sarah with a start, her heart in her throat. The Indian girl knelt at her side.

"Is it Kitto? Has something happened?" Sarah bolted upright in the lean-to and looked over to where Kitto lay awash in pale moonlight. He lay on his back, the rise and fall of his chest smooth and steady. Sarah breathed again. She berated herself silently for having fallen asleep. She told him she would watch over him!

That morning Van had held the red-hot head of an ax to Kitto's leg, where the shark had torn away his bent foot. Sarah had held Kitto down by sitting on his chest and pinning his arms to his sides. Van had set a stick in Kitto's mouth to bear down upon to keep from biting his tongue when the pain hit. And had it ever hit. Sarah shivered at the memory.

"*Quog quosh*," Ontoquas said and then translated. "We hurry."

"Is there something wrong? What is it?"

Ontoquas shook her head. "I did not know you *wawmauseu.*" Ontoquas frowned, wishing her English allowed her to say it the way she could in the language of her own people. "I see you with him today. You are a good mother. *Nitka.*"

"I do not understand, Ontoquas."

The Wampanoag girl's brow knitted. She reached out for Sarah's forearm and gave her a gentle tug. "You must come."

"Where?" Sarah bit her lip. She looked over at Kitto. "I do not want to leave."

"Please. He is not far."

He?

"Is there someone else on this island? Is there a ship?"

Ontoquas shook her head. "Please come." Sarah pushed herself slowly to her feet. This native girl was such a puzzle to her. Who was she? How had she come to live alone on this forsaken island? And was she truly alone? Sarah swore that she could sense some other presence, some other life, lurking in the dense jungle. All that day the girl had disappeared for stretches of time, sometimes returning with a freshly killed turtle or a split coconut or a bucket of fresh water, but other times with nothing at all save for a worried look.

From habit Sarah ran her hands along the front of her shift as if to smooth it, but the tattered and sun-bleached material was long past such ministrations. The dress that once covered it had been lost to the sea during the hurricane that nearly killed them all.

"For a moment, then," Sarah said, and followed the girl out of the lean-to.

It was a primitive domed structure, made by Ontoquas's own hands from woven tree limbs skillfully tied together with reeds, and broad palm leaves covering the frame and providing protection from the rains. Van slept on a pallet of palm leaves at one end of the dwelling, snoring lightly. Sarah stole one last look at Kitto. Were his cheeks truly that pale, or was it the moonlight? He looked peaceful enough. She turned back to the native girl.

Ontoquas led her along a narrow path that carved its way through thick foliage, heading deeper into the island. The way was slow going, with fallen tree trunks and patches where the thick undergrowth forced the path into wide sweeps. After a few hundred yards the ground rose up beneath them in a gentle hill.

How much farther? Sarah wondered. She stopped and looked back in the direction they had come. As she had since they first set foot on the island, Sarah felt now the eerie sense that somewhere in the dark wood there were eyes watching her. She turned back and chided herself. The girl had disappeared around a bend in the rising trail. Sarah was just about to call to her to say she could not go farther on, when Ontoquas came back around the bend. She beckoned to Sarah with urgency. Sarah pursed her lips, but made her way up the last several yards, surprised to see a flash of teeth on the Indian girl when she reached her.

She is smiling! Sarah drew closer. The look on Ontoquas's face was more than just a smile. The girl's face beamed with love and joy and pride so radiantly that it brought Sarah to a shocked standstill. The girl pointed toward the ground just a few feet ahead. There lay a tiny clearing in the wood, a circle bordered with stones, fallen logs, and brush shrouded in dark shadow.

Sarah peered toward the circle. In the middle of it, bathed in pale moonlight, slept a baby, a tiny African infant. The baby slept on his back, his arms up by his head. His stomach gently rising and falling with his breath. Sarah gasped when she understood what she was seeing.

"A baby! What is an infant . . . where did . . . is the baby yours?" Ontoquas held a finger to her lips. She knew the baby would be very angry if awoken in the middle of the night.

Now Sarah was even more confused. How did this baby come to be here? The girl was too young to be a mother, and even in the dim light Sarah could see that the two could not be directly related. The girl's lighter skin, her straight hair—she had to have been a native of the Americas. But the baby was much darker, with a thin layer of curly black hair and a wide nose that flared with each breath.

He was beautiful.

Ontoquas watched the *wompey* woman step over the barrier she had built to make sure the baby could not escape—not yet necessary since he did not crawl, but she could not bear to leave him in the open woods, even if this island had no animals that would show an interest. Sarah squatted down and scooped the child up expertly. The baby gave a startled jerk and his eyes shot open, but Sarah immediately rose and began to bob him up and down and run the tips of her fingers over his tiny black curls. The child's eyes drooped, then shut again.

"He is beautiful," Sarah whispered.

Ontoquas nodded. *"Weneikinne."* Sarah stepped about the enclosure with the child in her arms, bouncing gently with each rhythmic step. Ontoquas felt a pang in her stomach as she watched and knew it to be jealousy. Whether the jealousy was aimed at the baby or the woman she did not know. She felt pride, too. Without her, the tiny one would be at the bottom of the sea.

When she looked up again at the woman, she could see her cheeks were wet with tears. Ontoquas said nothing, but let the woman walk her little one around the circle, bobbing as she went. She knew the *wompey nitka* was thinking of the other child, the son of hers who they had said was somewhere lost out on the sea.

Finally the woman wiped the tears away and stepped close so as not to wake the baby. "He is so young. How have you fed him?"

Ontoquas shrugged. "I chew turtle in teeth," she said, pantomiming the words. "Then I . . . I kiss it to Bucket."

"Bucket? That is his name?" Sarah smiled.

"A bucket saved his life. And me."

Sarah looked back at the shining baby in her arms. "You have done so well, Ontoquas. He looks quite healthy. I would never have thought a girl of your age . . ."

Again silence won out.

"I helped my mother with my *netchaw*, my . . . brother. Before."

Before. Sarah nodded, wondering what horrors this child had faced. "Your mother taught you well. But I must know, Ontoquas, how did it come about that you and this baby are here together on this tiny island with no other soul in sight?"

Ontoquas sighed and lowered herself to a fallen log that formed one barrier of the pen. She puzzled, staring hard at the floor of matted palm fronds.

"It is long, our story. And my English . . ."

"Your English is excellent, young lady. Astonishing. You should be proud of it." Sarah looked back down the rise in the direction they had come. "Kitto is asleep and will stay that way long enough."

"You do not need to go back?"

"Tell me your story, Ontoquas."

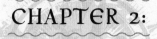

CHAPTER 2:

Slave Ship

JULY 1678, TWO MONTHS EARLIER

"The skin is cold on this one, captain."

The first mate pinched the woman about the forearm and relayed his message through the kerchief he pressed to his face. The woman in question, dark-skinned yet somehow frighteningly pale about the face still, clutched at a naked baby in her arms with the little strength she had left. The man examining her could scarcely believe she could stand.

"And the eyes, Mr. Preston. Note how sunken they are. Blast!" Captain Lowe grimaced as he made a mark in his precious ledger. He carried the book with him on deck each day, using it to calculate what little profit might be made from this journey gone awry.

"Make your way down the queue, if you please," Captain Lowe said, "while I decide what is to be done with this one."

"Aye, aye, Captain." Mr. Preston moved to the next

slave, inspecting a wispy dark man for signs of disease.

At the head of the line stood a girl not older than twelve. She stood out by virtue of her skin color and the texture of her hair. Her skin was the color of wet sand, her hair black as India ink and falling straight over her ears and forehead. It had been longer, but the slave trader in Jamaica had taken sheep shears to her locks to ward off the lice.

Unlike her fellow captives, Ontoquas had not hailed from Africa. Her people—the Wampanoag—had lived for thousands of years in lands that would one day be named "Massachusetts" after the people it had been taken from and the language they spoke. But she, too, was a slave.

The line of slaves formed a ragged arch along the outer rail of the ship's quarterdeck, so Ontoquas could clearly see the diseased woman and the tiny naked boy she cradled in her arms. Ontoquas remembered her little brother, Askooke. He was not much older than this baby when the *wompey* men came to take them away. She used to help Mother bathe Askooke down at the river. Whatever happened to him?

The woman with the baby sagged, and the baby nearly spilled from her arms. Ontoquas almost leaped from the line to save the infant from being dropped to the deck, but checked herself at the last moment.

They will beat me. They will stop my food as they did to the others.

Ontoquas turned away, a defense she had learned to save herself from witnessing the horrors that this life had shown her.

"This one looks well enough," Mr. Preston said, moving farther down the line. Ontoquas looked out over the rail and tried to conjure up Askooke's face in her memory. Somehow her brother's image had begun to fade.

From behind her came the sound of a heavy burden hitting the deck, followed by startled cries. Ontoquas turned despite herself.

The woman with the baby had fallen, pitching forward onto the quarterdeck's planks. Her last effort had been to protect the baby, turning so that her body cushioned the infant's impact. The baby, curled tight, rolled several rotations outward to the middle of the quarterdeck and came to rest on his back. He let out a tiny wail, and Ontoquas felt her heart might break, but none of the white sailors seemed to pay the child any heed.

"Mr. Preston!" Captain Lowe said. "See to that one." He flicked his pointed chin toward the collapsed woman.

The first mate returned to the sick woman, his kerchief again pressed to his face. The captain watched as the officer pressed his fingers to the woman's neck, then her wrists. Mr. Preston looked up with arched eyebows.

"She's dead, Captain!" he said.

"Dead? Are you quite certain?" Captain Lowe ran a finger down a column of numbers in his ledger.

"Aye, Captain. Keeled over right where she stood." The captain scowled and added another mark to his page.

"Very well, Mr. Preston. Toss the body overboard, if you please."

"Bowler! Simpson!" Mr. Preston barked toward two sailors nearby at attention. He pointed at the woman.

"You heard the captain. Put her overboard."

Ontoquas knew enough of the white man's language to know what they had said. Again she tried to turn away, but somehow she could not take her eyes from the pitiable baby lying on deck, kicking his legs out now and crying out for someone to pick him up.

The two sailors stepped forward and took hold of the woman, one by the wrists, the other by the ankles. They moved toward the rail and the line of slaves parted to make room for them. One woman in the line held her hands over her face; a man with wide eyes withdrew in fear, as if he might be the next to go overboard.

The sailors positioned themselves by the rail, one of them pausing to get a better grip. Then they swung the woman's slack body back and forth several times, as they would a sack of grain. In a moment she was tossed into the air and out of sight.

The men turned around and paused. They were looking at the wriggling baby lying on the quarterdeck, its empty howls being carried off by the wind. Mr. Preston followed their gaze. He, too, seemed puzzled.

"The wee one, Captain?" the first mate said. "What is to be done with that?" He pointed to the child. Captain Lowe, busy with the calculations of reduced profit this latest inconvenience had caused, did not want to be interrupted.

"Just toss it overboard as well," he said with a wave of his hand, his eyes never leaving the page.

"The baby too, captain? It appears fit enough."

Captain Lowe jerked his head up in frustration.

"I said overboard! Are you daft, Mr. Preston!" Captain Lowe pointed at the infant with the feathered end of his quill. "The miserable whelp should not have been allowed on this ship in the first place. It must nurse from its mother to stay alive, and now she's dead."

"So we throw it overboard?"

"Can you nurse a baby, man? There is nothing more that can be done!" the captain said. "And it probably carries the sickness as well. Get it over before the others fall sick."

"Aye, aye, Captain."

Again Ontoquas tried to look elsewhere, and this time she succeeded. In the two years since her enslavement in the Caribbean—so far from her home—she had seen horrors that haunted her dreams: men whipped until they fell and then whipped more, children succumbing to the smoke in burning fields of harvested sugarcane, human beings bought and sold at market in chains, families and loved ones torn apart.

Ontoquas did not want to watch them throw a baby overboard—this baby with the tiny feet it kicked in the air.

Several feet away knelt a boy no older than Ontoquas: a white boy in a plain sailor's shirt and pants cut at the knee. Captain Lowe had ordered the deck holystoned, and the ship's boy had been assigned the task. The stone lay in front of him as he sat back on his haunches, breathless, having stopped to watch the unfolding drama. Ontoquas wondered what he thought of it. *How could he look on so easily?* The stone was large, two hands wide. Beside it a large bucket made from the bottom third of a cut barrel held fresh water.

Ontoquas's eyes locked on the stone, but she turned when she heard the first mate speak.

"Bowler, Simpson, damn your eyes!" Mr. Preston said. "Do as you're ordered, men!"

The two sailors who had cast the dead woman over the rail without a care now stood eyeing the infant. They each stole a glance at the other.

"You quite certain, sir?" one of them said, risking a flogging himself.

"Oh, for the love of God!" said Captain Lowe. He tucked beneath one arm his treasured ledger and strode to the middle of the deck where the baby lay. He snatched the boy up by one leg so that the infant dangled upside down.

"Truly, Mr. Preston! You should be embarrassed, sir. Never have I known Englishmen to be so squeamish." The baby rocked back and forth as the captain strode toward the rail. Its cries grew louder.

Ontoquas spun away, pressing her palms against her ears. The baby's cries were too terrible! Her eyes fell again on the holystone. She remembered the words of her father, Chief Anawan, the last time she spoke with him.

"We will lose our lives in our fight. It has been foreseen. But if we do not fight, Little Wolf, then we are no longer a people. If we do not fight, then we are already ghosts."

Ontoquas lowered her hands.

If we do not fight, then we are already ghosts.

Ontoquas stepped from the line of slaves, and with that first step she was a slave no more and never would be again. She took three strides toward the boy who stared at the captain, and kicked him savagely across the cheek with the sole of her foot. He sprawled back in a heap, then turned an incredulous look upon the girl as she hefted the stone.

All eyes were still glued on the captain and the infant dangling from his hand. His back was to Ontoquas.

"Captain! Captain Lowe, sir!" the boy called out.

The captain did not turn as he approached the rail. "Silence, boy, or I shall have you flogged. This is the work of men." Ontoquas raised the stone high and charged.

"Captain!"

The wind was out of the west that morning. It swept steadily across the quarterdeck. Captain Lowe had handed his hat to the first mate before grabbing the infant, and the pressing breeze revealed a pale spot of scalp on his head. He had reached the rail now and drew back his arm to heave the baby to the sea.

"Captain, sir, look out!"

Ontoquas took a last step and drove the holystone for the spot on the captain's skull with everything she had.

I will fight!

The stone struck without sound. The captain's head snapped forward. The ledger he held fell, bounced once against the rail, and whirled off in a flutter. The captain slumped into the rail and slid along it until he dropped to the deck in a tangle of loose limbs. Ontoquas plucked the crying baby from the deck and tucked him beneath her arm.

There was an instant of shocked silence, and then

the line of slaves broke apart, everyone running.

"All hands!"

The ship exploded into chaos. Voices yelled out in all languages. The captives ran in every direction, some in terror, others in rage. One man hurled himself upon a crouched sailor who had just jumped from the ratlines, and the two struggled for a knife the sailor held. Others charged out blindly and struck at any sailor they could find.

"Get them tied! Get them below!"

Ontoquas ran across the quarterdeck away from the sailors, but Mr. Preston cut her off. She stared at the dark circle of the pistol's barrel the first mate leveled at her.

Then she dove and tumbled, holding the baby close and trying not to hurt him as she rolled. There was a terrific explosion, and a woman nearby crumpled against the rail with a cry. Ontoquas found her feet again and dashed across the deck.

"You little devil!" shouted the sailor. He raised a whip. Ontoquas dodged and the crack sang out just behind her ear. She clutched the little baby tighter.

I must save this baby!

The man's face contorted in fury. He reared back again. Behind him she could see a surge of dark bodies emerging from the main hatch, men howling tribal war cries.

Again the man lashed out with the whip. Ontoquas lurched to avoid it and lost her footing on the wet deck planks, falling onto her back and nearly dropping the wailing infant. The deafening crack resounded against the rail behind her. A hand clamped down on her arm.

Ontoquas bore down on it. The man howled as the girl's teeth crunched against bone, and then she reeled as the butt of the whip came down on the top of her head.

Somehow she still held the baby. He was part of her now, her own brother. She would do anything for him. Again Ontoquas rose, the first mate separated from her by a wrestling crowd of sailors and slaves.

The whip crackled the air. Many months before, Ontoquas had come to understand that she would die, and die young, but with the infant in her arms, living was an imperative. If she did not live, the baby, too, would die. Ontoquas charged at the first mate, who had made his way clear to her, and scooted under his arm. Across the deck she scampered, the snap of the whip chasing her. She ran directly at the ship's boy—crouched in terror— the infant still cradled tight in the crook of her arm. Next to the boy rocked the overturned bucket.

"Leave me be!" the boy wailed.

"Get that one!" Ontoquas heard a sailor shout. "Grab her!"

Ontoquas lifted the boy's bucket by its handle. She turned toward the rail, and she ran like she had never run. She leaped as she had never leaped. One bare foot lighted upon the rail. She thrust against it and was over.

Through the air they flew, Ontoquas and her new brother, the bucket held above her head by its handle. The endless arms of the Great Mother Sea rushed up to greet them.

CHAPTER 3:

Shark

TWO DAYS LATER

In an open and seemingly infinite sea the girl floated. From the vantage of a flock of white birds that passed high overhead, it would appear the girl was alone, but she was not. She clung to the sides of the bucket, keeping the rolling waves from tipping it and using its buoyancy to save her strength. Inside the bucket the tiny baby curled on his side and slept. In the late afternoon the wind ebbed to a gentle breeze, and Ontoquas was able to haul herself up and spread her body over the opening of the barrel without tipping it. In this way she protected the boy from the bright sun. From this position she looked at the uninterrupted horizon on all sides.

Now I cannot die. I must survive. I must find land for my brother.

In the language of her recently lost people the name *Ontoquas* meant "she-wolf." On the night before she was born her mother had a dream in which a wolf spoke of a daughter who would survive the death of her people to go off and begin the world again.

Ontoquas's mother, Shanuke, was an important healer; her father was the great Wampanoag Chief Anawan. But that was before the war and the killing. Anawan and his tribe had joined with a fellow Wampanoag tribe headed by the great Metacomet to fight a war against the white man: King Philip's War. Metacomet and Ontoquas's father led many raids on English villages, but then a man named Benjamin Church came hunting. With the help of an Indian tracker, Church led a silent attack before dawn on the grassy meadow where Metacomet and Anawan and their weary warriors had made camp.

The colonists' rage was not quelled with just the death of the men. Soon afterward the women and children of Anawan's village were rounded up and brought to the port of Boston. There they were sold into slavery and loaded onto ships heading south to distant islands where sugarcane grew.

For two years Ontoquas had known the whip of many masters. She had felt the searing heat of the boiling houses and smelled blackened death among the torched sugarcane stalks, burned before harvesting. She had watched men, women, and even children sink down into such fields from exhaustion. And she had come to care little as to whether she lived or died.

Ontoquas was twelve years old.

I thought the wolf had lied, Ontoquas thought, stealing

a peek into the shadows of the bucket where the little boy twitched as he slept. *Oh, please, please, let the wolf be right. I want to live again.*

The unlikely pair bobbed along between the rising and falling of the waves, the Caribbean sun blazing down. Ontoquas let her head hang. Sometimes she drifted into sleep, only to startle awake in time to steady her balance on top of the bucket. She awoke to measure how far the sun had moved along its descending arc.

Night would come. *What then?*

Before she had time to consider how she would survive the night, something rose slowly from the water—a fin. It formed a tidy triangle and it cut a straight line through the surface of the water. Ontoquas had watched dolphins swimming alongside her ship in the open sea, chittering and carving exuberant arcs through the air. She liked to think they were laughing at the ridiculous humans. But this fin was different. It had no curve.

Ontoquas pulled herself up onto the bucket as best she could, bending her knees to keep her toes out of the water. Supporting her entire weight and that of the baby, the bucket's lip sank to just a few inches above the surface of the water.

The fin carved a complete circle around Ontoquas. Then another.

"Leave us!" she shouted at it. Could sharks be scared away? Her heart thundered in her chest. No, no! This could not be. To have survived the ship, only to die now?

In front of her again, at a distance of perhaps fifteen feet, the gray triangle cut in sharply and came straight at her.

"No!"

Just a few feet before the fin reached her it lowered into the water. The great gray body swept slowly beneath her, so close that Ontoquas could see its mighty tail swishing back and forth as it propelled itself through the water. It was huge, perhaps twice as long as she was tall.

Ontoquas felt her chin begin to quiver. The baby beneath her stirred. He opened up his eyes and began to cry, his mouth stretching wide open.

I will save you. I will save you.

The triangular fin reappeared again at the earlier distance. Again it circled her, once, twice. And again it broke from its arc and came straight at her, this time toward her left side.

Ontoquas tried to pull herself up higher on the barrel, but there was nowhere to go. Closer came the fin, closer, and then the triangle leaned over and out of the water rose a gaping mouth of gray and white full of glittering teeth. The huge jaw snapped at the barrel, and its teeth found a purchase in the wood. The shark thrashed, nearly tossing Ontoquas from the bucket.

She could see the shark's black eye looking up at her. Again it thrashed, and this time Ontoquas slipped, and her legs and body slid out and onto the shark's snout.

No!

Rage filled her. Pure rage. Ontoquas reared back with a hand and punched the shark on its snout. The shark turned to try to get its mouth on her, but the bottom lip of the barrel got in its way. Again and again she punched, her eyes filling with tears. Again and again and again she struck. She could hear her voice shouting at the beast, but it somehow seemed far away, as if another voice were calling.

Suddenly the shark broke off and sank beneath the surface. Again Ontoquas watched it swim beneath her, and again it reemerged at its former distance.

The circles began anew.

How long can I fight it off? she wondered. She pulled herself up onto the bucket's lip again and saw that the knuckles of her left hand were wet with blood. Ontoquas knew little enough about sharks, but she had heard that the scent of blood drew them like ants to honey. She pulled her wounded hand in and rested it on her forearm instead, the wound dripping a drop of blood down onto the baby's leg.

The baby was crying now, crying loudly. So loudly! Ontoquas wondered how she had never heard the infant before today, but then remembered how loud it was in the hold of the slave ship, how many different cries of distress there were both day and night.

Ontoquas craned her neck around to watch the shark pass along the right hand side, still at a distance, when suddenly another fin broke the surface just inches from her. Ontoquas raised her fist to strike at it, but she did not bring the fist down. This fin was different; it curved back and came to a rounded point.

A dolphin?

Sure enough, a rounded gray snout broke the surface. The dolphin regarded her for a moment. She reached out, and the dolphin stayed still and allowed her to pet him.

"You must go!" she told it in her own language, giving it a push. "It is not safe here!" The shark had swum behind her now, and Ontoquas turned to keep an eye on it. Then, to her surprise, the dolphin broke from her, and it, too, began to make a circle around her, a tighter one, swimming between the shark and her barrel.

Before Ontoquas had even a moment to comprehend what was happening, another curved fin emerged next to her, then another. And another. In a breath's time there were more dolphins than she could count. Was it eight? Ten?

And before her disbelieving eyes, they formed a ring around her, floating just at the surface—all but two, and these two continued to swim along with the shark.

They are protecting us, little baby. They are saving us!

One of the dolphins swam just ahead of the shark and thrashed its tail in the water, creating a torrent of froth. The shark raised its ugly snout to snap at the dolphin, but the animal had already shot out of reach. Then another sped in, and it too thrashed at the water near the shark's head. Again and again it happened, and each revolution of the circular path the shark swam grew wider and wider.

And then, without incident, the gray fin lowered into the water, turned away, and was gone.

"Aaaaaaiiiiiiiiiiii!" Ontoquas shouted to the sky. *"I am alive! We are alive!"*

The dolphins had turned now, all seeming to seek her attention. Ontoquas reached out, careful to pat them only with her unwounded hand. She reached out and caressed each beautiful shimmering snout, each smooth gray head, telling each one how much she loved it and how they had saved her life and that of her brother. A triumphant smile lit her face.

The baby was crying again, though, and Ontoquas stopped to run her hands over the poor child. His skin was very dark, the color of rich earth, and cool. A layer of tiny black curls adorned his head.

He is so young, Ontoquas realized, *for he cries without tears.* She had six or seven summers when her brother was born, and she remembered that he cried this way too.

How old is this baby? She did not know. He did not sit up in the bucket; when she propped him up earlier, he had flopped onto his side. *When was it that Askooke could sit?* Her brother was born right when they had planted the corn. Ontoquas remembered this because there was one day when mother did not join her to plant the rows of kernels. And then the next day she had come, with the infant swaddled to her back with a long sash.

When we cut the corn down, he could sit. She remembered sitting him on the ground before her as she worked

a line of stalks. How he slapped at the green ears that
she piled up around him!

So this baby cannot be even six moons. Three? Four?

One of the dolphins shoved its snout at the side of
the barrel, nearly upending Ontoquas. She glared at the
animal, but reached out to pet.

"Are you jealous?" she asked. But the dolphin lowered its snout again and pushed at the barrel.

"Why are you doing that?" Another dolphin came to
the other side and it, too, began to push at the bucket.
With the two of them pushing, the cut barrel surged
through the water. Ontoquas knew the playful nature of
dolphins. Were they having a game with her? After several seconds the two stopped in unison, and one lifted its
head entirely out of the water and looked squarely at her.

"Ahhhhhhh!" It made a strange clicking noise with
its mouth wide open, then lowered and swam forward
a few feet so that its dorsal fin rubbed against the barrel. Thinking that the animal wanted to be petted there,
Ontoquas reached for the curved fin. As soon her hand
touched it, though, the animal heaved with its tail and
shot off a few feet. It turned around and swam back to
her, again lifting its head.

"Ahhhhhhhhhhhh!" it said to her.

What is it? What do you want from me?

Again it spun about so that the dorsal fin was positioned directly beneath her hand. This time Ontoquas
reached out and took hold of it. Immediately the dolphin
propelled itself forward and this time Ontoquas and her

barrel shot through the water after it, swift enough to make the water ripple around the barrel.

She held on, half alarmed and still unclear as to the animal's intentions. On either side of her she could see that the other dolphins were swimming with them too, all heading in the same direction. One dolphin shot ahead and leaped clear out of the water, carving a glorious arc in the air and landing with hardly a splash. Again it leaped, and again. Two more dolphins joined in the fun.

Then, after several minutes of being towed along this way, the dolphin whose fin Ontoquas held promptly dived deep into the water, forcing Ontoquas to release her grip. The bucket came to an abrupt halt. Before Ontoquas had time to marvel at what was happening, another dolphin broke through the surface just inches from her face. It opened its mouth and let out a similar bark, then positioned itself the same way the other one had with its dorsal fin next to the barrel edge.

Risking putting her wounded hand into the water, Ontoquas reached out and held onto this dolphin's fin. Sure enough, it shot through the water and all the other dolphins—there seemed to be even more now, at least a dozen—swam along with them, some cavorting with one another, others just swimming contentedly.

The idea was too good to be true. Ontoquas could hardly allow herself even to think it.

Could they be taking me somewhere? Could they be taking me to land?

One thing was certain: The dolphins had some sort of intention in their actions, because the towing went on for hours. The sun neared the western horizon. Ontoquas's hands ached. It seemed to her as if each dolphin had taken dozens of turns. She alternated hands every time, hoping her strength would last longer that way. The salt water had cleaned the wound that turned out to be nothing more than a small cut across the knuckles. She prayed for strength.

The sun set. The baby cried, probably from hunger and from thirst, Ontoquas knew. She had nothing to offer him but her hope.

The next time her dolphin dove Ontoquas lay her head on her hands and closed her eyes. Her throat burned with thirst, a familiar enough sensation aboard the slave ship, but at least then she knew someone would come along sometime and offer her a ladle. A dolphin pushed its snout against her cheek.

"Ahhhhhhhhhhhh!" it squeaked.

"I am tired."

"Ahhhhhhhhh!" it said again. Three other dolphins lifted their snouts and made similar complaints.

Ontoquas drew a deep breath and let out a sigh. The baby continued a weak cry, more of a moan. *If they are taking me to land, then I must hang on. How long can this little one last if I do not find him food and water?* She lifted her head and looked eye to eye with the dolphin.

"Yes, yes, I hear you. I can hold you now." The dolphin positioned itself and again they were off.

* * *

The night was dreadfully long. The infant slept in snatches and would awaken mostly to cry. Ontoquas would let go of whatever dolphin she held long enough to adjust the baby in the bucket so that he did not lie too long on any one side. He was so very tiny, so delicate. During one of the baby's crying jags, weariness and desperation and the darkness broke Ontoquas down. She stopped to weep, crying like the baby now, tearlessly. The dolphins seemed somehow to sense her distress. She let her hands drag in the cool water and rested her cheek against the bucket. The dolphins swam along in front of her, rubbing their smooth sides against her slack hands.

It is too much, Mother. It is too much to ask me to survive.

But then the weeping subsided, and an overwhelming exhaustion swept over her. Ontoquas closed her eyes and listened to the little boy's cries until they, too, went silent.

Did she sleep? She did not know. A dolphin prodded the top of her head.

"Aaaaaahhhhhhh!" it said.

"Leave me alone," she whispered, the effort of saying words stinging her throat.

"Aaaaahhhhhhhh!" it said again, more insistently.

Maybe it had been sleep, for Ontoquas felt the tiniest amount of energy left in her as she lifted her head and looked out at the bright stars above. Her grandmother had told her the stars were little tears in the fabric at the edge of our world, and that through those holes our ancestors would peer through to watch us and give us their strength when we needed it. Ontoquas wondered if her mother and father were together again up there, looking down on her.

I need your strength now.

The dolphin slapped its flipper on the water's surface, splashing water on Ontoquas's face. She smiled at the animal, then reached out with her hand and grabbed hold of its dorsal fin.

You win.

All nights, no matter how long, yield to dawn, and this one finally broke with breathtaking beauty. The light started in the east to Ontoquas's right side, the black of night leaking away into the darkest of blue that in turn faded with each rotation of the dolphins. The wind had picked up slightly, and the rolling waves through which Ontoquas and the baby-filled bucket were towed swelled enough to give her a better vantage by which to view the awakening world.

Atop such a swell, Ontoquas saw it. Just as the brilliant yellow of the sunrise seeped over the horizon with the same brilliance as the yolk of the quail eggs her mother and she would sometimes find when they went gathering in the springtime woods, Ontoquas saw it.

Far ahead—still a few miles off—a small but unmistakable mound rose above the northern horizon.

Ontoquas looked down at the sleeping baby.

Land, little one! They have taken us to land. We will live.

CHAPTER 4:

Uncharted Island

The island was quite small from what Ontoquas could discern once they had drawn closer—a mile in length at most. Its highest point was on the eastern end, which dropped off suddenly in a cliff face, and gradually sloped downward toward the west. Along that eastern section a ring of white water frothed around the island. Ontoquas knew it meant reefs. As the dolphins propelled them closer, Ontoquas began to worry that they would be led over those reefs, but the dolphins steered toward the western end of the island where the surf seemed less lively.

Ontoquas had no voice left with which to coo to the little infant, but when came the moment's rest as the dolphins rotated the duty of pulling their charge, Ontoquas would reach down and caress the baby's smooth skin. Sometimes the infant would open his eyes and look up at Ontoquas. Once she even thought he began to smile at her, but then he closed his eyes and went back to sleep.

Closer and closer they came, and the western cliffs rose up before them. Closer still they came. The cliff was not nearly as sheer as it had looked from a distance; in fact Ontoquas was sure that she could scramble up it if she had to, and she might need to do just that, as there did not appear to be a sandy beach along this end of the island.

When they were only a hundred yards from the rock face Ontoquas could make out details on the craggy tan rocks. Still the dolphins swam straight ahead, as if they would ram her into the cliff face itself.

Where is it that you are taking us?

The cliff bulged out at about the height of thirty feet, then curved in slightly, and as they drew to a distance of twenty yards, she could see that the color of the rock grew very dark in one spot quite close to the water level.

What is that?

Whatever it was, she would soon see it, as it seemed to be the very spot the school of dolphins had picked out. Ontoquas noticed that the larger group of dolphins had silently disappeared, and only five now surrounded her little bucket plus the one dolphin pulling her.

At just ten feet from the rock face Ontoquas could see that the dark spot of rock was actually some sort of a passage leading into the cliff itself. The opening was perhaps four feet wide and rose above the water level only a few feet. Ontoquas suddenly let go of the dolphin's fin. Something was coming out of the passage! She startled and reared up on the bucket, but then smiled. It was a large sea turtle, paddling its way into the aquamarine brilliance of the water.

"Aaaaahhhhhhh!" complained the dolphin at her side. One of the dolphins dove and shot into the passage. With her stiffened muscles crying out in complaint, Ontoquas pushed herself off the bucket, careful to keep it from tipping. She took a breath and lowered herself into the water in time to watch the dolphin come shooting out of the passage again, twirling its white belly up at the surface. It snapped its mouth open and looked at her, as if with a satisfied grin, and a tiny turtle scurried along behind it.

Ontoquas rose to the surface.

"Aaaaahhhhhhh!" Another dolphin streaked into the passage, was gone for several seconds, then sped out again. It was clear that the animals wanted her to go inside. Ontoquas puzzled over whether to do so. The passage looked dark and forbidding, and she worried that it might lead to a place where there was nowhere to draw a breath. Another turtle, one as large as a split pumpkin, paddled its way out at the surface, its head held daintily above the water. It turned to look at Ontoquas, then dove and swam off.

And then Ontoquas knew. She knew what might well be inside. Hurriedly she hoisted herself back atop the barrel and grabbed hold of the dolphin's fin. Ontoquas ducked her head against the bucket to avoid striking it on the rock as they entered, and she was gladdened to see that the passage opened up inside. The way ahead was dim, but a bright light pierced the blackness. It grew brighter until Ontoquas could see that she was emerging from a narrow tunnel into a small chamber, a pool several yards in diameter. Above rose an uneven domed ceiling. Light filtered through a long crack at its peak.

Beneath her the dolphin rolled. Ontoquas slid off and felt her feet touch a sandy bottom. She stood in water to her waist, and reached into the bucket to give the baby a quick pat.

Mother! Ontoquas remembered the prophecy her mother had bestowed on her. All her life the meaning of that prophecy had eluded Ontoquas, until now. She would survive. Her people were gone, but she had survived.

All six dolphins whirled about in the pool, swirling and playing and making their strange yipping noises.

Thank you.

Ontoquas ran her hand along the smooth snout of one dolphin that approached her. It wriggled its nose in the air as if to nuzzle her in return. Then it sank back into the water, and with a graceful flicker of its tail, it turned and swam back toward the dark opening of the tunnel. The other dolphins filed behind. The last dolphin lifted its head and turned to her.

"Aaaaahhhhh."

"May the Great One smile upon you," Ontoquas said in return, and then she and her baby brother were alone.

For several moments she stood there, luxuriating in the feel of sand between her toes and the gentle sound the water made as it lapped against the edges of the surrounding rock. The bucket bobbed lightly. Turtles of various sizes paddled past, ignoring her.

It was time to see if the idea that occurred to her was in fact true. Ontoquas pushed the bucket ahead of her through the pool to its far side, giving way to a particularly large turtle that did not seem interested in going around her.

On the far side of the pool rose a broad bank of sand. It teemed with turtles, hundreds of them: small ones the size of her palm, medium ones the width of her shoulders, and a few so large they must have outweighed her. They clambered about lugubriously, each seeming to move toward a different destination. One slid down the embankment and into the water with a plop.

Ontoquas hoisted the bucket to her hip and began to climb up the rise of sand. As she neared the top, she could make out a shimmering division in the collection of creatures, a groove in the sand that reached back into the blackness.

"Nippe!" She had been right! Animals need water, freshwater, and even sea creatures like turtles make their nests where they can have some access to it.

Ontoquas surged forward, nearly stumbling and dropping the bucket. Several tortoises spooked and threw themselves into the pool. Ontoquas set the bucket down as gently as her ebbing strength could manage and then fell facedown into the shimmering rivulet of water.

Nippe. Water, and though not as fresh as would have been the creek water she had known as a young girl, it was not the salt water of the sea.

The trickle gave her little to work with, but Ontoquas sucked desperately at it until she lifted her head at a small pool that glimmered deeper in the cave. She crawled over to it on all fours, then waded in. Though only a few inches deep, the pool was several feet long, and made for easy drinking. There she gulped and guzzled the slightly brackish water until breathless and bloated.

Netchaw. It is his turn now. Ontoquas considered for a moment, then pulled her shirt over her head. She plunged the weathered fabric into the water and drew it out dripping, then draped it over her neck and went back to the barrel.

"Come, *netchaw*," she said, and lifted the little brown boy at his armpits. The baby's head flopped back, and she turned to cradle him in the crook of one arm.

"I have something wonderful for you. *Cottatup.*"

She held a corner of the wet shirt to the baby's cheek. The baby rooted after it, turning his head and taking the fabric into his mouth. He sucked away greedily as Ontoquas bundled the fabric in her hand to squeeze more to him.

She looked back toward the empty bucket and smiled. She had been wondering what to call the little boy. He was not a Wampanoag, so she did not want to give him a name of her people, and she did not know his people or what he might have been called by his own mother. Seeing the cut barrel gave her the idea.

That barrel of the wompey, it saved your life. So I will honor it with your name, as I know how the English call it.

"You will be called 'Bucket,'" she said aloud. "Bucket, *Noe wammaw ause.*"

I love you and I always will.

After Bucket had drunk all he could hold, Ontoquas crawled to a spot of sand the turtles had ignored. She lay on her back in the cool sand and placed Bucket belly down on top of her. In little time the world slipped away from them both.

Hours later the cave glowed with bright light. The sun hovered directly above the narrow aperture in the rock ceiling, and the rippling waves of the pool threw a dance of sunlight about the walls. Ontoquas eased the sleeping Bucket from her chest and nestled him on his side into the warm impression her body had made in the sand. Silently she crept to the puddle again. She cupped her hands and drank from the water she collected in them. Full again, she pushed back on her haunches. Her body ached and her head pulsated with pain. It was the most wonderful pain she could imagine. She gave a broad grin.

I have survived. Kean nitka was right. My mother was right.

Gingerly Ontoquas pushed herself to her feet, crouching so as not to hit her head on the low ceiling. She looked back at Bucket, twitching in his sleep.

The main part of the cave was comprised of the larger pool to which the dolphins had delivered her. At the far end the ceiling swept low, forming the tunnel that led to the open sea. During her nap the tide had risen, and now the water had almost entirely submerged the tunnel. Ontoquas made the observation with some dismay. She had grown up near the ocean and understood that the water rose and fell nearly four times each day there. She hoped it would not rise so high as to fill the cave with water.

It will not fill up, silly nickesquaw. *That is why the turtles are here. It is their nesting ground. Here they find water and protection.*

She turned to look deeper into the cave in the direction of the stream's source. The light grew very shadowed there and it took her eyes a moment to focus. When they did, the eerie assemblage of shapes they beheld made her catch her breath. Her heart hammered. The shapes did not move, nor were they frightening in and of themselves, but they were arranged in tidy stacks.

Wompey sannup! White man.

Only the white men would take such care to be uniform. But what were they? As she stepped toward the shadows, the shapes became clear. Barrels.

Barrels. Everywhere the *wompey* went, there were his barrels. The traders who would enter the village to swap beads for furs had them. They hung from the sides of their horses. As a little girl she had watched her father conduct such a trading session with one of the white men. He had removed a barrel from his horse, opened it, and beckoned her to come closer. He showed her, taking a pinch of the white powder inside and dropping it into his mouth. When Father had nodded his approval, Ontoquas took a pinch as well, and the taste exploded in her mouth.

Could these barrels contain the white sand? She thought how happy Bucket would be to have a taste.

Each barrel stood to her waist. They were stacked two high in a tight formation that parted wide enough to allow the trickling stream to wind. It disappeared in shadow somewhere at the stone wall behind the stack. Little light reached this corner of the cave, leaving the barrels to lurk in dark obscurity. Something about them filled her with foreboding.

Maybe Abamacho lives inside them, she considered. Ontoquas scowled. *Only a little girl fears evil spirits in a wompey's barrel.* She would have more heart than that.

Still, when she stepped close enough to touch one, her fingers trembled.

"Sugar." That was the *wompey* word for it. Sugar.

She knew barrels held other things too, more useful than sugar: salt pork, dried fish, cornmeal. Her stomach twisted with hunger. When was the last time she had anything to eat?

When had Bucket last eaten? She turned a worried look back to him, but his peaceful stirrings quelled her worries.

Ontoquas grabbed the rim of the nearest barrel. It

balanced neatly atop an identical one beneath it. She wrestled it awkwardly, and it moved beneath her efforts. The barrel was heavy, but she found that she could rock it onto one edge and spin it slightly so that it shifted outward a few inches before settling flat. She yanked at it again, and again it curled out toward her. Ontoquas swooned from the effort, and she took a deep breath. She had little strength after the ship voyage, and nearly none after the long journey with the dolphins.

When her dizziness steadied, she heaved again. This time the barrel spun easily along the lid of the one beneath it, and Ontoquas had to step away quickly. The barrel teetered at the brink, overbalanced, and pitched to the stone floor. A loud *crack!* filled the air when it landed askew.

Ontoquas righted the barrel and saw that the ring of copper fitted over the top had come loose. She pulled at it, and the rusted tacks that held it gave way. She cast it aside and pulled at the staves.

Nothing. No movement. She pressed one palm against the far lip and pulled at the nearer one, gritting her teeth and straining.

Please please please!

Still nothing. She just was not strong enough. But she could not give up.

She cast her eyes about the gloom for a rock, but seeing none, she moved along the edge of the stacks, skimming her hands along the tops of the barrels.

"*A quit, nees, nis . . .*" She began to count them aloud

THE DAGGER X

but gave up after a few dozen. She figured perhaps fifty barrels were in the stacks all told. As she moved back down the line of barrels to the spot where she had begun, her fingers pushed against something hard. There was a scraping sound, and then some object tumbled in the space between barrel stacks, rattling its way to the ground. Ontoquas jumped backward in surprise, then crouched and reached into the darkness between barrel stacks. She withdrew the object slowly and held it toward the light.

It was a hammer, its steel head obscured by a thick layer of orange rust. Again she smiled. The hammer had a long wooden handle and a weighty metal head, wide on one end and narrow on the other.

"Nenetah ha!" She warned the barrel she had pulled free. Holding the hammer with two hands she scratched a mark in the center of the lid with the narrow end of the head.

She raised the hammer high and brought it swinging down with everything she had.

CHAPTER 5:

Sharpshooter

"Kitto! Truly, I do not believe you are ready for this."

Kitto leaned against Van's shoulder to keep balance on his good leg.

"I cannot lie here forever, Mum," he said. The wounded leg hung in midair. He looked down at it, draped now in the new pair of pants Sarah had stitched for him. Sarah had found a bolt of well-preserved sailcloth in the trunk inside Ontoquas's shelter. It was the same trunk with the pewter hardware in the shape of a dolphin that Kitto had identified as belonging to William Quick the morning after they had landed on the island. The trunk was what told them they had made it to the very island where William Quick had stashed his treasured nutmeg. Rich as kings, that spice could make them.

Kitto watched the eerie flapping of the pants leg with nothing to fill it—no shin, no ankle, no foot.

My clubfoot is gone, he told himself, and the admixture of emotions the thought gave him made his head hurt.

His memory of the incident was clear now. He had

nearly made it. He had pulled Van from the water—saved him from drowning—and just as he was about to climb into the rowboat, the shark had struck. It had taken hold of him below the knee, and the impossible ferocity of the shark's jaw power combined with the razor edges of its myriad teeth allowed it to sever Kitto's shinbone near the top of his calf muscle before it dragged him down to the depths. And then his mum had jumped in after him and hauled him back to the boat.

I saved her life, and she saved mine, he thought.

Today was not the first attempt Kitto had made to stand or to walk, but he intended now to test the crutch Van had made him, and he was nervous. Any contact with his wound—even when the wind picked up and the sailcloth pants rippled against the tender skin that formed an oozing and uncertain scab, fiery tendrils of pain shot through his entire body.

"I need to learn to get about, or little Bucket will be walking before I am."

Bucket lay cuddled nearby with Ontoquas on the palm-frond pallet inside the lean-to, sucking a thumb knuckle. Ontoquas, too, wore new clothing: a shirt, also made of sailcloth by Sarah.

"Two weeks is not a long time for healing," Sarah said. Thirteen days had passed since Van had burned him with the flat of an ax head held over a fire until it glowed a faint red. The burning heat of the ax still haunted Kitto. When he was awake, he seemed always to be thirsty, and Ontoquas had to fetch freshwater two and three times a day to satisfy him. She would disappear with the cut barrel that had once carried Bucket, and return later with a few gallons sloshing in the bottom. None of them knew where she procured it. Van had offered to help her, but it seemed that to reach the freshwater he would need to swim, and Van had no interest in ever doing that again.

"Here, Kitto." Van plucked the crutch from where it leaned against the sea chest. Using Kitto's dagger, Van had fashioned it from the branch of a tree. "If it's too tall, I can whittle it down in a trice." Van held it out to him, hopeful that Kitto would be pleased. He had come to accept his guilt at the living nightmare he had helped to visit on Kitto and his entire family. Van needed money to carry out his dream, which was to be reunited with his sister, whom he had not seen since she had been taken from the orphanage many years ago. He fed Captain John Morris and Spider the information they needed to follow William Quick from New York to Falmouth in exchange for payment. And once in Falmouth, Van had told the men where Kitto lived. Morris wanted to silence Kitto's father, and to take revenge.

Van had traded a man's life for a small bag of silver, and now that too was gone, heaved into the sea by Sarah after Van confessed to his role in her husband's death.

Kitto jammed the crutch in his armpit. Van had carved it from where a thick branch split into two smaller branches, forming a crook. Ontoquas had wrapped the crook with a layer of reeds to provide padding.

"It feels good," Kitto said, lying only a little. He settled his weight into the crook and took a very small hop-step. His wound throbbed, but he tried not to show his discomfort.

"Here I am wishing I had my old bent foot back," he said, astonished that it was true. For how long—how many hours adding up to days, months—had he stared at that clubfoot, hating it and wishing that it were gone? Now it was gone, and he couldn't help feeling that his body was no longer whole. Part of him was missing.

"Just a few steps, sweetheart," Sarah said.

"No. I want to see the beach. I would like to make it that far." Kitto steeled himself and lurched forward another step.

Van waved him on. "It's not but fifty yards or so. You can make it." Van collected the bundle of pistols and shot and wadding at his feet. Ontoquas had led Van a week ago onto the rocky peak at the island's southeast corner, and there showed him two more of William Quick's trunks that had been hidden away in a deep depression. Inside it were several pistols and short muskets wrapped in oilcloth, as well as enough powder and shot to hold off a small army.

"Van, no. Let's leave that," Sarah said.

Van shrugged, a trace of a smile on his lips. "Now is a good time, ma'am, don't you think?"

Kitto thought some strange message was being communicated between them, but he could not attend to it. Each step brought intense pain, and Kitto clenched his teeth and swallowed a groan. He took another step with the crutch, then gave a bit of a hop to catch his good leg up. Crutch, hop. Crutch, hop.

You can do it. Just one step at a time.

They reached the edge of the small clearing, and Ontoquas, Bucket in her arms, walked ahead. She swept her arms across the leafy foliage, exposing the narrow path her feet had carved during the months she had lived on the island. Ontoquas felt there was something different about these *wompey*—these white people. They differed from the ones who had sent her into slavery. Although she could not say quite why it was she felt she could trust them, it was a delicious feeling. So long it had been since she had felt connected to anyone. The white masters had seen her only as an instrument of labor, and the other slaves had kept their distance from her because she looked different than they did. This wounded boy, his mother, and the strong older boy, they were the first people who seemed interested in knowing her.

"That's it, mate. You're nearly running now," said Van, behind Kitto now with the pistol clutch under his arm. The statement was not remotely true, but Kitto was settling into a rhythm. Crutch, hop. Crutch, hop.

"Is the pain quite bad?"

"Always a burning." Kitto shook his head in frustration, beads of sweat standing out on his brow and darkening his curls. "Maybe the water will do it good, you think?"

"Sure it will."

After ten minutes and three falls in the loose sand of the beach, Kitto had the answer to his question. A smile of pleasure that had hardly lighted his face since his father had died did so now, and the sight made Sarah weak with relief as she watched from higher up on the beach. Kitto lounged in the surf, balancing his hands against the bottom and floating in the eighteen inches of water, his legs aimed out to sea.

Sarah sat in the sand with Bucket propped upright against her now, his feet kicking as he watched Kitto in the foamy wash.

"Not too deep!" Sarah said. Kitto hardly heard her. The cool water was unbearably delightful.

Sarah let her eyes drift seaward, out to the ever empty horizon.

Oh, sweet Elias. Where are you? Are you safe? Can you feel my love reaching out for you?

Sarah swept a strand of hair behind her ear. Her skin had not been so dark since she was a little girl. She had tanned deeply in the weeks since their arrival, mostly due to the long hours she spent out on the beach, scanning the horizon for a sign of either Morris's or William's ship. Not knowing whether her young son was safe or even alive was an exquisite torture that was wearing her nerves threadbare, as the sun and salt did to the bedraggled shift that clung to her.

Sarah suddenly became aware of Ontoquas at her side, solemnly reading her features. Sarah shifted Bucket to her other arm and reached out to take the girl's hand. Their fingers interlaced. Ontoquas looked up at the *wompey* woman and smiled at her.

"The water is good," Ontoquas said. Her English was improving rapidly now that she had a chance to practice it again. Saying the words made her remember a time long gone when her *noeshow*, her father, would sit her down with an English fur trader, and the three of them would point at the objects around them and say the words in English and in Wampanoag.

Kitto pushed out deeper, the froth of the surf washing over his head. He cycled his arms, propelling himself through the water.

"Oh! Oh!" Sarah cried out.

"I watch him." Ontoquas pried her hand free and ran into the water on light feet, leaping the waves until it was deep enough to dive. Ever since the days of digging for *suckis suacke* in the great water, she had loved to swim. Ontoquas caught up to where Kitto floated on his back twenty yards from shore.

"The water is good for you?" she asked.

"Yes." He lifted his head to look at her. "Your English. It is better already."

"Your Massachusett?"

Kitto grinned. *"Nippe!"* he shouted, and slapped the water.

Ontoquas splashed water at him, then stopped short. He was not a brother. "The water *is* good for you." Ontoquas looked back to the beach where Sarah stood motionless with Bucket in her arms, watching them. "Mother is scared."

Kitto didn't answer. He turned away to the sea and let the rising waves lift him high.

"I would like to go to the cave. To see the barrels," he said into the wind. He turned to see if Ontoquas had heard.

"You are ready?" she said.

"Any time the bad men might be back," he said. "I need . . . I need a plan."

"But Mother scared."

Kitto nodded. "We won't be long," he said.

"Come." Ontoquas turned from him and paddled toward shore.

Van waded out to hand Kitto the crutch when he reached the shallows. Kitto cursed quietly as the crutch sank into the wet sand, requiring even greater effort to make progress up the rise of beach.

"See any sharks?" Van said, smiling.

"If I didn't need this crutch for walking I'd slap you with it," Kitto said.

Van smirked and pointed up the beach. "Oi. Have a seat up there. I have something for you to see." He gestured to Sarah.

Sarah rose and approached with a wry expression on her face, Bucket propped on her shoulder.

"I do not think this is the time, Van," she said. "Bucket is frightened by the sound."

"We're all here," Van said, as Kitto took his last labored steps and threw himself on the sand next to where the unraveled clutch of weapons had been laid. Sarah passed Bucket to Ontoquas.

"What on earth are you talking about?" Kitto said. He swept aside his wet curls.

Van looked at Kitto, then up at Sarah. "She has something to show you, your mum does."

Kitto squinted up at Sarah. The sun was high in the sky behind her, casting her face in shadow. He could not see her face well enough to read it.

"Mum?"

Sarah bent and picked up a pistol. Kitto's mouth dropped open, stunned. He had always known his mother to detest weapons. She straightened and turned the pistol slowly in her hands.

"You know, Kitto, that I . . . I am a member of the Religious Society of Friends. A Quaker, you would say." Kitto nodded.

"My father knew George Fox, who started the movement, and he brought it to Falmouth. That is how I became involved."

"You have told me that before," Kitto said.

"A central principle among Friends is that of peace." Sarah looked down warily at the weapon in her hands.

"And for that reason you never tolerated guns in our home," Kitto said. He remembered times when she had marched tradesmen straight out of the shop because they had entered with pistols in their belts. Sarah took a slow and deep breath and raised the pistol. She sighted along its barrel, aiming down the beach.

Kitto felt alarmed. "What are you doing?"

Van stepped away swinging a medium-size turtle

shell in one hand. He ran several yards down the beach and turned.

"Here?" he said to Sarah, grinning broadly. Sarah nodded with a look of resignation. She took a step away from Kitto.

"You are going to fire it?" Kitto said, even more astonished now. "Do you even know how?"

Ontoquas held up her palm toward Van to tell him to wait, then retreated up the path by which they had come, pressing Bucket's turned head to her shoulder to cover the baby's ears.

"Right, then!" Van said. "Here goes!" Van drew his arm behind his back and then whipped it forward, sending the shell hurtling outward over the surf. Kitto barely had time to comprehend what Van intended before Sarah's pistol exploded in her hand and recoiled. Instantly the shell shattered into a thousand shards and tumbled into the white foam to vanish.

Kitto, incredulous, pointed to the spot in the air where the shell had been.

"How? But . . ."

Sarah carefully returned the pistol to the oilcloth and draped the excess over the guns to keep the sand from them. She sat down next to Kitto.

"My father taught me. In secret, of course."

Kitto finally found his tongue. "So you . . . all this time you have known how to shoot?" Sarah nodded.

"And all this time I have greatly been opposed to weapons and to violence." She hung her head a moment.

"And still I am." She took Kitto's hand. "You will remember the words I have told you all these years, that what you see in your mind's eye and deeply believe, you can make come true?" Kitto nodded. How could he ever forget that lesson? Who might he have let himself become without it?

"Those are not just words for me. They run deep. My father taught them to me, taught me that notion." Sarah let go Kitto's hand and stood again. She bent over and took up the musket. "They run deeper than the teachings of Friends."

Kitto had forgotten the burning pain in his stump. "I do not understand, Mum."

Sarah reached down to Van's pile of shells, snatched a largish one up and cast it toward Van who caught it neatly. Van grinned, turning and walking down the beach again.

Sarah set her feet in a wide stance and lifted the musket to shoulder level. She lowered her eye to the site and pulled back the hammer.

"Morris will be back. He has my boy. I know it. And I will be ready to do whatever a mother must, no matter how it might imperil my soul." A long way down the beach now, Van hurled the shell out over the surf. Kitto watched Sarah's body tense. The musket bucked, roared, and a plume of smoke drifted off in the breeze. Kitto turned in time to see the last shards of turtle shell scatter into the white foam.

Sarah sat down next to Kitto, but Kitto edged away.

This was all too much: his clubfoot, this island, a baby . . . now this. *His mother knew how to shoot!*

A long moment of silence passed between them until Van charged up and gave Kitto a slap on the shoulder.

"Is that not something? Your mum could best the king's own marksmen!" Van's bright teeth flashed in the sun. "What a wonder, eh?"

Sarah silenced him with a look. "You are upset, Kitto," she said.

Kitto grabbed Van's shoulder to hoist himself to his feet, crutch in one hand.

"I do not know what I am," he said, meaning it in many ways. He took a few hobbled steps along the beach. He spun around and nearly lost his balance.

"Lies," he said, glaring at Sarah. "Lies! Father had plenty. Never told me my name, never told any of us his past. And you, Mum"—Kitto steeled himself—"you had your lies too. I never . . ." His thought eluded him and he shook his head violently. "And you treat me like a child, like I was Duck! You never trusted me to know any of this."

"That is not true, I simply—"

"Is there anything else, Mum? Anything else I should know about you?" Kitto's tone had taken on more than a bit of venom.

Sarah stood, her face flushed.

"No, Kitto, I should think that one dark secret is all that I have."

Kitto looked down, suddenly ashamed. But there was more he felt he needed to say.

"I am not a child, and I will not be treated like one any longer." He spun away again and hobbled his way down the beach.

Van and Sarah watched Kitto go.

"Shall I stop him?" Van said.

"No. When he is upset, it is best to leave him." Sarah turned out toward the sea and scanned the impossibly distant line of the horizon. Her brow furrowed, and her eyes moistened with tears.

CHAPTER 6:

THE CAVE

"How much farther is it?" Kitto said. It had been ten minutes since Ontoquas had caught up to him as he hobbled along the beach, seething with an anger he did not fully understand.

"Soon." They were now just coming upon a rocky rise that jutted out into the water. The island here did not slope steadily from forest to beach as it did elsewhere, but instead tumbled sharply from a hundred feet up at the island's pinnacle to a jumble of craggy rocks upon which the waves thundered and sent up wisps of spray. Kitto's stump burned from the effort of the walk.

"It is here. There." Ontoquas made a sweeping gesture with her hand that indicated they were going around the promontory.

"Do we swim, or climb over?"

Ontoquas stepped into the water and motioned for Kitto to follow.

"Good," Kitto said, and tossed his crutch high up on the beach where it would be safe from a rising tide. He hopped into the wash, then lowered to hands and knees and crawled his way into the surf.

Ontoquas was out deep enough to swim now, and Kitto made for her. He welcomed the flow of the water along his body. He had always loved to swim; it was one of the few physical activities that he could do as well with his clubfoot as any other boy. And he found now, even without the last ten inches of his leg, his body could still glide gracefully along. After several strokes he caught up to Ontoquas. They had come just far enough so that Kitto could begin to see around the rocky promontory. It bent along for a good stretch, then eventually gave way to a smooth beach beyond.

"Where are we going?"

Ontoquas pointed toward a place along the rocky expanse, perhaps forty yards before the sandy beach resumed. The rocks at the water's edge seemed shrouded in shadow.

"That is the cave?"

"Yes. You like cave. I show you." Ontoquas continued on, swimming a path that paralleled the island for some time. Kitto kept pace easily, careful to keep his kicks gentle. Shortly, Ontoquas began to angle toward the dark outcropping of rock. Closer they swam toward the crag. Closer.

Kitto pulled up from his stroke to better look. They were now only ten yards from where the waves washed up against the rocks, and sure enough he could see the top of a dark opening just above the lapping water.

From farther back it looked simply like dark rock, but this close he could see that it formed a kind of tunnel. A strange feeling passed over him, sending goose bumps up his spine.

I know this place, he thought. Was that possible?

He paddled forward to come alongside Ontoquas just at the opening. She still treaded water but held one hand against the lip of rock that formed the mouth of the tunnel. Her long black tresses fanned out in the water and draped her shoulders.

"In there?"

Ontoquas nodded. "Have care," she said, tapping herself atop the head. Kitto understood. Here the water did not so much crash against the rocks, as the waves had already broken on the rocky tumble that reached out behind them, but still the water rose and fell several inches. It would be easy to strike one's head inside the tunnel.

Ontoquas had just turned from him and was about to enter the shadowy gloom when a dark movement in the water below Kitto gave his heart a flip. Something was there, swimming just below their feet.

"Watch out!" Kitto cried and clutched at the rocks above as if to pull himself out of the water, the terror of the shark coming back to him in an instant. Ontoquas heard him and ducked back out into the sunlight.

She gave a toothy smile. She reached out and patted his arm.

"No! Not shark. No sharks here. Turtles. Many, many.

See!" She lowered her head below the surface. Kitto did the same, his cheeks aglow with embarrassment. His eyes open underwater, he could see the entire entrance to the tunnel. It descended several feet to the sea floor and was perhaps a yard or so wide. As Kitto looked on, a turtle about the breadth of two hands paddled its way straight through the middle of the tunnel, swam beneath Ontoquas's kicking feet, and flippered off into the open sea. A moment later two more followed, smaller, swimming one just behind the other.

He looked up to see Ontoquas smiling at him. He returned a smile of his own, struck by the rarity of the expression on the girl's face. Together they broke the surface again. Ontoquas swept her hair from her eyes, her high cheekbones and angular jaw aglow in sunlight. Kitto saw her as pretty for the first time.

"You are ready?"

Kitto nodded. "I think I am."

Ontoquas took a deep breath, turned from Kitto, and went under the water. He followed suit, paddling himself through the water just behind her kicking feet. Dozens of white air bubbles swirled about her toes and rose slowly to the surface.

Within a few strokes Kitto and Ontoquas swam in near darkness. The light from outside the tunnel lit the way dimly, but the farther they went, the darker it grew.

Kitto felt a dull panic beginning to rise.

Just stay with her. Trust her! He startled when a dark form moved below him; he squinted and made out the outline of a large turtle swimming in the opposite direction. Again the strange sensation struck him, the familiarity of the place.

After several yards it grew lighter again, and with a few more strokes he could see Ontoquas settle her feet on the sandy bottom. Kitto carefully raised his head and came to a stop beside her, balancing on his one foot. He began to tip over, but Ontoquas reached out and grabbed him about his arm and shoulder and pulled him upright. Kitto put a hand on the girl's shoulder to keep himself steady. She was slight of frame, but somehow still very strong.

"You are scared," she said. Kitto felt his cheeks burn. He cast his eyes downward and nodded.

"You are brave to swim again, after the shark," she said. Her dark eyes glinted in the light that flickered along the rippling water. Their eyes met for a moment, then Kitto turned away to take in the surroundings.

They stood in a pool the size of a small room. The ceiling rose in the middle to a height of perhaps twelve feet, and at the middle a slim crack in the stone revealed the blue sky above. Indirect sunlight lit the cavern in a dreamlike glow. A small splash sounded at the far end of the pool, and Kitto turned to see turtles, dozens and dozens of them. Some of them sat motionless on the sandy embankment at the far end of the pool, others climbed sluggishly into or out of the water. A small turtle swam right toward them, its little head and shell shiny and dark above the water's surface. Kitto and Ontoquas moved apart, far enough for the creature to paddle between them. Kitto laughed.

"This is amazing!" he said, looking around again. The cavern was still and quiet, the wash of the waves outside barely audible. There was something comforting about the little cavern.

"The water, to drink, it is here." Ontoquas started forward. "You walk?" Kitto leaned on her to hop forward until the water grew more shallow, at which point he bent over and scrambled along with his hands and one foot.

Ontoquas emerged first from the water onto the sandy expanse. Kitto followed awkwardly, self-conscious of his pathetic need to crawl like a wounded animal. He was used to walking oddly, but this animal-like shuffle left room for no shred of dignity. He wished he had brought the crutch. As he scrambled up the rising embankment, a very large turtle half the size of him glowered down from the crest. Its neck telescoped outward, and the creature opened a fearsome beak in Kitto's direction.

"Good Lord," Kitto muttered, caught between alarm and amusement. Before he could decide how to get past the turtle, Ontoquas appeared behind it with the bright smile again.

"He will not bite," she said. She grasped the turtle by the edges of its shell and with a few heaves scooted it out of the way.

"Not you, maybe, but he looks ready to take my

nose off." The turtle lowered its head and padded down the sandy bank into the water.

"He is the big one," Ontoquas said. "He is the father, the chief."

Clearly the sandy beach on which they now stood was a nesting ground for the turtles. Small mounds speckled the area, indicating where eggs were buried. The ceiling sloped downward here, too, and came very low toward the back of the sandy expanse, some yards off. Between Ontoquas and Kitto, at their feet, a tiny rivulet of water cut a groove in the sand and flowed into the pool they had just left.

"Do you see?" Ontoquas pointed toward the back right part of the cave, where the beach was somewhat more elevated and the ceiling stooped. "White men," she said.

Kitto looked in the direction she pointed, but at first he could see nothing but obscure gloom. As he stared, the shadows took form.

"Barrels!" he shouted, and his voice reverberated through the cave. He let go of Ontoquas's shoulder and scrambled forward.

Barrels! Dozens of them, not the huge kind used for water, but smaller ones maybe three feet high and eighteen inches in diameter at the top. They were nestled along the back wall three deep and two high. Kitto reached out for the first barrel he came to and steadied himself next to it. He ran his hand along the stave edges and the top. It felt dry. That was good. Barrels like these would not keep well in the damp for seven years. *This has to be the nutmeg,* he thought. Kitto withdrew his hand, and could feel a dusty residue on his fingers. He brought his fingers to his nose and sniffed hesitantly. Then he breathed in deeply. He smiled and lifted his head.

Now he remembered. He had been here! So long ago . . .

Kitto spun around, a look of wonder and shock on his face as the memories came flooding back. The light playing off the pool's surface, throwing flashes up on the craggy ceiling . . . the turtles' incessant marching up and down the embankment . . . the smell . . .

"What is wrong?" Ontoquas took him by the shoulders, a look of alarm on her face. "Are you sick?"

"No. I . . . I remember. I have been here before! And there is more here than just barrels!"

CHAPTER 7:

Spice and Sin

"You? Here?" Ontoquas said, confused. She said something in Wampanoag to the effect that the boy was losing his mind.

"Yes. When I was very young." *But how? How could that be?* And then it came back to him, those obscure comments that William had made back on the *Blessed William* about Kitto's shoulders not being too broad yet. He and his father had come to the island with his uncle to hide the nutmeg first. Father had lost his leg in the firefight with Morgan when they fled, so likely he had not even gotten off the ship when they reached the island. But Kitto had. He had been so young he had forgotten it.

My uncle brought me to this cave! But why was it? He had a job for me to do, something only I could do . . .

Kitto traced his eyes along the rivulet of water that he had first noticed at the embankment. Midway up the beach it split. One branch went toward the left. Several feet away Kitto saw a small pool glisten in the dim light. Water dripped down into the pool from the rocks above.

That would be where Ontoquas gets the water, he thought. But this other branch. The one to the right, that headed toward the barrels. There was something important about it.

I was small. I could fit. The other men could not!

"This way. It is this way!" Kitto hopped along the rows of barrels, squinting down at the tiny rivulet that cut through sand down to a stone floor beneath. It wound about deeper into the cave, then turned sharply into the rows of barrels themselves. Kitto's breath quickened.

"Help me, Ontoquas." Kitto needed to move the barrels. He needed to get at what was behind them. Ontoquas joined him, and together they wrestled with the first barrel. It was stout but not too much for them to manage—perhaps four stone—but they were able to spin it out on one lip and lift it from the barrel on which it was stacked. Then they pulled away another barrel. And another. In little time they had removed three layers of barrels and Kitto could see what he knew had lain hidden.

The rivulet of fresh water emerged from the wall itself through a low-slung passageway the water had dug through the stone over thousands of years. He pointed.

"Do you see it? *Do you see?*" Ontoquas did see, but she did not yet understand until Kitto got down on hands and knees and peered into the opening. He dragged himself forward on his elbows until he could poke his head into the darkness.

"I am going in," he said. Kitto dug his forearms into the sand.

Ontoquas did not like the idea, but it was obvious there was nothing she could do to convince this boy otherwise. She did not know Kitto well, but she knew instinctively he had a fiercely determined spirit. No sooner could she prevent the tide from rising than keep him from going on.

Wrestling awkwardly with his toes and elbows, Kitto propelled himself forward until he had entered the tunnel up to his shoulders. The streamlet of water wet his right elbow, cool enough to give him a chill as·it soaked into his shirt. The tunnel smelled clean and dry, not musty. Not that it mattered. What he was after did not mold, did not tarnish even.

The passageway was perhaps three feet in width but very low to the ground, so low that while Kitto was able to get his shoulders through quite easily, once up to his chest he could feel the rock snag along his back. Was he too broad after all? He remembered his uncle making odd comments aboard the ship about Kitto's size. This is what William had meant.

"I can barely fit!" Kitto gasped. He wiggled vigorously back and forth, the rock raking along his spine as he moved. A thin layer of sand beneath him was pushed aside by his efforts, just enough to allow him to shimmy himself forward to where the passage opened up. Ontoquas grabbed his good leg at the knee and pushed from behind. In a moment his entire body was swallowed up in the darkness.

Ontoquas knelt down and peered into the shadows.

"Are you well?" she said, frustrated that she could not communicate better in English. The words she needed eluded her. *Aren't you terrified to enter such a dark place? What do you expect to find back there?* She thought of what Kitto had said, that he had been to the island before. She thought he was mad, or that she misunderstood him, but how could he have known of this hidden passage otherwise?

When Kitto did not answer her calls but disappeared farther into the blackness, Ontoquas resolved to enter herself. She lay down at the opening and scooted forward with her palms and bent knees. Being somewhat more slight than Kitto, the way was easy for her and she entered quickly.

Up ahead of Ontoquas, now perhaps ten feet into the passageway, Kitto extended his hand to the ceiling. Yes, there it was. High enough for someone Duck's age to stand.

I remember standing here, he thought. *I remember that I had been given a torch. I remember the yellow light and the feeling of pride at being allowed to hold the torch by myself.*

Kitto pulled himself into a sitting position. He reached a hand out beside him. His fingers found the cool rivulet, and he traced its passage upstream. It curved off to the right. *Yes, here is where it disappears into the wall.* His fingers felt a moist crack in the stone.

Just a little farther.

Kitto scooted along on his bottom, keeping his bad leg carefully aloft. He continued back several feet until his stump bumped into an uneven wall, igniting his whole body in agony. Kitto gritted his teeth until the spasms of pain diminished.

"Please, wait!" Ontoquas called behind him.

Reaching out with his hands now, Kitto felt the wall ahead of him. He reached to his left and where there had been a wall was now open space.

This is where it is. Right here.

Slowly Kitto reached out with his left hand, leaning into the emptiness. His fingertips brushed along the bare stone floor. Kitto bent farther, straining against his lean frame. Farther . . . a bit farther.

There. Something solid, but not rock. Kitto scooted closer to it and reached again.

He felt a corner, neat and square. It was wooden, with metal hardware. It was a chest.

Kitto edged closer and fumbled with the two latches, feeling his excitement grow. One of them broke off beneath his fingers and clattered to the stone floor. The other creaked loose. Kitto rested his hands on the chest's lid as Ontoquas appeared behind him.

"How are you?" she asked, hearing but not seeing Kitto.

"Right here," Kitto said. The chest was smaller than he remembered. But he had been so young then. It could not have measured more than eighteen inches along its face. Kitto pushed at the lid, but it did not budge. He gave the lid a sharp whack with the palm of his hand and tried again. This time the hinges responded, and he could feel the lid rotate backward with a creak.

"What is it?" Ontoquas said, her hands reaching out and brushing against his along the wooden chest.

Kitto set the lid all the way back against its hinges. He reached down into the box slowly, and when his fingers struck the cool contents, a tiny jingling sound greeted his ears.

"Did you hear that?" Kitto said. He took Ontoquas's hand in his and pushed them down into the chest. They each clutched a handful of what must have been coins. Kitto lifted his hand a few inches and let the coins fall from his grasp and clink with an unmistakable jangle into the chest. Ontoquas rubbed the coins in her hand against one another.

"Gold?" Ontoquas said, and she felt her breath quicken. She let the coins fall from her hands, then picked up a single disk and brought it to her mouth. She bit down on it and could feel the metal give beneath her teeth. She knew the *wompey* valued gold above all things. Her people did not prize it particularly, but sometimes they came by gold coins in their trades with colonists.

"Rich as kings," Ontoquas said, remembering what Van had said weeks back when Kitto had identified the chest in her lean-to. She gave a small laugh, and to Kitto's ears it was a sweet music. He laughed too, and plunged his hand down into the gold.

"There is more here than we could ever spend!" he said. "And this is only a small part of it. Watch your hand." He pulled hers away and lowered the lid.

"Reach over it." Kitto took her hand in his and guided it over the top of the chest. They each scurried a few inches farther into the darkness. Together they felt something, also wooden. Another chest, small again. This one flipped open easily, and their fingers plumbed through the odd collection of shapes inside.

"This is not gold," Ontoquas said. "What is it?"

"Jewels," Kitto said, but Ontoquas did not know the word. Her fingers found something quite thin, a tiny chain. She withdrew it slowly from the chest and pulled it to her. Something hung from the chain, something small. It was a necklace. Ontoquas's people made necklaces from the shells they collected, and from the beads they traded for with the white people. She knew necklaces. Her thin fingers separated the strands, and she draped it over her head.

"See this," she said. She found Kitto's hand and pulled it to her. *Why do I find it so easy to touch him?* she wondered. She led his hand to the chain, and pushed into his palm the small medallion that hung from it.

"'Tis a cross," Kitto said. That much he could tell, but there was some other knobbylike protrusion at the bottom that did not make sense to him.

Ontoquas understood. "Jesus Christ," she said.

"Yes. Do you know . . . about him?" Kitto let go of the medallion.

"Yes. Men come to my people to tell us of him. Man and God. But we have our own gods."

Kitto turned back to the chests. The tunnel was

wider, and he felt that there was room to move to one side of the first chest. He did so and reached farther back. He felt a third chest. There were at least five if his childhood memory served, and then some loose large items toward the back. He pivoted into a crawling position and painstakingly clambered deeper into the tunnel. Ontoquas stayed where she was, running her hand through the contents of the second chest.

"How did you know this place?" she said. Moving forward, Kitto felt a fourth chest, then a fifth.

"When I was a little boy, I dragged all of this in here."

"You?"

"Yes." He lurched forward a length, and reached beyond the fifth and last chest. His hands rested on something smooth and flat, like a broad bar.

"I was the only one who could fit in here," he said as he ran his hands along the bar that lay flat on the floor. "I remember it was all so heavy, but I had to get them around this corner so they could not be seen from the outside if someone had a torch."

"Why . . ." The words eluded Ontoquas. *Why did these have to be hidden? Wasn't the cave hiding place enough?*

"I am not sure," Kitto said, understanding her confusion. "But there was something about this gold, these jewels. Something very special, and almost no one knew about it. My uncle, I remember he told me it was a secret. A 'family secret,' he said." Kitto's hands bumped against something resting on the bar, something solid but odd in shape. He ran his fingers along it. *What is it?*

He edged closer. The object was heavy, but with considerable effort he was able to lift it up and run his hands along its bumpy surface. It, too, was hard, certainly made of metal. Gold? He did not know. It was perhaps two feet tall with a central section and then two parts that reached out, one to the left and one to the right.

"A cross," he said.

"What is it?"

It was not the cross part he held, Kitto knew. That was the smooth bar on the ground. In his hands was the figure of Jesus Christ, arms spread out in the position of his crucifixion. The figure must attach somehow to the cross on the ground. Kitto ran his hands along the top and felt the sharp points of the crown of thorns at the figure's head.

"More of the same," he said, not sure how he could explain it. Effortfully, Kitto lowered the figure gently back to the ground. It certainly had the heft of gold. *But if it were gold, what would the value of something so large be?* He could not fathom it.

"I am coming back," he said. A few moments later his hands found Ontoquas's in the darkness where she reached out to help him. Kitto pulled himself beside her.

"Do you still have the chain?" Kitto said.

"Yes. You want me to put it back?" Ontoquas ran her fingers along the bauble at the end of the chain at her breast. She did not know why, but she very much wanted to see it.

"No," Kitto said. "But . . ." He hesitated.

"What is wrong?"

Kitto was not sure. *Should this place remain a secret?*

"This tunnel. I do not think we should tell the others," he said finally.

"Not your mother?"

Kitto considered. Was it some sort of revenge, keeping it from Sarah? And why not tell Van? *Because he has betrayed me in the past?* A possible answer, but that was not it. He knew Van toiled with his guilt.

"Not just yet," he said. "Please do not ask me why. I do not know, but I think I am right."

"I will not tell," Ontoquas said, and Kitto knew he could trust her.

Together they headed back out the way they had come, Ontoquas in the lead this time. She took care to tuck the cross of her necklace into her tunic to protect it before crawling out the opening. As soon as she emerged among the barrels that stood over the tunnel like stern sentinels, she scrambled for the main chamber and the bright sunlight that now shone directly through the crack in the ceiling. She was still inspecting the necklace when Kitto limped over to her.

"Can we sit down?" he said, one hand holding Ontoquas's shoulder for balance. The muscles in Kitto's left leg throbbed. Ontoquas lowered herself and Kitto to the ground, then held out her hand before them. The necklace draped across her palm. The chain was gold, untouched by its dubious storage, as shiny and perfect as the day it was forged.

"Beautiful," she said. The chain was quite thin, with delicate gold links, elegant enough for a fine lady. But the crucifix was truly remarkable.

"May I?" Kitto said. He reached over and plucked the chain from her palm.

"You want me to put it back?" Ontoquas said for the second time, but Kitto shook his head. His brow thickened as he inspected the piece.

Back in Falmouth, Kitto attended church each week with either Sarah or his father. At Sarah's meeting house there were no crosses whatsoever, but at his father's church there were both crosses and crucifixes adorning the chapel. Kitto expected to see a similar image here, with Jesus impaled on the cross with a crown of thorns on his head.

"I have never seen one like this," he said. There was a cross, plain enough, but at the base of the cross was a figure, a kneeling figure. A woman, her head covered in some sort of veil, but her face revealed.

"Who is she?" Ontoquas said. Kitto rubbed at the image with his thumb as if that could reveal an answer to her question.

"I assume . . . well, it must be the Virgin Mary."

"Who is this?"

"The mother of Jesus Christ."

Ontoquas shook her head in confusion. "He is God, and he has a woman mother?" Kitto shrugged. Christianity might well sound strange to someone who did not know it. The girl reached over and pointed carefully at a detail of the kneeling figure.

"She cries."

Kitto peered closer, then ran his thumb over the

piece again. The kneeling woman was portrayed in profile, her palms pressed together in front of her as if in prayer. Sure enough, a tiny teardrop of gold descended from her eye.

"Why does she cry?"

"Because the Romans, they just killed her son."

"He is God, and he is killed?"

Kitto smiled at her and wagged his head. "It is a bit hard to explain."

Ontoquas accepted this answer. Much about the *wompey* made little sense.

She took the necklace back from Kitto and held it out with both hands so that the dangling cross and figure glinted in the light.

"I would like to wear it," she said. She was not sure why she felt such a compulsion. Maybe it was because of the mother, weeping over her child. It made her think of her own mother who must be somewhere very far away feeling sad for Ontoquas. She knew she would never see her mother again. The white soldiers had made sure of that. They burned the village, stole the horses, and sold them all off to different slave traders, splitting mothers and grandmothers from their children, sisters from brothers—unless the brothers were old enough; those were taken away and never heard from again.

"Yes, wear it." Kitto said. "It is yours." Ontoquas handed the necklace to Kitto and bowed her head low. It took him a moment to realize that she meant for him to put it around her neck. He did so, feeling all thumbs.

She raised her head and placed her palm at her chest over the cross.

"Remember," Kitto said. "'Tis a secret. Keep it hidden."

"The barrels, too? They are secret?"

"No. That we can tell them about. We should tell them now."

CHAPTER 8:

Pirates

THREE WEEKS ON THE ISLAND

"Your mother can barely keep from crying when she looks out to sea," Van said. He and Kitto leaned back against the trunk of a palm tree, taking a break from the hot sun. Kitto whittled at a stick with his dagger, appreciating how easily the patterned Damascus steel stripped the bark away. The last hour he and Van had devoted to shooting practice on the beach, as they had done every day since Kitto had been able to limp to the beach with his new crutch.

"I know it," Kitto said. "She worries for Duck." They were quiet a moment, each considering the chances that the squirrely six-year-old would have been able to keep himself hidden on a ship overtaken by killers. Neither spoke his thoughts. Kitto flicked a few nicks of wood from the stick onto the matted leaves beneath them.

Van shrugged. "She is a strong one, that mother of yours. We'll break before she does." Van had never met a woman like Sarah, never knew that a person could be both gentle and loving and yet strong as steel.

A cooling breeze stirred the leaves of the little glade. Kitto stabbed at one and speared it with the dagger. He lifted the leaf up to inspect it absently.

"I wish my father would have told me," Kitto said.

"Told you what?"

"About my past. His past. My uncle. My mother. Any of it if not all."

"He never did?" Van said. Kitto shook his head.

"Hardly. I knew I lived in Jamaica when I was very young. And I knew my mother died, though not the real reason why. He let me go on not even knowing my real name."

"Maybe he was just trying to protect you." Van tossed a stick out onto the sand.

"I am sure that's what he told himself," Kitto said. "But look at what my life was." Kitto pointed the dagger tip toward the wrapped stump of his leg, tracing the point in the air as if outlining the clubfoot that was no longer there. "A cripple, an eyesore everywhere I went. A shame. Would have been something to know I had a mum who loved me but was murdered, or that I had somehow been involved in ripping off the great Henry Morgan." His lips curled into an ironic smile. He tore the leaf from the dagger's blade and flipped it aside. "And I wonder who this Henry Morgan is?" He shook his head in wonder. "Everyone seems so afraid of him. My uncle told me he almost drowned me when I was very young."

Van's eyes darted to Kitto for a moment, then looked away. Kitto did not notice. There was something Van had overheard about Henry Morgan—and about Kitto—back in Falmouth, from William Quick's lips. But he must have heard it wrong. It could not be possible.

"He's a very powerful man," Van said.

"Powerful . . . and evil," Kitto said. "And before all is said and done I believe I will come face to face with him."

Again Van fought the urge to tell him what he had heard. *Should I?* he thought. *No. Of course not.* He decided to change the subject.

"Too bad your mum never taught you how to shoot," Van said with a smile.

"No," Kitto said. "She had good enough reason to keep it secret. Likely my father did not know she could shoot either. I am not angry with her." Kitto paused in thought. "Mad, I suppose, but I think I have never stopped being angry with my father. It feels terrible to say that aloud, now that he is dead, murdered right before my eyes. All he wanted in his last moments was to get me to safety." Kitto drew a deep breath. "But it *is* true. I've been angry at him a long time."

"Since when?"

Kitto shrugged. "Probably since the time I really understood that I could never spend my life at sea, and that instead I would be chained to the dull life of a cooper."

"I've spent my life at sea, mostly," Van said. "I think I

would have traded places with you." Van held no romantic notions of the bitter and often vicious life of a common sailor.

"Maybe when you know you can't have something, it becomes the thing you want most of all."

Van plucked a blade of grass and stuck it between his teeth.

"I hope that don't mean that the thing you want most of all is the thing you can't really have," he said.

Van's syllogism left them quiet. Kitto thought about what he most wanted as he scraped the flesh of his thumb across the razor-sharp blade of the dagger: Duck and Sarah safe—and William, too, he realized, if still his uncle lived—making a life somewhere together with the fear of Morris and Spider and Henry Morgan far behind them.

Van pondered the thing he desired most of all, to find his sister Mercy—wherever she was—and be able to offer her a life far from whatever drudgery had become hers after she had been taken from the orphanage so many years ago.

To consider that such futures might be impossible was a depressing notion to each of them. They were due another round of shooting, but instead they remained in the shade of the broad palm leaves and let the cool breeze wash over them.

Kitto closed his eyes and found his thoughts drifting back to life in Cornwall. How hard it had seemed then. . . . Bullies like Simon Sneed tormenting him in the alleyways because of his clubfoot, people crossing cobbled streets so as not to pass him by, and all the while the mind-numbing future of being a cooper looming over him. Somehow the struggles that had defined him for so long seemed petty and selfish to him now.

So childish I have been, haven't I? How little time has passed, but I feel . . . changed, somehow. What I most desire now is not for my own benefit, but for those I love. Is that what it means to be a man?

It was a puzzling question, and after muddling it for some time, Kitto's tired brain gave up the struggle. He had drifted into a dreamless sleep.

Kitto awoke to the painful sensation of something pointed and hard thrust into his left nostril. He startled and whipped his arm up as he opened his eyes, but a hand caught him at the wrist and held him in an iron grip. Before him stood a man, a grinning man with a single gold tooth that glinted smartly, and pale blue eyes so wide—and with such tiny pupils—that Kitto thought a madman had emerged from the jungle.

"Where . . . what?" Kitto said, terrified, the words tangling in his throat. *Am I dreaming this?* No, the pain in his nose was too real for fantasy. His free hand swept about the mat of leaves on which he lay.

Where did I drop the dagger?

He could not find it.

The figure leered above him. The man wore a weathered black frock coat and a tricorne hat, and a thick black beard strung with colorful beads dangled from his chin. Kitto craned his eyes downward and saw that the man had no right hand, and that the thing inserted into his nose was the hook end of the appendage that stood in its place. The man jerked his arm up, wrenching the hook end of the instrument deeper into Kitto's nostril. Kitto gasped and started to reach up with his other hand, but the man kicked out with a boot and pinned Kitto's arm to the tree against which he lay.

Oh, God, please don't let him kill me!

"I am not a learned man, I admit," the man said in a thick accent. "I speak the English, along with the French and the Dutch, but they tangle themselves to knots in my mouth." He winked and leaned in closer to Kitto. "But this brain I have! Many questions occur to me, and my mind—it is so very inquisitive! I must know the answers. I must! It is like an itch from a mosquito that never goes away." Kitto craned toward Van to see that a burly man pressed the barrel of a pistol to Van's eye socket. Van gritted his teeth in anger and fear. Now other figures were stepping into the glade behind them.

"Please! Please don't hurt us!" Kitto's heart pounded, his breath catching. "We can tell you what you want to know," he gasped.

"*Oui, oui, oui.* Of course you will," the man said, his voice rising in pitch. "You like this nose that God gave you, ah? I do not blame you! I was admiring it myself while you slept!"

"*Ja,* you will tell me everyzing. Like how you and

your friend found yourselves on zis lonely island?" He looked down at Kitto's stump. "I can see there must be little food here, ah?" The man jerked his head toward Van. "Did that one over there get hungry and eat your foot?" He wagged his finger at the older boy. "Not very gentlemanly of you!" The man's grin vanished. He turned back to Kitto.

"How many more of you are there?" The man peered out toward the beach. Kitto swallowed heavily and his Adam's apple bobbed. He said nothing, his mind spinning.

Should I tell them? What might they do to Sarah and Ontoquas? And Bucket?

The man's smile grew wider, wilder. He giggled. It was a high-pitched twitter, almost like a little girl's, and it made Kitto quiver with fear.

"You are not quick to answer my questions, are you? That leaves me with *more* questions! But do you know what my favorite question is, right at zis moment?"

"No, sir," Kitto said, his voice weak.

"I will tell you. My questions is zis: If I lift you up with my hook, here, all zee way in zee air, will zee hook tear through your flesh, or is zee nose strong enough to hold your weight? An interesting question, do you not think?"

"Please, sir! Don't hurt me!" Kitto said again.

The man shrugged. "The flesh of the nose . . . who knows the nose? I tell you, zis question burns me. And like all important questions in life, it can probably be answered with a little experimentation. Let us try that now, ah!" He jerked the hook higher. Kitto's nostril stretched out unnaturally and he let out a whimper.

"Please!"

The ugly bear of a man jamming the pistol in Van's eye had turned to watch the comedy.

Van bared his teeth and shot up with his left arm, ramming it against the pistol. The weapon fired and the ball sent a splintered chunk spraying out from the tree. Van kicked savagely with his right leg, knocking the man's feet out from under him. In an instant he scrambled up and lunged for the man accosting Kitto, but before he ever got there a blur of speed intercepted him. Van was thrown backward, falling into the brush unconscious. The man who had struck him stepped over him to assess the damage. He was naked from the waist up, tan skinned, and though short in height, his body was wide and muscled. His head was shaved bald, and it, along with much of his shoulders and torso, was covered in tattoos, mostly a series of squares connected at the corners like a chessboard grid. He turned back toward Kitto, his face flat with a wide nose and narrow eyes.

"Quid! I hope you did not kill him!" the man said, and for a moment Kitto thought he was genuinely concerned. Then he turned back to Kitto. "Let me guess . . . zat one is the fighter, but you are the smart one, ah?"

Kitto's panic mingled now with anger at seeing Van so abused. "I have done nothing to you! Now get your bloody metal finger out of my nose." This brought chuckles from the men looking on from the edge of the glade, pistols and cutlasses leaning on their shoulders.

"*Ja, ja,* you are right. After all, I need to eat with zis thing!" The man withdrew the hook end and lowered the boot that held Kitto's arm. "May I?" he said, but before Kitto understood what he intended, the man had bent to grab the tail of Kitto's shirt. He let go of Kitto's other arm so that he could polish his hook. Kitto used the moment to wipe at his nose. His knuckles came away bloody.

"Out to the beach with these fine lads," the man said, waving his hook. "Zee other jolly boat should be along soon." He reached down and picked up Kitto's crutch. "After you, monsieur!" He spread out his left hand in the direction of the beach in a dramatic sweep, his gold-toothed smile returning. Kitto struggled to his feet with the help of the tree behind him, and as he did so, he caught sight of the dagger on the ground by his foot, half hidden in leaves.

I must hide it!

Kitto gave the knife a surreptitious kick as he reached for the crutch. The knife skittered underneath the cover of fallen leaves.

Someone has reached the island! But it is neither William nor Morris! Have we escaped one danger just to find ourselves in the midst of another?

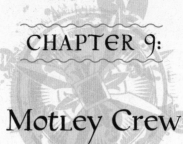

CHAPTER 9:

Motley Crew

The beach on which Van and Kitto had been practicing stretched wide and flat in the low tide. The pistols and ammunition they had used for practice lay in a tidy pile covered in oilskin. Kitto hobbled toward it. Two other men beat him to it. Both were clearly of African descent, very dark, one hardly any older than Van. Their clothes were ragged and their hats looked so salt worn that a stiff breeze might tear them apart. One of them picked up a pistol and sighted down the barrel.

Oh, please don't kill us! And please, oh, please, stay hidden, Mum!

The men gathered themselves in a loose circle around Kitto and Van, who the tattooed man had deposited gently onto the sand at Kitto's feet. Van stirred, his eyes blinking.

The gold-toothed man was obviously the leader of the rabble. He stepped forward. Kitto allowed his eyes to travel along the curious figure before him. The man's beard was a wild collection of colorful beaded braids that jangled slightly when he moved, an adornment

Kitto had never before seen. The shirt beneath his frock coat was cut with the traditional ruffles, but the material had an intricate pattern of flowery blooms that looked— well—feminine! A rich woman in Falmouth could have worn something like it, and likely paid a fortune to do so. The man's eyes were as pale blue as the Caribbean seawater and they seemed to protrude slightly from his head, adding to Kitto's impression that he might be mad.

The man fetched a brown satchel from his belt, and poured from it a small pile of brown beans that Kitto did not recognize. The man pinched one with his fingers and popped it into his mouth. He crunched on it and closed his eyes with pleasure.

"Ah!" He hefted the bag in his hand. "My supply. It grows light!" he said. He eyed Kitto for a moment, then extended his palm out to Kitto. "Have a few! I feel badly about your nose." Kitto wiped it again, but the blood seemed mostly to have stopped.

"What are they?" he said, looking dubiously at the odd collection of beans.

The man looked down on them, then back at Kitto, eyebrows raised.

"You do not know?"

"No."

The man withdrew his hand. "Then I take back. I share with those who can appreciate. They are coffee beans, of course!"

Kitto had heard of coffee. He believed it to be a

Dutch drink. He had never seen it in Cornwall, just heard it mentioned occasionally down at the quay where all manner of goods came and went.

"I thought you *drank* coffee," he said. The man stuck his tongue out and blew a raspberry. Kitto had never seen anyone older than Duck do such a thing with his tongue, and he would have laughed were his whole body not shaking with fear.

"Who has the time? The time to sit and drink? What for, zees? Just eat it, and feel alive!" Again he gestured his collection in Kitto's direction. "Go on!" he ordered.

Just do as the madman says, Kitto told himself. He reached out a shaking hand and pinched a few beans from the man's palm, then lifted them to his mouth. He chewed, unable to contain a revolted expression when the bitter taste struck. The men in the circle chuckled.

"You do not like?" Kitto spit a few flecks from his mouth.

"Of course he don't like your rabbit turds, X!" said one of the men. "Nobody but you does."

The man shrugged. "More for me!" He giggled again. Next to Kitto, Van struggled to stand. He got halfway up and then sat down again groaning and holding his head.

"Ow," Van said finally.

"Quid, he has a big fist. Like a hammer! But I see your jaw is still attached to your head. Consider yourself lucky!" He twittered. "Double lucky, even, for Fowler shot a tree instead of you." Van glared up at the man, squinting against the bright sun.

"Who are you?" Van said.

"I could ask zee same of you, ah?" the man said, arching his eyebrows down at Van. "They call me X." The man drew himself to a dramatic stand of attention that Kitto could see was meant to be ironic. "I am the captain of these fine men!"

"Not for long," said Fowler, turning and spitting in the sand. X rolled his eyes.

"I found the island, did I not, you filthy pig?" X said. "You want to vote. Fine. We vote, just as soon as my sweet Pippin is brought to shore."

They vote on who their captain is? Kitto thought it the strangest thing he had ever heard. Van knew what it meant.

"So you are pirates," Van said. Kitto looked at the faces around him worriedly, fearing they might take offense. *Don't get us killed, Van!* Mostly the men seemed not to have heard.

X pursed his lips comically. "What you want me to say, man-boy? 'Yes, I am a pirate'? No one who is a pirate says he is a pirate! Pirates would not do that, would they?" He threw his hands out wide in exasperation. "*Oui, oui, oui,* some people, they would call us zees. I prefer 'sea dogs.' It has a nice ring."

Pirates. *Men who steal and kill for sport are here, on the island. But how did they get here?* Kitto wondered. He cleared his voice and decided to risk asking.

"Do you have a ship?" Kitto said, wondering if the idea that was occurring to him had occurred to Van.

The man called Fowler spoke up with a haughty tone. "Aye, X, do we have a bloody ship?"

X ignored him. He let out a long sigh. "Alas, a ship we do not have. We had a ship, but she has sunk."

"From an attack?" Kitto said. The more this strange man talked, the more his fear lessened. After all, if they were going to kill them, would they not do so quickly?

"No, it was not the navy. It was the worms."

"Worms?"

"Shipworms." Now X turned to spit. "Devil-loving shipworms. The ship we . . . borrowed . . . from this fat little Spaniard piglet, it was full of them! But we did not know this when we traded his ship for our own. Two weeks later and our new ship is sinking beneath us."

"So how did you get here?" Van asked.

"Shut your hole, you," Fowler said. He spat again, this time quite near where Van knelt.

"Jolly boats, but nobody jolly in zem. Two, and we have been rowing with the current the last eight days to find this island—or another one like it."

Kitto's heart sank. A ship would have meant the possibility of freedom. It was hard to imagine that such men could be allies with them against Morris and Spider and the rest of the crew, but any assistance could have made a difference. X could see the disappointment register on his face.

"*Oui, oui, oui.* Not such good news for you two, ah? But let me introduce my fellow dogs. The mutt here, the ugly one, that is Fowler." Fowler gestured rudely at

X. "The one who is all squares, that is Quid. There is Pickle and Xavier." The two young men toying with the pistols looked up and raised a hand to their hats. "That one we call Pelota, and this savage here is Black Dog." X pointed to a glowering man at his elbow. He had a stony, dark face and long straight black hair, much like Ontoquas's, and Kitto assumed he must have been a native of the Americas. Black Dog stared at Kitto with a baleful look that made goose bumps run up his spine. He turned away.

It occurred to him as he looked over the pirates that very few of the men were European. In fact Fowler and X himself were the only two with skin as fair as his own. Pickle and Xavier were dark enough to be Africans—as were the other two men whose names Kitto had missed— Quid from the Far East perhaps, Pelota dark and indeterminate. Kitto was accustomed to seeing a variety of peoples spill off the ships that came to dock at Custom Quay in Falmouth, but never in such concentration.

Kitto and Van introduced themselves, first names only.

"Kitto," X said, making a funny popping sound with his mouth. "I have heard this name before. What was it . . ." His puzzling ended when Fowler hailed out to a rowboat that came into view.

"Splendide!" X said. "My Pippin has arrived."

The jolly boat was paddled right up onto the sand, a handful of men leaping into the surf and hauling the boat the rest of the way up the beach.

"How is she?" X called, rushing for the boat. "Have you kept her watered?" The grumbling men assured him they had. "Little John, help and get poor Pippin out of zere."

An enormous man in the boat waved back.

"You need to set the stake first," Little John said, his accent indicating that he hailed from England, though not Cornwall. He tossed a long metal rod with a loop at one end to X, who snatched it up and walked farther up the beach with a heavy mallet.

In a moment he was pounding the stake into the sand a few yards from Kitto and Van.

What is a Pippin?

Two men held the jolly boat steady while Little John braced his feet on the sides and reached down to where Kitto could not see. When he came up, he had his huge arms wrapped about a massive crocodile, although Kitto did not know that name. He thought it to be some sort of overgrown lizard. A thick leather belt wrapped about the creature's snout. Little John arched his back, trying to clear the crocodile's thick tail over the gunwale.

"Careful! Careful!" X said, and too late.

The beast writhed its tale savagely, whipping it back and forth. Little John lost his balance. The huge man and the crocodile both tumbled headlong out of the jolly boat, knocking into the wash one of the men who had been steadying the boat.

The three figures fell in a thrashing heap shouting

a fusillade of foul language. X had commenced to shrieking, incensed with worry about the crocodile who scuttled off down the beach at a terrific speed. It stopped short thirty yards away.

"Pippin! Pippin, my sweet!"

Kitto watched in astonishment. Somehow in the fall, the belt clamping Pippin's jaws closed had slipped off. Pippin opened his jaws wide, displaying a frightening array of teeth. He snapped them shut with a clack that could be heard over the breaking surf. X turned back on the men.

"Robbie, the fiddle! Give it to me!" A young man sprang to the leaning jolly boat and dug about its contents. Shortly he produced a wooden case, which he opened, revealing to Kitto's surprise a violin, its polish glinting in the sunlight. Robbie raced it to X, who continued to call to the crocodile.

"I am coming, my darling! Do not be upset. Daddy is coming!" The captain tucked the violin under his chin and immediately launched into a lullaby, a slow melodic strain. Kitto and Van looked at each other in wonder.

"Do you think he is mad, Kitto?"

"I don't know. They vote him captain. Must say something." A thought came to him. "Do you think there is enough of them to take Morris's crew?" Van shook his head.

"Shut up, girls." Fowler stood over them with his pistol bared. "Scheming, that's what the two of you are doing. Scheming." He pulled back the hammer on his pistol. It clicked. "Open your mouth again, cripple, and I'll fill it with lead."

The pistol flew from Fowler's hands in a blur, its pieces scattering in the wash beyond them as the sound of a shot rang out from somewhere indeterminate in the thick jungle.

CHAPTER 10:

Pippin's Run

The men shouted in alarm, and suddenly every pirate had his hands on a pistol or a cutlass or both. Several scrambled behind the beached jolly boat for cover. Only X ignored the shooting, slowly walking down the beach toward the crocodile, never missing a note.

Pelota raised his arm and fired a shot into the greenery. Whether he knew the direction the first shot had come from Kitto could not tell, but the other pirates joined in, dispensing a hail of fire toward a bend in the beach fifty yards away. Kitto looked on breathlessly, but he could see no sign of either Sarah or Ontoquas.

X turned. "Idiots! Idiots!" he shrieked.

Pippin bolted again, but rather than heading farther away down the beach, the crocodile had sprinted past X and back the way it had come. It stopped ten yards short of the men huddled behind the jolly boat reloading their weapons.

"Shoo! Shoo!" Pelota waved at Pippin with his dispensed pistol. "Somebody shoot it!" X ran toward them, sawing madly at his violin.

"Anybody shoots my baby I cut his heart out!" he said in a singing voice to match his notes. X drew closer.

The music did seem to work some sort of magic on the crocodile. Pippin flexed his jaws several times in a lazy way.

"*Oui, oui, oui,* sweetheart!" X cooed. "You are so thirsty. Too long you have not had a swim. Just a few moments longer." He played a few more bars.

"Robbie, the harness and belt!" X sang, trying poorly to match the tone of the sweeping melody. The young man fetched the belt from the sand and tossed it over the crocodile to land at X's feet. The men finished reloading their weapons, but they could not decide where to point them: out at the unseen foe in the jungle, or at the crocodile that might any minute attempt to devour them.

Robbie rummaged in the leaning rowboat and produced another contraption of leather and iron. He held it up toward X.

"Come and get it!" Robbie said, fear in his eyes. X shook his head at the man's stupidity.

"If I stop playing this song, you idiot, you are going to be a snack for poor Pippin. Now bring it here and put this strap on!"

Robbie replied in foul terms that he would not do so. Fowler called out from behind the rowboat. He pointed with a new pistol at Van.

"You! Get up and take it over there."

"Me?" Van looked up. Kitto could see the fear in his eyes, perhaps the first time he had noted it in Van.

"What do you think?" Van hissed to Kitto.

"Try not to get too close."

Van shook his head, but he got up slowly. His jaw still throbbed and his first few steps were wobbly, but he made it to the rowboat. The man called Robbie handed him the leather bundle.

"Go on!" Fowler said from behind the boat. "Take it over there. X will show you how to put it on her." Van glared before answering.

"Her?"

"Aye, Pippin's a girl. But she ain't no lady," Fowler said, his lips parting to show a tangle of brown teeth. "Go on and take it."

"What is it?"

"A harness," Fowler said. "Now get on."

"Why don't you?"

"Because I've got the pistol, now don't I?"

Van turned with the harness, and making a wide and slow arc up the beach, he walked around the enormous crocodile and came to stand at X's side. X was into his fourth or fifth verse of the melody now, but Pippin did not seem to mind the repetition.

"Here," Van said, holding it out toward the pirate. X scowled.

"You have to put it on her!" X hissed. "I cannot stop playing. She is very upset!" Van shook his head disbelievingly.

"I ain't touching that lizard."

Kitto watched, his mind spinning. Seeing over a

dozen hardened sailors—bonafide pirates, even—had inspired a vague idea that had not yet taken form but that he could not quite shake. *We could use these men, perhaps! But why would such men allow themselves to be used?*

Kitto took a few jerky steps toward Van and X, leaning on his crutch. The crocodile, still enraptured by the music, chose not to notice him. Kitto took a few more, following the path of Van's footsteps in the sand. In a few moments he stood beside Van and the pirate.

"How does it work, the harness?" he said. Van threw him a stern look, but X launched into a musical explanation of how the two pairs of longer straps wrapped around the creature's midsection, one pair just inside each set of legs.

"Just slide zem under her belly, very gentlelike," the captain said. "She will let you do it." X pursed his lips in disapproval. "She is usually much better behaved. . . ."

"Come on, Van," Kitto said, turning to him. "We can do it."

"You are as mad as this pirate!" Van said. X giggled. Van and Kitto locked eyes a moment, and Kitto tried to communicate how important he thought this could be for them. Van scowled fiercely but stepped forward with Kitto.

"Stupidest thing I ever done!" he said under his breath.

Pippin's back was to them as she eyed the motionless men at the jolly boat whose heads pivoted back and forth between the jungle where the shots had been fired and the terrifying beast. Kitto angled toward the reptile's left side, Van to the right, carrying the bundle. They stepped over the massive tail, its very end tracing a small arc in the sand.

"If he comes at us, jump on top of it," Van hissed. "I don't think they can get at you that way."

"She!" X shouted, then cringed at his own words. "Pippin is a girl!" he spat.

Kitto did not reply. He reached the midsection of the crocodile. A simple spin and the beast would be upon him with that hideous mouthful of teeth. Kitto beckoned for the first strap, which Van produced from the bundle. He pointed to the creature's side, indicating for Van to slide that end under the animal. Van scowled fiercely, but he edged closer.

"Pet her!" X said behind them. "On the top of her sweet head. She likes zis very much."

Kitto and Van looked at each other. Van jerked his head to Kitto, assigning him that task. Kitto reached out and ever so gently stroked the crocodile on the top of her bumpy skull, just behind the eyes. Pippin jerked her head up a few inches.

"Yes, yes," X said. "Keep doing that, a little harder. With the fingernails. She will stand for you."

"This is insane," Van said.

"Hush." Kitto petted a bit more vigorously, bearing down with his nails to scratch at the scaly armor. Sure enough, Pippin's whole body shimmied, and then the crocodile pressed its weight up onto its four diminutive legs, lifting its entire ponderous belly off the sand.

Van wasted no time. He fed one belt under the crocodile's belly where Kitto was able to grab it—while making sure never to stop petting—and send it over Pippin's back for Van to work the buckle. In no time Van had moved to the reptile's hind legs and repeated the action, this time able to do so without Kitto's help.

"*Oui, oui, oui. Splendide!*" The two belts were connected to each other by a thick leather strap that ran along Pippin's spine, and at its center was sewn a hefty metal ring. "Now for the tether." X lifted his bow from the fiddle.

"Little John! The rope. She is ready—" Irritated that the music had stopped, Pippin convulsed, her massive tail sweeping wide and knocking Van at the ankles. He spun through the air and landed flat on his back on the packed sand. Kitto petted the crocodile harder.

"Keep with the music!" Kitto hissed. X's strings gave a squawk and resumed the melody. Pippin lowered her snout and belly again to the moist sand. Van picked himself up slowly and retreated behind X.

Back at the boat Little John retrieved a stout rope and handed it to Pickle.

"Not me!" Pickle said. "Fiddle or no fiddle." Little John turned to Fowler next, who glared angrily and shook his head. Without another thought Little John heaved the bundle into the air. They all watched in fascinated horror as the rope uncoiled as it spun along its momentous arc. Kitto scratched and petted even more fiercely on Pippin, but held one hand over his head to protect himself.

"Imbécile!"

The mass of rope landed directly on Pippin's skull, and one of the metal locking hooks attached to each end thumped the beast squarely on the eyeball. Pippin went berserk. Emitting something like a roar, she thrashed her head and tail. X—who had stepped closer when Little John threw the rope—was knocked backward by the tail, his hat and the fiddle bow hurtling off with the wind.

"Run!" X screamed as Van yanked him to his feet. It was good advice, too, because Pippin had spun and lunged in their direction and snapped her jaws in the air where X had been sprawled an instant before. X and Van ran pell-mell down the beach, X's violin waggling in the air. Pippin shot off after them, abruptly stopped, then turned around slowly, the bundle of rope splayed out over her body.

Kitto looked at Pippin. Pippin looked at Kitto. The beast's eyes were two slits of black. Kitto tensed. His natural reactions told him to run, but he had seen how fast the crocodile could move, and he knew he stood no chance.

"Get out of there, lad!" called one of the pirates from the jolly boat behind him. Kitto held his crutch out in front of him as if it might provide some defense.

And then Pippin charged. The crocodile raced

straight at Kitto, its huge reptilian grin growing wider as it neared. Sand flew out beneath her claws. Without thinking Kitto stabbed the crutch into the ground and vaulted himself into the air just as Pippin reached him. He flew over the reptile's snapping jaws and landed on her back. Pippin whirled about, and Kitto found himself clinging to the metal ring of the harness along the crocodile's spine. Again Pippin thrashed, writhing her head in an attempt to get at the boy.

Kitto clung to the harness for dear life. Pippin went still finally, and Kitto took the opportunity to get a good grip on the leather strap as well as the ring.

Behind him Van and X were half watching Kitto and half desperately trying to find the fiddle bow, which had gotten lost in the wash of waves.

"Zere it is!" X yelled, pointing into the water. "Go and get it."

"I don't swim!"

"Neezer do I!"

With Pippin still motionless, Kitto had time to see that one end of the rope with its steel locking hook lay just inches from the metal ring of the harness. Kitto risked releasing one hand to grab the hook and neatly attach it to the ring with a click. No sooner had he done so than Pippin whirled again and charged the men at the jolly boat.

The crocodile was amazingly fast, covering the distance of thirty yards in just seconds, even with Kitto weighing her down. Little John, Fowler, Pickle, and two other men leaped gracelessly into the jolly boat, which teetered on its keel and tipped back to its port side, nearly dumping the men right into the approaching predator. Little John heaved a leg against the beach and the jolly boat swung up onto its keel again and flopped to the starboard, exposing the hull of the boat to Pippin in time for the reptile to crack her head on the bleached planks. Kitto still clung tenaciously to the animal's back, his knuckles white and his eyes wide.

Momentarily Pippin's rage was foiled, but then her slitted eyes saw the retreating figures of Quid, Pelota, and Xavier higher up on the loose sand next to the pile of pistols.

"No, no," Kitto said in as soothing a voice as he could muster. "Good lizard . . . no more running."

Pippin was unconvinced. She took off like a launched arrow toward the running men, Kitto flopping along astride her now as if she were a horse. The men scrambled for their lives and were fast enough to gain ground on the crocodile, who stopped after several seconds and gave up the chase. When Pippin turned again, Kitto saw the stake X had pounded into the beach. It lay a dozen feet off, the hoop at its end just a few inches above the sand. Kitto scanned about the bundle of rope caught up beneath him and found the other hooked end of the tether dragging in the sand to his left. He reached out for it, but Pippin whirled again, nearly upsetting Kitto's grip. Kitto risked reaching out with one hand to scratch at the crocodile's skull.

"'Tis okay, Pippin. Sweet Pippin. Good Pippin." The beast lowered its head. Kitto let go of the ring—his last firm grip on the crocodile—and leaned toward the hooked end of the rope in the sand. He retrieved it without incident, and now eyed the loop end of the stake in the sand, several yards away.

It is too far! Kitto thought. Too far to reach while still on Pippin's back.

"Come on, lad! You can do it!" called Little John.

"Secure that latch!" said Fowler.

Up the beach, X had goaded Van to wade into the water to fetch the fiddle bow from the tumbling waves. Van ran with it through the shallows to the pirate. X put it to his instrument to play, but the wet bow would elicit nothing but a squeak. Cursing, X withdrew a scrap of cloth from his cloak and feverishly scrubbed it against the horsehair.

The crocodile turned to face the four men huddled in the tipped jolly boat.

"Oh, rot," Fowler said, and as if on cue, Pippin shot forward. Risking it all, Kitto rolled off the reptile's back, still clutching the hooked end of the line in his hand. If Pippin noticed her unburdened state, she did not show it; she charged at the men who were now screaming at one another, trying to coordinate their actions and tip the boat over again, increasingly frantic as the distance between them and the crocodile rapidly diminished.

Kitto scrambled across the sand on hands and knees toward the stake. The slack from the rope was paying out very quickly, the loops hissing in the sand. Fowler jumped atop the jolly boat, thus frustrating the efforts of the other men to flip it up. The other two men tried vainly to find protection behind the rowers' seats.

Kitto reached the stake and slapped the hook down onto the loop. The rope snapped tight and the stake jerked in the sand. Pippin strained at the rope, snapping her massive jaws not more than a foot from Little John, whose face had gone ashen. Fowler, standing with the jolly boat between him and the crocodile now, broke out into a lusty, bellowing laugh. The laugh spread to Quid and Pelota and Xavier who walked back slowly from up the beach, and even the men cowering in the jolly boat started to grin too, when they trusted that the stake would hold.

Kitto felt a swell of relief and pride.

I did it.

Quid called out in heavily accented English. "Little John make big mess in pants!" Little John did not find this funny, but the others did.

Pippin spun around again in the direction of the voice—which also happened to be in Kitto's direction, and instantly the feeling of relief that had washed over Kitto vanished.

I am standing at the stake! I am not safe! He swallowed hard.

"Lad, I think you best get moving," Fowler said.

His crutch nowhere in sight, Kitto took one crawling step up the beach.

Pippin clacked her jaws together and made for him. *No! No! No!*

"Run, Kitto!" Van screamed.

Kitto crawled forward and then half stood on his left foot, throwing himself forward and falling, the loose sand conspiring against his efforts. Closer and closer and closer rushed the crocodile. The distance was down to only ten yards when out from a thick stand of leafy undergrowth burst Sarah. She ran onto the beach toward Kitto, musket in one hand and three pistols shoved beneath her waistband.

"Kitto, get down!" she wailed, unable to shoot with Kitto standing between her and the animal. Kitto dove for the sand, and Sarah raised the musket.

"Please do not shoot!" X said, but the musket's report rang out. The ball crackled inches over Kitto's head and struck Pippin squarely on the snout. The crocodile dug her claws into the sand and stopped dead in her tracks. She shook her head and snorted as if sneezing.

Kitto seized the chance by scrambling forward again, off at an angle so as to give Sarah a better vantage. Again Pippin bolted. Sarah had already dropped the musket to the beach and now held a pistol in each hand, which she discharged in rapid succession, one ball striking Pippin square atop her thick skull, the other on the front right leg. This time Pippin stopped for good, settling down on the sand, her great chest heaving. Kitto crawled farther until he was sure he had exceeded the crocodile's range.

X rushed forward, holding the fiddle over his eyes to block the sun's glare.

"A woman! You are a woman? Did I see zees with my own eyes!" He pointed accusingly with the fiddle bow. "You shot my crocodile, you Medusa!" he raged.

Sarah dropped the spent pistols and pulled the third from her sash.

She aimed it at the pirate who now strode toward her angrily.

"I did shoot it," she said. "But it lives, which you shall not if you come any closer." She pulled back the hammer. X stopped. The men behind the jolly boat had retrieved their pistols and trained them on Sarah.

"Just give us the word, X, and Medusa is crocodile food!" Fowler said.

Ontoquas leaped out now from the jungle just a few feet from X, so that he stood between her and the men at the rowboat. In her hands was the bow she had made, a crude arrow with a sharpened rock at its tip nocked against the string. Slung to her back in a tight swaddle of sailcloth hung baby Bucket, peacefully craning his neck about to look up at the sunlight playing in the palm leaves.

"Your men shoot her, I shoot you." X turned an incredulous look on the girl, his mouth gaping open.

"No!" Kitto exclaimed. "Please! No. No one needs to shoot anybody. I did just save some of you your lives, did I not?" Kitto said toward the men in the boat.

"True enough," Little John said. Bucket let out a

happy cooing noise as he watched a white tropic bird sail over the treetops.

"*Est-ce que un bébé?* Turn around!" X demanded, pointing at Ontoquas. She answered him by pulling back the bowstring a few more inches. Again, Bucket cooed.

X turned to Kitto. "You have a baby and a savage on this island!" Ontoquas took a step closer to him.

"*Nenetah ha!*" she shouted, her voice shrill.

"*Nenetah ha?*" The pirate called Black Dog stepped out from behind the rowboat. He tossed his pistol to the ground and strode forward. "*Kean wawtom! Kean wawtom!*"

Ontoquas never thought she would hear her own tongue again, but this man was telling her that he understood her words. She lowered the tip of her arrow. Black Dog fiercely waved at his companions to lower their pistols.

"Black Dog! What the devil are you doing?"

"You are Wampanoag?" Ontoqaus called out to the man. He shook his head.

"Pokanoket," he said, naming a tribe a few days journey from her village. "*Wuneekeesuq.*"

Ontoquas smiled and returned the greeting. "*Wuneekeesuq.*"

The man strode to Ontoquas, his long black hair streaming in the wind, a bright smile cracking his chiseled features. He reached out and put his hand on Ontoquas's shoulder. Rather than lower her head as would have been customary for a woman to do, Ontoquas dropped her bow and reached out to place her hand on the arm Black Dog extended to her. Black Dog smiled, then turned to X.

"These people. They are friends. We will not fight them."

"Lovely!" X said, thoroughly disgusted.

CHAPTER 11

Articles

Now that Black Dog had declared the island's five inhabitants "friends," the rest of the pirates deemed them unworthy of their interest. Sarah turned a few heads when she would pass by, bobbing Bucket, and the men would tip their hats to her or to Ontoquas when the girl returned with their jugs, filled with fresh water. The entire band of men—sixteen in all—pondered their grim situation as they lolled about in the shade of the palm trees overlooking the beach.

Kitto caught Van's eye and gestured with his head toward the path that led back to the lean-to. He crutched off in that direction, and soon enough Van caught up.

"What do you think of all this?" Van said when he had reached him. Both boys cast wary looks along the path they had come. The jungle obscured their view.

"I keep having an idea," Kitto said.

"Oh, dear."

"Shut it and listen, Van. Do you think there is any chance these men could help us?" Kitto said.

"Help us!" Van scowled. "They are pirates, Kitto! Said so themselves."

"Are we not wanted by the law as well?"

Van shrugged. "True enough."

"What if I proposed a trade? They help us, we share the nutmeg with them." Kitto stared intently at Van as he said these words. He knew Van would not like the idea, but his heart told him there was something to the notion. He watched Van's cheeks color.

"You do that, Kitto, you tell them about the riches on this island, and for sure they will cut our throats!" Van was red to the tips of his ears, the pupils of his blue eyes narrowing to a pinprick.

Kitto took a deep breath. He matched Van's stare.

"What about that Black Dog fellow? You heard what he said."

"Fine," Van said, nodding. "Ontoquas gets spared, the rest of us get run through."

"I do not think so."

Van gritted his teeth, and the words came out in a hiss. "Kitto, you've got more in here than the deadwood I've got, I'll give you that," he said, tapping his forehead. "But I'm the one who knows the life of the sea, not you!" He thumped his chest. "I've been around men not so different from these most of my life. I don't trust them, I watch my back, and I get away from them as soon as I bloody well can!"

Van took two steps backward and spun around to head back to the beach, and in so doing he nearly ran straight into Black Dog. The pirate stood tall and stern, his dark eyes taking in the boys with a deep intensity, one hand at his side and the other resting on a large knife in his belt.

"Excuse me!" Van said hotly and stepped around the towering figure. Black Dog did not flinch as Van maneuvered around him and tromped down the path.

Kitto looked up at the man. Their eyes locked for several seconds. Black Dog had high cheekbones and a broad forehead, and stood with a bearing of pride and strength. There was little to read in the expression, but Kitto was sure it was not simply hatred or anger coming from his eyes.

Can we trust you? he wanted to say, but didn't. Instead, he leaned forward on the crutch and took a step as to move around the man. When Kitto and he were shoulder to shoulder, Black Dog extended the palm of his hand. Kitto looked up.

Black Dog's voice was soft, like the whisper of wind through the palm trees.

"Be . . . careful," he said.

When Kitto returned to the beach, he made his way toward the pirate captain, who lay on his back at the edge of the jungle, dangling his foot over the slight drop-off down to the beach. Van sat several yards away, scowling and dragging a stick through the sand. He stopped short when he saw Kitto approach the captain and toss himself to the ground nearby. X lifted the tricorne hat he had tipped over his eyes to block out the sun.

"You are not going to ask me for more coffee beans, are you, crocodile boy?" he said.

Kitto snorted. "Not likely."

"Good." X pawed through the satchel that balanced on his chest, procured a single bean, and dropped it into his mouth. As he crunched down upon it, the colored strands of beads in his beard gyrated along his chin and neck.

"What is it like," Kitto said, "being a pirate?" X coughed, turned, and spat out a fleck of bean. He pushed himself up onto an elbow and looked at Kitto with a crooked eyebrow.

"I associate with fat men, stupid men, smelly men," he said. "It is quite blissful."

"Do you trust them?" Kitto said, and his eyes darted to Van for an instant, who glared at him with jaw set.

X took a moment to look out over the assortment of men splayed out in the shade. All looked to be asleep but for Black Dog, who stood some distance off, watching them.

"With my life," X said. "Many times over."

"But why?" Kitto pressed. "Why, if they are pirates—as are you—would you not just steal from each other when it suited you?" X giggled at this and fished in the bag for another bean.

"You have a very low opinion of people in my line of work," X said. "We are not animals! We work together to help each other, to protect each other, to make ourselves wealthy. And we have a contract."

"A what?"

"A contract. An agreement. A promise to one another."

"Written down, do you mean?" Kitto said.

X sat upright, his hat tumbling to the floor of palm leaves. "Would you like for me to show it to you?"

"Well, yes! Very much, thank you."

X reached inside his grimy frock coat and produced a small oilskin pouch. He tossed it to Kitto.

Kitto scooted back to lean against a nearby palm tree and unfolded the oilskin and the parchment it contained. He cast a quick look to Van and mouthed the words, *Come here*.

"It is our Articles of Doghood," said X, looking up as Van approached. "Without it we would perhaps, as you suggest, simply steal from each other and kill each other."

Kitto held the unfolded document up before him and Van. The hand that had written it was skilled. The document consisted of a list of statements, numbered in roman numerals. A series of scrawled signatures littered the bottom section, most barely legible.

"What's it say?" Van whispered. Kitto turned to him in surprise.

"Can you not read?"

Van flushed, shaking his head. "The orphanage was not so particular about schooling," he said. "Most of what my parents taught me I have lost." Kitto did not know why the admission surprised him. If anything, it was rare for a boy Kitto's age to know his letters as well as he did.

Kitto read over the articles silently and then summed them up for Van's benefit. They outlined a set of rules for deportment: that none would steal from the others, that none would show cowardice in battle, that none would strike another of the company, that all men would share equally in prizes but for the captain who would receive one share plus a half, that all taken goods be given over within a day at the end of a successful raid, and that the assignation of captain was to be settled by vote but never during an engagement. One rule stood out to Kitto.

"What is this about slaves?" he said. "It says here that 'no man shall take a slave as a captive, and any slaves encountered on any captured ship shall be liberated or welcomed into the crew.'" Kitto lowered the document to look at X. "I would think slaves had a great value to men like you, to be traded for gold."

X made a wry face, then thumbed toward the men about the beach.

"Take a look, *jongen*, at our skin. You will have your answer." Kitto did look, and what he saw was a great variety in appearance, as he had noted before. Some of the men were quite dark in complexion, nearly black, a few tanned but fair like Englishmen, and then there seemed to be every shade in between.

"Do you mean . . . your men were slaves?"

X wagged his head. "Some of us."

"You?"

"No. Only the Irish in these parts. But I was, how you say, 'indentured.' Not so very different."

Kitto looked back to the document. Each statement except for the last ended with the following: *He who is found in violation of said rule shall be subjected to Moses's Law on the bare back and marooned.*

"What is Moses's Law?" he said.

"Forty stripes on zee back with zee company whip," X said, pointing toward Fowler, who lay on his back in slumber, a coiled whip tied to his belt. "So you see, I do not zink you would like to be with us, eh?"

"I did not say I would," Kitto said, startled that the pirate captain had anticipated the suggestion he was considering despite Van's warning.

"We do not sign boys, and I would never tolerate a girl or a woman aboard my ship," X said, "no matter how well she shoots." He pointed off to the beach where Sarah and Ontoquas played with Bucket.

"You don't even have a ship," Van said. Nearby, the pirate named Pickle, overhearing, chuckled loudly. X stuck his tongue out at him.

"I will admit this has put a damper on our prospects," X said.

Kitto cleared his throat and spoke loud enough for all the men nearby to hear.

"But what if I could get you a ship, and more than that, make you all rich men? Would you agree to sign us on then?" Several pirates nearby turned to look over at them.

"Blast it, Kitto!" Van said underneath his breath.

In moments, it seemed, nearly all the sailors had come to sense that something important was taking place. Several sat up and a few others inched closer to where Kitto sat. X giggled.

"Let me guess," he said. "You are actually a merman, *ja?*" He pointed to Kitto's stump. "That is not a missing foot you have, but a magical fin that transforms when you are in the water! And you can swim into the sea there, and guide a ship right to us, ah?"

"If I could do it, what would you say?"

"And what was that about making us rich?" Fowler was sleeping no longer. He stood a few feet behind Kitto and dug at his dirty fingernails with a dagger tip. "What is it you ain't saying?"

"First your answer," Kitto said, turning back to X.

The captain snickered again. This was all quite entertaining.

"Men!" he called out, sweeping an arm wide. "Can we agree, zis boy gets us a ship, we allow him to sign our articles?" Grunts of approval sounded around the glade.

"Anyone to speak against?" Silence.

"Well, merman," X said, "you have our attention. Be quick. Fowler breaks wind when stories run too long."

"Kitto . . . ," Van said again.

"Let him speak, Van," Sarah said, having returned

soundlessly from the beach, Bucket asleep on her shoulder.

Kitto composed his thoughts a moment, and in so doing he let his eyes run down the articles to the squiggled signatures at the bottom of the parchment. Most of the names were a scrawl of ink, but one was neat and plain. He froze.

Alexandre Exquemelin

Exquemelin!

That name, that last name, Kitto knew where he had seen it before. It was the name written on the rolled slip of parchment that Duck had discovered hidden inside the dagger his father had given him. That dagger lay obscured by the leaves not thirty feet from where he sat. *Could it be?*

"Which one of you is Alexandre Exquemelin?" Kitto said.

"The stupid one," Fowler answered, pointing his dagger in X's direction. Kitto turned to X.

"It *is* you?"

"'Exquemelin' is too long of a word for men like Fowler to say. They call me X, but yes, my name is Exquemelin. Why? Do I owe your father money?" He readied himself to toss a coffee bean into the air.

"My father is dead," Kitto said. Kitto felt his heartbeat quicken. "Did you know a man named . . . William Quick?" Now all the men sat up and leaned forward.

The coffee bean X had thrown caromed off his nose and fell to the ground. He did not bother to retrieve it. Instead he glared at Kitto, all trace of impishness vanishing.

"The Pirate Quick. It is to ask me if I know my own brother!" he growled. "Why do you ask me zis?"

"Because he is my uncle. And without your help he is sure to die."

CHAPTER 12:

Dagger Tales

The sun had dipped behind the forest of palm trees. Ontoquas blew on the smoking pile of dried leaves and sticks, starting the fire that would cook them a meal of barbecued turtle.

With the exception of Exquemelin, the band of seamen had made camp in the glade near the beach. Although they had had to abandon their stolen ship before it sank, they at least had time to load the jolly boats with such provisions as they saw fit to carry: various tools, tarps, sailcloth, a few barrels of salted fish and jugs of cider and rum, not to mention powder and shot and slow match for the flintlocks. Some busied themselves with setting up the tarps as tents, while Fowler and Quid and a man named Ox rowed the jolly boats out in the direction Ontoquas had pointed out for hunting sea turtles.

Sarah sat with Bucket at the firepit in front of the lean-to. She teased Bucket by dragging the tip of a stick in the dirt before him, which Bucket would try to grab, smiling broadly. Van had left to search for more firewood.

Exquemelin and Kitto sat together on two adjacent rocks near the fire. X turned Kitto's dagger in his hands. He had insisted on seeing it when Kitto mentioned it in his explanation of all that had happened over the last month, and together they had retrieved it from the woods at the edge of the beach. Exquemelin whistled a high descending note.

"My past. Never do I seem to escape it," he said.

Kitto sat beside him, his stump propped up on a large rock near the fire.

"You recognize it, then?"

Exquemelin traced his finger along the grain lines of the Damascus steel blade.

"You say this was your mother's. But not this woman?" X gestured with the tip toward Sarah.

"I call her my mother, but by birth, there was another woman." X nodded and began to fiddle with the dagger's pommel. In a few moments he had wiggled it in the way Duck had for the first time back in their home in Falmouth. The metal pommel popped as it withdrew from the handle, revealing the hidden chamber inside.

"How did you know about that?" Kitto asked, but X did not answer. Instead he tapped the hollow handle on his palm. Out tumbled the rolled scrap of parchment, dry and undamaged. X unrolled it. He read, giggled, then rolled it back up and returned it.

"This is how you knew my name," he said. Kitto nodded.

"And later I asked my uncle about you."

"Did William curse me?" X grinned.

"Not at all. He described you as a good friend."

X grunted in approval. "Zis surprises me. I would have thought he blamed all his old comrades, us little fingers of 'The Hand.'" X lifted his right arm up, rotating the brass hook attached to his wrist before him with a lost look.

"The tattoo . . . of a skeleton hand. Did you have one as well?" Kitto said. X did not answer, but instead fixed Kitto with a stern stare.

"Your foot, *jonge* man. Before it was gone like it is now, from a shark . . . was it bent?" Kitto felt his face flush.

"How did you know that?"

"So, it is true, then," X said. He grinned and shook his head in disbelief. "The world is so very small! Is it not?"

"I do not understand, sir."

"Yes, I had the tattoo you ask about. You know what it meant?"

"That you were Morgan's man."

"*Ja, ja.* I was Morgan's man. Your uncle, too." X scratched the flesh of his thumb across the blade of the dagger. He eyed Kitto again from the corner of his eye, hesitating to go on.

"You can tell me. I do not think you could say anything that would shock me," Kitto said. So many surprises and disappointments he had survived in just a short time.

"I think you are wrong. But we shall see." X handed the knife back to Kitto.

"Sometimes we did things to people, we members of 'The Hand.' Things that leave me with no pride. We did these things always to protect our interests and our silver." X tugged at his beaded beard. The beads rattled. "A customs man would need to be convinced he would lose his ears if he did not listen better, or a merchant underselling us on broadcloth might dangle from a second-story balcony by his ankles."

Overhearing, Sarah aimed a worried glance at Kitto. He looked back at her steadily, nodding. She turned her attention back to Bucket, who slapped at her hand.

"You tortured people," Kitto said. X shrugged.

"I say I am not proud. I am ashamed even. But there was worse," he added, pausing yet again before continuing. "Like with your mother."

Kitto felt his throat constrict. He forced himself to take a breath, demanding that he be steady before attempting to speak.

"You murdered my mother?" His voice had cracked. Kitto and the pirate stared at each other for a few long seconds that drew out like an eternity. Kitto wondered what he would do if this man were to admit to committing the crime that forever changed his life.

X pinched the bridge of his nose and closed his eyes. "Morris summoned me, through that vile creature of his, Spider, who was barely out of boyhood at the time, but vicious like a beaten dog. In the darkness of an alleyway

Morris handed me a small bottle. Some sort of dark liquid it contained. From Henry Morgan, Morris told me."

"What was it, in the bottle?" Kitto whispered.

"Poison. He told me the home, behind the shop of a young cooper." X tugged at the beads again. "I was to pour it into the stew pot. Simple as that."

A small silence followed. Kitto finally broke it.

"And did you?"

X grabbed furiously at the pouch at his belt and took a moment to extract a small handful of coffee beans. He held them in his palm a moment. Kitto could see that his hand shook. Disgusted, X squeezed the beans in his fist and hurled them into the fire.

"I made it to the alley behind the home, and I saw the stew pot through a shuttered window." Kitto held his breath. X continued. "I saw a woman tending it. A *woman*! She had a spoon she dipped into the stew to test it. A woman . . . Never had I . . . only men before, you understand.

"I began to walk away, up the alley, but then I turned back around. To disobey, to refuse . . . I knew what it would mean for me. Maybe the woman deserved it, I told myself. So I went back and resolved to be done with the task quickly."

"Did you kill her?" Kitto whispered. X looked at him, letting his eyes travel down Kitto's body to the stump propped up on the rock.

"I intended, yes. I looked in again, through the shutter. This time I see the woman again. She dips the spoon into the stew and holds it out to a young boy, perhaps five years. The boy sips at the spoon, but the stew is hot and he hops about waving his hand in front of his face."

Kitto turned away, embarrassed at the tears filling his eyes. "And the little boy, he had a clubfoot?"

"*Ja, ja.* He did." X cleared his throat. "And that little boy was you. I have never felt shame like that, standing there in an alleyway, thinking of murdering a woman and a little cripple. I, who had lost my own *moeder* when still I was a boy."

"So what did you do?"

"I rapped on the shutter, and after a time, I convinced the woman to open the window and speak with me. I told her my name. I told her what I had been charged with doing and who had instructed me. I showed her the vial I carried."

Kitto took a deep breath, willing down the tears. "And what did she say?"

"She gathered the little boy—you—into her arms and brought you to me. 'This is my Kitto,' she told me. 'He is the world to me. Nothing less.'"

This time when the tears came, Kitto did not try to hide them. They rolled down his cheeks. Exquemelin pretended not to notice.

"And then she showed me something. She left for a moment and came back holding this dagger." X turned the knife in his hand. "She showed me the name inside it. Henry Morgan had given it to her, with a promise: If she were to make it so that blade met with my heart, then he would allow her to leave Jamaica and he would see her no more."

X stood abruptly, swept off his tricorne hat, and scratched at his graying hair with the tine of his hook. He stared up at the sky bleeding red toward the west. He did not wish to tell the boy too much. Not yet.

"And why did Morgan want you dead? Why then?" X dared not turn around when he answered.

"He had his reasons. That is all."

Kitto took the opportunity to sweep away his tears.

"So, essentially, you and my mother agreed not to murder each other?"

X giggled, turning around. His goofy grin reminded Kitto for a moment of Duck. "Does not sound like a difficult agreement to come to, eh? But, *oui*, that is what we agreed. And we each paid for this agreement."

Kitto sat up and swung his stump to the ground gently.

"I know how she paid. With her life. What did you pay?"

X raised his right arm into the air. "Spider and Morris came for me, with two other men. They dragged me off to the woods. Spider took my hand from me with an ax while Morris looked on, telling me I could not even be buried with the tattoo still a part of my body. I had dishonored my brethren."

"So they were to kill you, then?"

"*Oui, oui.* Of course! They took the hand, but not all the fight in me. I took a pistol from one of them and shot Morris. Good enough to grant me escape, not good enough to send Morris to the hell he deserves. I ran to the beautiful mountains of Jamaica, and they did not catch me."

"How did you survive?"

Exquemelin smiled. "My life was saved . . . perhaps my soul as well."

"A priest rescued you?" Kitto said. To this X let out a falsetto squeal of laughter that went on for several seconds. Finally he composed himself and poked Kitto in the shoulder.

"No, thank Jesus. I was saved by slaves, runaways. They took me with them deep into the mountains, where I met the most intriguing and beautiful woman the world has ever known." X closed his eyes and smiled sweetly up at the paling sky.

"You fell in love, then?"

"Oh, *ja*. And I made a whole new life. As a pirate."

CHAPTER 13:

Barrels

Exquemelin gave out a long whistle. Seawater dripped from the strings of beads at his chin, making them sparkle in the cave's glow. He stood atop the rise of sand beyond the main pool, turtles moving around his boots. Kitto struggled up the rise behind him with his crutch, and Ontoquas, Quid, and Pickle stood silently in the pool.

"*Ongelooflijk!*" he muttered. "Not to be believed. Sometimes the silly stories the buccaneers tell are true after all."

"You had heard about the nutmeg, then?" Kitto said.

"I heard about stolen treasure. Every one of the raiders of Panama did. We all spoke of it, bitterly, when we recrossed that jungle back to our ships with hardly enough silver in our pockets to even notice its weight." He stepped forward to caress the first neat staves.

Kitto hobbled over to the barrel that Ontoquas had broken through a few months before. He scooped up a handful of the nutmeg pods and offered his hand out to Exquemelin. The captain plucked one and held it toward the light.

"Men are stupid," X said. "I take this turd to Europe and turn it into gold. But here, it is just a turd." He placed it back into Kitto's hand. "Do not drop them." Kitto smiled.

"I think there are enough to spare."

"One or two, perhaps. How many barrels?"

"Sixty including this one, which we shall have to transfer out by bucket to keep them from getting wet."

"The other ones, they can take to the water?" X asked.

Kitto gave a firm grasp to the lip of a barrel nearest him. "We should check each before lowering it into the water, make sure it's sound, but yes, I believe they will hold up fine."

X nodded, but he did not look pleased.

"Should we start moving these bloody turtles out the way, captain?" Pickle asked, scratching at the tangle of matted hair atop his head.

X scowled. "Think, think. We must think this through!"

"We cannot leave the nutmeg here," Kitto said. "Morris will know about this cave. William will have told him to save the lives of his men."

X stepped away from the barrels toward the pool. He turned and sat on a large turtle as if it were a stump. The turtle withdrew his head in alarm and did not attempt to move.

"Where do we put the barrels, ah?" He flicked his fingers at his beard beads, making them dance. "Morris arrives, drops anchor somewhere. He and twenty men, perhaps, come ashore. It is then we must take the ship. He has how many you say, ah?"

Kitto shrugged. "At least thirty, I would say."

"We have twenty, counting the woman and the girl, neither of whom is useless."

"But we have surprise on our side," Kitto said, hopeful the captain would not back out of their arrangement.

"The jolly boats will ride low enough with our nineteen. No room for barrels."

Kitto saw the problem.

"Can we make more trips, perhaps? We take the ship first and then go back for the nutmeg?"

X stood up from the turtle—which immediately began to crawl away—and approached the barrels again. He tugged at one of them.

"Two boats rowing out in the night to the ship, that smells like danger to me. What if the watchman on Morris's ship gives a warning shot? The men on shore, they hear it. We cannot go back for barrels then. They will guard them from the rocks above. No."

"So we cannot leave the barrels behind in the cave, since Morris would then have them, but we have no way to bring them either."

"*Exactement.* Exactly."

Kitto felt a growing frustration at their predicament. No ideas were coming to him that would end up with both the barrels and them on Morris's ship unharmed. His mind a stew, Kitto leaned on his crutch and hobbled over to the smaller pool of freshwater.

Toward the back a steady trickle flowed off a bulge of rock, and Kitto lowered his mouth to it. The water was cool and refreshing. It made him think of Pippin. X had told him that crocodiles do not take to saltwater; they can swim in it but prefer freshwater for lounging about in. Kitto sloshed his crutch through the pool's water.

"What about Pippin?" he said aloud before considering.

"Eh?"

Kitto felt his heart skip a beat. "Pippin!" Kitto spun and hurried back over toward Exquemelin. "Could not Pippin stand guard here in the cave?"

"Stand guard over the barrels?"

"No, stand guard over nothing!" He explained his idea to the sea captain while X savagely tugged at his beaded beard.

"We remove the barrels and hide them somewhere."

"Where?"

"It does not matter. The far side of the island perhaps, where they will not be found. Why would Morris look for them if he knew they were located in this cave?"

X nodded, his blue eyes growing wider. "*Ja, ja,* keep going!"

"Morris arrives and puts himself and most of his men ashore. They try to get into the cave right away, but they can't because there is this terrifying lizard in the cave that attacks them!"

"Pippin is a crocodile. Not a lizard."

Kitto ignored him. "So they lose time trying to solve their dilemma, at least one night, and during that night we take the ship."

"What if there is more than one ship?" X said. "William's ship. What if they pursue us in her?"

Kitto waved a hand at the possibility. "Never. Even if the *Blessed William* is still afloat after the battle, William himself admitted the *Port Royal* was a faster ship."

"And what of Pippin? Will she be hurt? I do not want her hurt." Kitto thought it through, staring from the cave passage to the pool where he imagined Pippin would happily lurk when she was not making a feast of turtles.

"How would they hurt her?" he said. "My mum shot her, and that did little."

"She has nasty scratches," X said, shaking his head.

"Even so, getting weapons into this cave? It would be next to impossible to do without wetting the powder or the pistols . . . And even then, it would not be enough to kill Pippin."

X paced, nodding. "*Ja, ja.* I know Morris. He would be patient. He would wait until Pippin left the cave, or he would lure her out."

"All we need is one night!" Kitto said. "Morris would find out in a day or two that the cave held nothing, but by then we would be far to sea and they would not know how to follow us."

"And William? We must take him with us."

Kitto agreed. "And the other crew, at least the loyal

ones. And my brother Duck." X threw Kitto a look. He had been told about the boy but had kept to himself his estimation of how long it would be before Morris pitched him overboard.

X chased away the grim thought by slapping Kitto on the back hard enough for it to sting. Kitto grinned.

"*Briljant!* If I did not know better, I would say you must be of William Quick's blood!"

Kitto laughed, shaking his head at the pirate's error. "But I am! I told you he is my uncle." X stopped laughing abruptly. A moment of confusion clouded his features for a moment. Then he rapped himself on the forehead and smiled.

"Of course! I am a fool." X turned to snap in the direction of Quid and Pickle. "Why is it we stand here! *Venez, les petites filles!*" he shouted, beckoning with the sweep of his arm. "Move the bloody turtles, we have work to do and not so many moments!"

CHAPTER 14:

Waiting No More

The work of moving the barrels took all day. Only a handful of the pirates could actually swim—a fact that still astonished Kitto about most seamen—so working in pairs the swimmers would start out in the cave, wrestle a barrel out into the pool, then shove it along out the tunnel and into the open surf. The barrels were buoyant, though barely: Only three or four inches of oak showed above the waterline when they were rolled into the pool. Once through the narrow passage the way was difficult, as the rolling waves pushed the barrels back toward the cliff face. The task required both swimmers to push and prod the barrel ahead of them, round the rocky head, and make for the beach about fifty yards beyond, where the rest of the band waited to fetch the barrels and haul them to a new hiding place Quid had picked out on the opposite end of the island.

Kitto and Ontoquas teamed up to assist with the swimming crew. Kitto knew he would be useless at the overland tasks, and he could not bear the thought of watching while everyone else maneuvered the nutmeg barrels that had had such a profound effect on the course of his life. Over the next several hours he and Ontoquas had transported a dozen barrels from the cave pool to the party of sweating men waiting at the beach, Van among them. Sarah worked back at the camp, cooking up strips of turtle meat over an open pit fire and keeping Bucket at a safe distance. Periodically she came down to the beach with Bucket in one arm and a bundle of browned meat in the other to distribute among the grateful men.

X and Fowler spent the morning out in the jolly boats, surveying the island to get a better sense of where Morris—or any approaching ship, for that matter— would likely drop anchor. When they returned after several hours of rowing, the answer seemed clear to them. The island was difficult to access; on all sides but one it was ringed by a series of reefs ranging from a quarter to about a half mile out. Only a stretch along the southeast end was clear. Certainly an approaching ship would drop anchor there, quite near to the entrance to the cave, in fact, and send in boats to the wide beach nearby.

The barrels now huddled in a dense stand of palm trees and various greenery at the northwest end of the island, draped in layers of cut brush they had secured with stones and rope. If all went according to plan, the company would steal a ship and sail off, returning in the middle of the night to the other end of the island, where they would make quick work of retrieving the nutmeg.

* * *

Kitto stood with his crutch at the edge of the beach when X and several of the pirates—including Little John—returned in the jolly boat after depositing Pippin at the mouth of the cave entrance.

"Did Pippin not go inside?" Kitto called to them. X splashed down into shin deep water from the bow, his expression pinched.

"Eh? Oh, *ja, ja*. My sweet Pippin was very brave."

Pulling up the boat nearby, Fowler rolled his eyes. "Aye, very brave. Took one look at a juicy turtle heading inside and took off after him like she went after Little John the other day."

"I worry about her. She has not been in the wild for a long time." X chewed on a knuckle and looked out to sea. "I wish my nanny was here. She says the right thing to stop this mad brain from spinning."

"Pippin will live like a queen in that cave," Kitto said. "Maybe you are worried that she will like it better than when she was under your care."

X made a sour face but then nodded. "Perhaps you are right. And she is one of us, after all. She must do her part, ah?" X slapped Kitto on the back. "Do you think this will work?"

If there was one quality of X's madness that Kitto truly appreciated, it was that he held no regard for status of any kind. X would comically insult any member of his crew should he feel they had stepped out of bounds. No one was untouchable, not even Sarah, who he teased now and again for her steadfast optimism. Likewise, X would seek advice of those he respected regardless of age—including Kitto—something Kitto's father had never done, nor even his uncle William.

Kitto rubbed his chin. "I think we will get our chance if Morris arrives. Our night, I mean. The part that worries me more is getting aboard the *Port Royal* without being seen."

X smiled. "That!" He shook his head. "That is child's play. You wait and see."

After three days on the island X had munched his way through the rest of his coffee beans. His mood declined precipitously, and he spent much of his day with his hat clenched in one hand and a fistful of his madly tangled locks in the other, as if considering whether or not to tear out his hair. Even Fowler, who seemed always ready to challenge X on any point of discussion, steered clear.

A watch rotation had been set up: one on the island's high point at the southeast, another on the northwest beach. Between those two points Exquemelin was certain they could see any approaching ship in plenty of time to make ready.

The days passed with painful slowness, and with each one Sarah's brow seemed to furrow deeper. Kitto would often join her down at the beach, holding her hand and looking out to sea. Sometimes they would speak of Duck, of the silly exploits he often got himself into, and over and over they would tell themselves that the little boy was a survivor—like Bucket, he would find a way into hands that would help him.

On the sixth day since Exquemelin and his band had arrived on the island, Ontoquas and Kitto were serving watch at the island's northwest end just before noon. Kitto had insisted that he, too, serve on the watch, but since his difficulty in hobbling around on the crutch meant that he could not spread an alarm quickly, X relented only when Ontoquas volunteered to serve with Kitto. The two of them, then, spent a few hours together each day. They filled the time by sharing stories about their lives as young children as they strolled the beach at the island's far tip. Kitto helped Ontoquas with her English and did his best to master a few words in Massachusett.

"Does it still hurt?" Ontoquas said. She and Kitto sat on a shelf formed by the edge of the forest and a small drop-off down to the sandy beach. Kitto had kicked up both his legs and was inspecting them against the brilliant white of the sand below.

"Sometimes. Mostly I just cannot quite believe that it is gone."

"Are you happy for this? You told me that the boys *tunketappin* beat you."

"Yes. And that was not the worst part." Kitto remembered the stolen glances from the adults. "Looks of pity were worse."

"Pity?"

"People on the street, they would look at me and

show sadness in their faces. They all thought my foot meant I was somehow tainted—bad or evil, in some way I could not help."

Ontoquas nodded.

"But you are not happy the foot is gone?"

Kitto shrugged. "Sometimes I am. Even if I am clumsier than I used to be, people won't look at me like they once did. They'll just see someone who got in an accident."

"Not someone who is evil."

"Yes. And I do not know why, but that just burns me." Kitto knew he was less able now than he had been with his clubfoot, yet he would be seen from here on in a better light by the world. He always knew how wrong those looks were, those beatings. . . . But once they were gone? Their absence would be a constant reminder of how bent the world was.

Can I stop myself from growing bitter? Perhaps my father's bitterness took its root from the same place. Kitto turned to Ontoquas.

"Is it like that with your people? Do those with bodies that are . . . not well made . . . are they scorned?"

Ontoquas looked at Kitto through her black bangs. She considered how to tell him that the ways of the *wompey* were strange, unnatural even. She knew a boy who was born with six fingers on one hand. People said that he had been blessed.

"No. It is not that way." She sat up and stared out at the crashing surf. "Was not," she said, her improved

English helping her to understand the implication in the verb tense.

For several minutes the two of them stared out to the blank horizon.

"If this all works, if we get away from this island," Kitto said, "where will you go? Will you try to go home?"

Ontoquas shook her head. "Home is gone. No home is left." She dragged a finger through the sand. "In Barbados I heard slaves talk about people like me in a place called Florida. Do you know it?"

Kitto shrugged. "Sounds Spanish."

"Yes. In Florida there are those who look like me, other People of the Sun, but different. Maybe I go there."

Kitto hoped not to offend his new friend, but he wanted to offer.

"If you would like, you could stay with us. With Sarah, Duck, and me. For as long as you like. If we live through all this, I mean."

Ontoquas turned to look at him. *Did she blush?* Kitto wondered. There was something soft in her look before she turned away.

"The other *wompey*, they will not like it," she said. It was true, of course. Kitto could not deny it. He laughed.

"I stopped caring what they thought a long time ago."

Ontoquas tried to imagine it, living as a Wampanoag among *wompey*. She had lived for years now among *wompey* who treated her like an animal. Could other *wompey* be as different as this boy here with her now? It was a decision for another day.

"What about the gold?" she said, avoiding a direct answer. "The gold and the silver and jewels we found. Deep in the cave. You do not want to tell this X about it?"

Kitto narrowed his eyes. "That part is odd. It is such riches, but Exquemelin does not seem to know about it at all. I am not sure that I should tell him, at least just yet. William never planned on all of this. If we can meet up with him again . . ." Kitto did not bother to finish his thought.

"Morris cannot get the gold?" Ontoquas said.

Kitto shook his head. "You and I could barely pass through that opening. Van could not even fit. And there was no boy on Morris's ship, just men. Even if they make it into the larger cave, they shall be none the wiser."

Kitto ran his hands through the sand. There was one part of this whole plan that still irked him.

"If we should succeed," he said, "—unlikely, but possible—have we not just succeeded in stealing? The gold, after all, was stolen from the Spanish."

Ontoquas shook her head. "No. The gold was stolen from the people of those lands. And they are dead."

Ontoquas's eyes froze toward a spot on the horizon out to sea. She stood suddenly and pointed.

"Ship!" she said. She reached a hand to Kitto and helped pull him to his feet. Kitto extended the spyglass that Fowler had handed to him when they relieved him of his earlier watch. He balanced one forearm on Ontoquas's shoulder so that he could peer through the instrument without falling over. The ship approached from the northwest, its masts aligned in almost a straight line, the bow pointing almost directly at the island. He could clearly make out the sails of the foremast and the great sail billowing behind it on the mainmast.

"Square rigger," he said. "And just one. I see no sign of a second ship."

"Is it this man, Morris?"

"I believe it is, yes."

After the first day on the island the pirates had moved their camp farther inland, wanting to make sure that when Morris arrived, there would be no sign on the beach of their occupation. That is where Kitto found them all gathered, along with Van and Sarah, who bobbed Bucket in her arms nervously while the boy sucked on a shard of coconut as big as his fist. Bucket's knuckles were grimed with white ooze. Ontoquas stood nearby, having run ahead of Kitto to relay the information. She gave him a smile from across the circle, glad that he had made it back.

They all formed a ring around Exquemelin, who had cleared the undergrowth away and drawn a rude sketch of the island in the dirt with the stub of a stick.

"Best check on their progress," X said, handing the spyglass Ontoquas had carried back with her to Black Dog. The towering man stepped forward and accepted the instrument wordlessly, then disappeared through the leaves toward the beach.

X squatted on his haunches and marked a spot just off the island's shore on the diagram.

"We hope they drop anchor roughly here and make to the shore with their boats. We count what number arrive to shore. It will likely be three parts out of four of how many crew total, which tells us how many to expect when we take the ship."

Fowler broke in. "We take it in the dead of night, aye?"

"*Ja, ja.* We take the ship in the night and we sail off."

"And we come back for the barrels?" Van said. X flicked his fingers at the beads on his beard again in thought.

"This part I do not love, but *oui*. We sail off. Morris watches his ship disappear, believing that never will he see her again. Then we return, very early perhaps. We row the jollies past the reefs and fetch the barrels, gone again after two trips at the most." X looked up at his men. He grinned his gold tooth at them.

"Is anybody else ready to be rich?"

X trained the spyglass to his eye. The *Port Royal* lay at anchor in gently rolling waves, its spars bare.

"Have they launched a boat?" Kitto asked. X handed him the instrument.

"Into the water it goes. Very exciting, no?" He poked Kitto's ribs. What Kitto felt could not be called excitement—something closer to nausea would be more accurate.

Kitto squinted through the spyglass, balancing his elbows against the rocks, being sure to let as little of himself show as possible.

"Oh, Kitto, do you see him? Can you see Duck?" Sarah said from behind him. He turned to watch her chew at her lip, her face tight with anxiety.

X, Van, Kitto, and Sarah huddled together atop the craggy rocks close to the crevice that shed light into the cave below. Kitto scanned frantically for some sign of Duck, but in all the deck activity of dozens of men, he could see none.

Duck, where are you? Still hidden?

"He is not there, Mum," Kitto said. "But that might be a good thing!" he added.

Sarah chewed on a knuckle now and willed herself not to cry. "Yes, it might be a good thing."

I do not see William, either," Kitto said finally. "I would have thought he would be on deck." His eye caught sight of a small, dark figure moving about, hauling a bucket with him.

"Akin! I see Akin!"

Now Van snatched away the telescope and peered through it. "It *is* him!"

"Stay down, lower to the rocks," X counseled.

"Now why is Akin the only one not locked away?" Van said.

Kitto held a hand to his brow. Without the telescope he could just make out the blur of activity on the deck.

"First boat is down in the water. Men are climbing into it." One of the men wore an oversize hat. Could that be Spider? Van handed the spyglass back to X, but Sarah stepped forward and snatched it away before he could take it. X scowled.

"I thought I was the captain here!" he said, but did not reach for the instrument. He turned to Van and Kitto.

"Please, boys. Check on my baby. She is there still, eh?"

Kitto motioned for Van to follow and together the two of them clambered over the rocks to the crack that looked down into the darkness of the cave below. While Kitto had served watch that day, Quid had fashioned a wooden leg for him out of a tree limb and the split bottom of a coconut shell. He attached straps to it with materials taken from the jolly boat stores, and with these Kitto had been able to put it on in little time after he had returned. The straps around his thigh and leg were not comfortable, but Kitto adjusted instantly to the contraption, and found it made movement a bit easier. He still carried his crutch, too, as he worried that putting all his weight on the healing stump would be both painful and detrimental to the healing process.

The crack was quite narrow, just wide enough for Kitto to pass through. He doubted that Van could fit. It was roughly six feet from end to end, and perhaps ten inches wide in the middle. The boys lay down on their stomachs and craned their necks.

"Don't fall in," Van advised.

"Good idea. There! Look at all the shells," Kitto said, pointing. He and Van had inched forward to poke their heads into the opening. It took a moment to see in the dim light, but once his eyes adjusted, Van too could see the wreckage of broken shells littering the sandy bank toward the back end of the cave.

"Pippin's been eating like a queen."

"Can you see her?"

"Hold my legs, will you?"

Van held while Kitto wriggled himself farther into the crack so that his shoulders passed through and he was able to peer deeper into the dark recesses of the cave. He squinted into the gloom.

Was that Pippin? There was a shiny something toward the back of the cavern, but whether it was the crocodile or just the pool that reflected the light he could not discern. Then Pippin made it easy for him by waddling out into the light.

"Hello, Pippin!" Kitto called. The reptile held a half-crushed turtle in her jaw that dropped to the sand when Pippin lifted her head to look up at Kitto with a dull curiosity.

"No, I am not coming in," Kitto said. "But be sure to eat anyone who does, right? Especially Morris or Spider. And chew slowly."

Kitto reached back for Van, who pulled him back roughly.

"Pippin there?"

"And looking tired of turtle."

"My baby!" X called. "She is well?"

"Yes, Pippin is fine. Any sign of Duck?"

Sarah still had the spyglass trained on the ship. Her sober look told Kitto enough.

"Have they lowered another boat?" X asked her.

"What? Oh . . . yes, they have. Still I cannot see Duck, though. Or William. Where can they be?" she fumed. X reached out for the instrument but Sarah pushed his hands away. X stuck his tongue out at her, then furrowed his brow.

"We shall not have long to wait now," he said. "If they know about the cave, they should make for it directly."

"I hope Spider goes in first," Van said. X settled his hat tighter onto his head.

"Bad for Pippin's digestion, that trash, but I think she could survive."

After an hour X was still hunkered low to the rock. He had finally cajoled the spyglass from Sarah. The boats had reached shore and the men had unloaded supplies well up from the cave entrance. Kitto and Van and Sarah awaited news.

"Jolly boat coming this way! Three men, is it? Two, and a boy."

"Boy?" Sarah sat up expectantly.

"A dark one."

"Oh."

Kitto risked a peek over the rim of rock. He could see the boat approaching, and from the looks of it, Spider was at the oars.

"Ah, yes. John Morris, the pig!" X spat. "He sits in the stern. They are rowing directly for the cave entrance." X turned to Van. "See how close you can get, but do not be seen," he said.

"Aye, aye, Captain," Van said, and turned to scrabble his way along the scree closer to the edge that overlooked the water. The wind swept his blond locks back as he crept along, agile and sure.

"I have waited a long time for this, Spider," Morris said. He dabbed a kerchief at the holes of his severed nose, then pulled back the fabric to glare disapprovingly at it. "A long time."

"Aye, Captain, that you have, sir," Spider said between strokes. "We have all waited for this day. I believe it when I sees it for myself."

Morris swept roughly at the sleeve of his black frock coat. "You saw Quick, Spider. There was no fight left in him after we took his ship. I do not believe he could have lied."

Spider turned to spit, intentionally missing Akin by only a few inches. "Aye. I think he was sweet on that woman, too. The one lost to sea. And the cripple. He kept looking out for them when we had him up on deck and transferred him to the naval frigate."

"No doubt they ended up with the sharks," Morris said. He pointed toward the base of the cliff. "That was a fortunate encounter with the HMS *Portsmouth*, Spider. A ship of the line of her size will not have any problems to contend with between here and Port Royal, a perfect escort for the *Blessed William*."

"Aye, sir. No Spanish ship would dare take her on."

"I do hate it that Quick is not here to watch us retrieve his pilfered treasure, though," Morris said. "He was a beaten man when we left him, yes, beaten but not broken. Seeing the barrels full of nutmeg come out of hiding and into our hands . . . I think that would have done the trick."

"And the other treasure, sir? The . . ."

"Ssst!" Morris hissed in warning. He raised a hand to his lips. Morris pointed a bony finger at Akin. His gaze turned to the cliff.

"There, Spider. That dark part of the rock there, just above the waterline. That is precisely how Quick described it. Row in as close as you are able."

Spider pulled away with the oar in his left hand, veering the rowboat in the direction his captain had indicated. A minute later they had drawn to within ten feet of the cliff.

"That is it. Remarkable. How is the depth here, boy?" Morris called up to Akin.

Akin stood at the bow and peered over the side into the water. "Ten feet, Captain! Deeper even."

Spider exchanged a meaningful look with Morris, then turned to Akin. "Look again, boy. I ain't wanting to run aground here and scratch up this fine boat." Spider eased one oar out of the oarlock.

Akin could see the bottom clearly and knew his first

reading to be accurate, but he wanted to look as compliant as he could. That was important. He had been the model of obedience since Morris first granted him the chance to be his cabin boy after he had promised that he detested William Quick and his horrid crew. With his freedom he had been able to keep Duck supplied with food up until Akin had been assigned to the *Port Royal* after they had met with the frigate.

Duck . . . Akin stared down into the clear water, wondering how the little one had fared, hidden in his barrel, bound for Jamaica.

Alone.

"I am looking, sirs. I see . . . I see . . . a turtle?" Spider lifted the oar free, turned it in toward the boat, and with its tip he jabbed hard.

"Take a closer look!" Spider said with a laugh. The oar blade struck Akin in the buttocks, knocking him forward and over the bow. He landed with a splash, then came up sputtering. He glared daggers at Spider while he treaded water.

"Well, look who knows how to swim!" Spider said, grinning widely.

"I have told you that I know how . . . *sir!*"

"Now, boy," Morris said to Akin. "Time to show your mettle, lad. That is a tunnel there in the wall. You see it?"

Akin turned in the water. He could see it easily, though how far back it went or where it led he was afraid to consider. "Aye, Captain."

"There is a cave inside, boy. A cave. Quick said there

would be enough daylight to see by. Head back into that cave and have a look around. There should be a collection of barrels. Find them, then come back out and give us the news."

Twenty feet above them, cowering behind a bulge in the crag, Van rolled over to look up at the heavens.

Oh, no!

CHAPTER 15:

Akin

"Kitto! Kitto! There's something wrong!" Van scrambled back over to where his companions awaited him.

X waved angrily at him. "Would you not scream it out, boy!" he hissed. "Quiet!"

Van ignored him. "Kitto! It's Akin."

"What? What of him?"

"Spider pushed Akin into the water. They just told him to go in first." Kitto blanched, then hurried over to the crevice and peered in. Nothing.

Think. Think. He looked up at Van.

"Quick now. Run back and fetch a rope."

"What for?"

Kitto looked down into the darkness again. Still nothing. "Akin can fit through this crack for sure. We can pull him out." Van nodded, then took off, clambering madly over the crags back to camp.

"Mum, please."

"What is it, Kitto?"

"Would you go too? You can get the pistols."

"No pistols!" X said. "Are you mad?" He eyed Kitto,

158

surprised at such a ludicrous suggestion. Kitto ignored him.

"You might need to shoot at Pippin to keep him from Akin." Sarah nodded and ran off in the direction Van had now disappeared.

X said nothing until Sarah was out of earshot. He cocked a head toward Kitto.

"I am not so quick as you, Kitto Quick: boy who would lie to his mother." Kitto shot X a look. X wagged a finger at him. "Boys, they should not lie to their mothers," X said with a rueful shake. "She cannot use the pistol. Not only would it hurt my baby, but it would announce our presence to Morris."

Kitto lowered his head down into the hole. Still no sign of Akin. Pippin's shadowy figure twitched at the edge of the freshwater pool. Kitto lifted his head out again.

"I am the only one of us who can fit through here," he said.

"And this your mother could not tolerate," X said with a nod of respect.

Kitto held out his crutch to X. "Perhaps you could lower me part of the way," he said.

At that moment, below the rocky outcrop that hid Kitto and X, Akin was weighing the importance of obedience. He treaded water outside the passage.

"You are sure, sirs?" he said brightly, feigning a smile. "This is the correct tunnel? I cannot see a cave inside," Akin said. He gripped the rock above his head.

"If we was sure, we wouldn't be asking you to go in, now would we?" Spider growled. "Get in there like the captain said!"

"Yes. Aye, aye." Akin turned around to face the darkness of the passage that wound toward blackness into the rock. He gulped. What were those old prayers of his people? He wished that he could remember one, but it had been too long. Akin reached out to paddle forward into the gloom when a sudden movement inside the passage stirred the water. Akin startled and pushed off from the wall, eyes wide in panic, until he saw the source of the movement. A tiny turtle a few inches across swam toward him, then dove down into the water and disappeared.

"Turtle!" Akin said, breathing a deep sigh. "I am not frightened of turtles," he told himself. He put his head down and started swimming forward into the darkness.

Above, Kitto lowered himself legs first with X's help as far into the crevice as he could go. X gripped him about his shoulders. With one hand Kitto reached about, dragging his fingertips along the stone below the lip of the opening. His fingers chanced upon a deep groove, and exploring it hastily, he found it fit most of his hand.

"There is a hold here," Kitto said to X. "I am going to try it."

"You want for me to let go?" X said in surprise. "Are you so brave, or a bit mad, too?"

"Just hold the crutch down to me so that I can grab for it if I need to," Kitto said. "Go ahead and let go," he said. X shook his head in disbelief, but slowly pulled away his fingers. Kitto lowered himself through the crack until his arms had straightened and he was dangling in empty space over the shining pool below.

"You are good?" X said, but Kitto did not answer. Instead, he scanned the sloping walls of the cave in search of a climbing route. He heard a faint splashing noise come from what seemed to be the passage leading out to the ocean. He twisted about to look down at Pippin.

The crocodile had heard it too. Pippin's head raised a few inches off the sand, but she remained otherwise still. Kitto risked unwedging his left hand so that he could run it along the dark rock face in the hopes of finding another hold. Above him X dangled down the end of his crutch, watching him and chewing the corner of his lip.

If I can find a way to climb down, then Akin can climb up. There must be a way!

His fingers felt something. *Yes!* Sure enough there was another crack, not quite so deep as the first, but still ample for a good grip. Kitto reached for it, and in so doing his body pendulated open to face the cave. He looked down, and saw that he hung perhaps eight feet from the surface of the water in the larger pool.

X pulled out the crutch and stuck his head into the crevice.

"What a stallion!" X said with undisguised admiration. "Better yet, a monkey!" He turned to Pippin, whose head had perked up at the sound of X's voice. "Hello, my pretty baby, baby, baby," he cooed. "You don't want to eat any skinny English boys today, do you, pretty baby? No, no, no. You save your appetite for the smelly Irishman, yes. He be here very soon, baby."

Akin swam through the passage and emerged from the darkness into the relative light of the cave. Quite a sight awaited him when his feet found purchase in the sandy bottom. To his left, hanging in space, was Kitto, spread-eagled, and farther along on the ceiling the head of a strange man with a tangle of a beaded beard emerged from a fissure of light and whispered sweet nothings toward something unseen deeper in the cave.

Akin rubbed the water from his eyes, then looked again. A smile of intense joy spread across his face.

"Kitto!" he said, flashing an incredulous smile. "Kitto, is that you? Why are you in the air?" He splashed closer to Kitto, away from the passage and into the center of the pool.

The speaking head at the ceiling spoke more loudly.

"Yes, Pippin, the stupid boy is talking, and making you think you are hungry. But no, you are not hungry."

"Akin!" Kitto hissed. "There is no time to explain. There is a crocodile back there. A crocodile!"

"No, Pippin. No, Pippin, dear!" The crocodile took three decisive steps forward so that she now stood in a bright patch of sunlight at the edge of the sandy bank overlooking the large pool. Akin looked up at the huge beast atop the rise. His eyes, wide with surprise and joy, now widened further with terror, the whites seeming to shine in the dim light.

Crocodiles have excellent vision, but the bright sunlight streaming down on Pippin left her dazzled for several moments, and the only movement she could see came above her in the form of Kitto's gently swinging foot and stump.

"I gave my love a cherry," X sang in a rich vibrato, *"that had no stone. I gave my love a chicken—"* X never finished the line, for just at that moment, Spider, who had swum underwater through the passage, came thrashing up at its entrance a few feet from Akin.

"What the devil!" Spider said, as the first thing he noticed was Kitto hanging from the ceiling. "You're alive!" he hissed. He sloshed in Kitto's direction just a single step, then he turned to look up at the sandy bank to his right.

Both her appetite and her curiosity truly piqued, the massive reptile launched herself forward. Pippin slid down the sandy bank on her belly and into the water, leaving a groove in the moist sand behind her. Before her front feet had entered the water, both Akin and Spider bolted for their lives. They dashed madly through the thigh-deep water in Kitto's direction.

Distracted by a tumult of bubbles underwater, Pippin's attention was drawn away for an instant by a large turtle that had chosen an inopportune moment to return to its breeding ground. Pippin whirled on the turtle, her massive tail sweeping out and knocking both

Akin and Spider off their feet and into the water.

Kitto looked on in helpless terror. X spat off a series of orders without realizing he spoke in Dutch. Spider found his feet first and grabbed Akin by the arms, holding him out like a shield in the direction where he thought the crocodile might surface.

Pippin's head broke through at the far end of the pool. In her mouth was half of the turtle, shell and all, shards jutting out between her teeth. Pippin whipped her head and the turtle hunk flew off and clattered against the wall of the cave. She eyed Akin and Spider with an expression that bore an uncanny similarity to a smile. Slowly Pippin lowered her head so that just the top of her snout and her eyes were above the surface, and she began to swim slowly toward the two figures at the far side of the pool.

"Let me go!" Akin struggled against Spider's terrible grip, but the man's crushing strength—fueled by his own terror—easily outmatched his. Closer inched the crocodile. Closer.

"Pippin, my sweet. Eat the big one! Very juicy, Pippin!" X called from above. Spider whirled about in confusion at the sound of the voice seeming to come from nowhere. He knew that voice . . . .

Kitto could watch no longer. He could see that Akin's life hung in the balance. He arched his back to swing his legs as best he could, and then as momentum brought them forward again he launched himself out into space. Kitto flew through the air just as he had intended, landing on Spider's back. Spider gave out a cry as Kitto's weight slammed into him, launching him and Akin in opposite directions.

Kitto plunged into the pool, disoriented. He opened his eyes beneath the water, trying to get his bearings in the torrent of bubbles, when Pippin's snout grew distinct right before him. Pippin launched himself at Kitto with terrific speed.

"No, Pippin!"

Kitto pushed himself backward with his good leg, breaking the surface. He kicked out with his wooden leg at Pippin. The crocodile clamped down on it and thrashed her head, whirling Kitto back and forth through the water. Kitto felt the false leg tear away from him and he threw himself in the opposite direction, finding himself at the bottom of the sandy rise quite near Akin. Pippin whirled about with her jaws clamped down on the stump, not yet realizing it no longer connected to flesh.

"Come on!" Kitto yelled, scrabbling up the sand. Akin followed him, and Spider, who had ended up on the far side of the pool, hesitated a moment, considering whether to swim out the passage or follow the boys. As making for the exit forced him closer to Pippin, Spider chose the latter.

Kitto and Akin reached the top of the rise together, just as Pippin hurled the splintered stump across the water. Akin pulled now at Kitto, trying to help him to stand, horrified to see that Kitto had now but one whole leg.

"Back there!" Kitto pointed past the single cracked barrel the pirates had left behind in the sand, and the two of them scrambled in that direction. Spider made it to the bottom of the rise and began to claw up out of the water.

In a moment Kitto and Akin had made it to the narrow crevice at the ground through which he and Ontoquas had crawled a week earlier.

"Go. Go in!" Kitto screamed, grabbing a fistful of Akin's hair and shoving him down toward the opening. Akin understood Kitto's intention and scurried in as quickly as he could. Spider reached the top of the rise, Pippin scratching her way up the slope a few steps behind. Kitto looked down to see Akin's ankles disappear into the tunnel.

Kitto crouched down to follow, but Spider reached him. He grabbed Kitto by the arm. Kitto spun and hurled out with his fist, a fierce blow that struck Spider square in the nose. Spider's grip slipped from Kitto, and again Kitto dove for the crevice.

Spider turned to see the crocodile racing toward him with frightening speed. He gave out a cry and snatched up the half broken barrel at his feet. He threw it at he approaching beast. The barrel plummeted down and landed on top of Pippin's head, stopping her cold for just a moment. Pippin twitched, and the empty barrel flew off and clattered against the wall. Not daring to crawl after the boys, Spider retreated deeper into the cave, desperately looking for a place to hide himself.

Pippin stepped forward, her head snapping to the left to see Kitto's good foot disappear into the crack at the bottom of the wall. Pippin launched herself at the crack.

Kitto got through the opening just in time, yanking up his legs inches ahead of Pippin's snout. The crocodile jammed her head into the crack, and inside there was just enough light for Kitto and Akin to see the full head of the crocodile enter into the dark passage with them.

Akin screamed in terror. Pippin whirled about, her mighty tail whipping back and forth as if might propel her wedged body deeper into the tiny crevice.

"She can't fit!" Kitto said, pushing at Akin to go deeper into the passage. "There is no way."

Spider, seeing the crocodile momentarily distracted, charged forward to leap over Pippin, but the beast's gyrating tail lashed his foot midair, and Spider fell forward in a heap. Pippin felt the contact and sensed that the quarry in front of her had already escaped, but the larger one behind was not yet out of her reach. Spider found his feet and ran.

X, still witnessing the chaos from above, watched as Spider reached the top of the sandy bank. "Pippin!" X called. "Get over here, girl! Come eat this ugly devil!" Spider's attention diverted for an instant, dazzled by the sunlight above him.

Pippin's great claws dug into sand and rock now, forcing herself backward out of the crack. In a trice she was free.

"Exquemelin!" Spider howled in midair as he dove headlong into the large pool, then thrashed away for his life.

"Get him, Pippin, my love! *Krijgt die schoft!*"

Spider had just reached the tunnel by the time Pippin was gliding herself down the sandy bank on her belly.

Within the cave, Kitto clenched his eyes. *Oh, please, God! Spider cannot make it out! He will warn the others!*

CHAPTER 16:

Disarmed

Waiting on the rowboat, Morris sensed that something had gone very wrong. He could hear the muffled cries of a great battle, but could not imagine what transpired within. He drew a pistol in each hand and stood in the rowboat, the barrels aimed at the dark passage, when Spider shot out into the open screaming, his fiery hair plastered down over his wide eyes.

"It's coming!" Spider wailed, his arms revolving wildly in the water. Morris trained the pistols toward the half-submerged tunnel.

"What is coming, man?" Morris said, ready to fire at whatever emerged. But Spider could not answer. Quite suddenly Spider was gone.

Morris rushed to the gunwale, bewildered. He leaned over the water, the sunlight playing on the blue surface obscuring his view. Sure enough, he could make out a dark swirl of activity. Morris dropped both pistols into the bottom of the rowboat and lifted one oar from the oarlocks. Would it be long enough? Morris flipped the handle end high into the air and drove the oar blade down into the water, letting the shaft run through his open hands so as not to lose it. The blade struck something, but he could not tell what. Again Morris drove the oar down into the water. Again.

The shape rose up, and as it became more distinct Morris could make out Spider's upturned face, the whites of his eyes wide, his orange locks streaming back.

Spider broke the surface wailing in pain and terror just a few feet from the rowboat. He reached out and by luck grabbed hold of the oar shaft. Morris heaved, tumbling backward into the boat. Spider's grip held true, and he was yanked from the water and over the rowboat's gunwale.

"What has happened to you, man?" Morris said. Spider seemed to be bleeding from all parts, his blood brightly staining the bleached bottom of the rowboat. Morris dropped the oar and reached down to turn the man over. Was he too late?

As he righted Spider, he could see one gash along his side, probably the point he had been struck first and pulled under the water. But Morris had seen his share of battle wounds, and this one looked endurable. As he continued to turn Spider onto his back, though, a grievous injury came into view: Spider's right arm was gone, ripped clean off at his shoulder. Dark blood surged from the wound.

"God, man!" Morris flipped Spider again so that the wound might be pressed against the bottom of the rowboat. Spider moaned, trying to say something.

"X . . . ," he said.

Morris ignored him and chanced a look over the gunwale again to see what could have caused such an injury, but whatever it had been was gone.

"Do not move, Spider!" Morris said. He lifted the oar back toward its oarlock. Suddenly a mighty and unseen force collided with the rowboat, throwing Morris onto his back in the bow. He barely had time to lift his head before he saw Pippin's enormous snout come up over the gunwale. The crocodile opened wide a mouthful of huge triangular teeth and snapped down on the metal oarlock and the wood to which it was fastened.

Morris could hear the wood splintering beneath the beast's strength. He leaped up and charged at it, rearing back and delivering a withering kick with the toe of his boot. The crocodile took the strike without notice, wrenched her head to one side, and the entire oarlock— along with a chunk of wood to which it was connected— splintered off from the boat. The rowboat tipped dangerously, then righted. Pippin slipped silently below the water.

"Come back here, you devil!" Morris reached for his discarded pistols, found them, and leaned over the side. At that precise moment Pippin shot up out of the water and snapped her jaws down on the two pistols. Morris squeezed the triggers of both weapons, and they exploded. He reeled back, falling, and landed again in the bottom of the boat. The beast was gone. Morris lifted his hands before him, grimly happy to see they were still both attached to his body.

Again he stood and looked over the side—with more caution this time. Obscured in the shadowy blue waters, a dark reptilian form glided swiftly in the direction of the cave entrance. Morris lost it in the reflection of the bright sunlight on the surface.

Exquemelin nearly wet himself, so hard was he laughing. His eyes streamed with tears that ran down his face. This was too good. Too good. Van scrambled toward him, a coil of rope over his head and shoulders, Sarah just behind with a pistol in each hand.

"Where is he? What has happened, you madman!" Van said, breathless. X lurched and writhed with hilarity, unable even to take a breath. All he could do was point toward the crack leading down into the cave below.

"Where is Kitto?" Sarah said, peering down into the hole in a panic. X gestured again, the woman's anxiety taking just an edge out of his enjoyment.

"Kitto . . . he is fine," X managed, then crawled over the rocks toward where he could risk a peek at what was happening in the rowboat.

Van lowered his head through the crack.

"Kitto! Kitto!" he hissed. He turned an ear inward. Did he just hear a call of response?

Van stood to shrug off the coil of rope. Sarah peered down into the crack and came up with a smile of relief.

"It is Kitto! Quickly, let us get him out of there."

Kitto and Akin had begun to extricate themselves from the tunnel as soon as Spider had fled with the crocodile on his heels. Just moments after they had emerged again they heard Van's voice calling. Now the dangling end of a rope was being lowered into the cave.

"Quick, now!" Kitto said. "Let's get out of here." He looped an arm over Akin's shoulders and hobbled toward the rope.

"Your foot? Has the beast taken your foot?" Akin said, looking down at Kitto's stump.

"No. I shall explain that later." Akin reached out and took the offered rope in his hands, a smile spreading on his face when he looked up and could make out Van above him.

"Grab hold, Akin!" Van said, continuing to feed the rope down. "I'll get you out of there in a trice." Sarah stood just to the side of Van, widening her view of the scene below. She was the first, then, to see the movement at the far end of the pool by the passage leading to the ocean. It was no turtle she saw.

"Kitto! The crocodile! It is coming!"

Kitto turned away from the rope just long enough to see that Sarah was right. Pippin was swimming toward them, her sinuous tail curling through the water.

Van had lowered several yards of rope down now. It coiled into a small pile on the sand at the boys' feet. Kitto and Akin grabbed two fistfuls of rope each, but the rope was too thin to attempt to scale it.

"Van! Get us out of here!" Kitto said. Pippin's tail whipped. Her half-submerged head aimed straight at the boys, the black slit of her pupils bearing down on them. If she had been wounded by Morris's shots, Pippin did not show it.

Van heaved with all he had, feet braced on either side of the crack. He lifted both boys from the ground and managed to work one hand before the first so that Kitto and Akin hovered a foot off the ground. Sarah leaped in, grabbing a handful of rope below Van's hands.

"Exquemelin, damn your eyes!" Sarah barked. "We need you!" Sarah's back straightened, lifting the boys another foot just as Pippin's groping claws struck sand at the bottom of the bank. Van worked his hands around Sarah's—leaving the entire boys' weight in her grip for a moment to do so—and grabbed another section of rope.

X's laughter died on his lips. He sprang across the bouldery cliff top with the agility of a monkey. Pippin had propelled herself just to the top of the embankment as X shouldered his way between Van and Sarah to get a handful of the line.

"Hang on, Akin!" Kitto said. "Lift your feet up!" The boys could see that the crocodile was craning its neck upward, her huge mouth a chaos of teeth set in mottled gray and pale flesh. The boys lifted their legs so high they were practically above their heads. Pippin snapped her jaws shut with a clack.

X heaved with a groan and the boys shot upward, but then jerked to a stop. Pippin had shifted, and now all three hundred and more pounds of her flesh had settled onto the rope.

"Weer!" X said. "Again!" Van and Sarah grabbed

below and strained against the hemp. Akin and Kitto rose another foot, the tight line sliding slowly beneath Pippin's leathery belly and along one side of her skull.

Seeing her prey disappear, Pippin snapped again, this time at the stretched rope. Her teeth sank into the fibrous hemp. Pippin pulled, backing herself down the slanted embankment. Akin and Kitto sank several inches toward the sand.

"Pippin! No, my sweet! *Ma bien-aimée!* Let go the rope!" X groaned. The black slits in Pippin's eyes widened a fraction, and the crocodile pulled back another six inches. Van and Sarah were knocked aside as X lost his balance and was dragged headfirst into the crack, sending Kitto and Akin plummeting downward another two feet. Akin let out a scream, thinking the end had come.

X's body was jammed into the crack, the rough crags ripping through the elbows of his frock coat. His grip held true, but then Pippin pulled back another step, and the rope began to slip through his hands.

"You must climb! Climb to me, lads! *Rapidement!*" Akin's grip was higher than Kitto's, and he scrambled hand over hand up the rope, the rigid line making climbing just possible. Kitto moved up more slowly, jostled and abused by Akin's kicking legs. In a moment Akin had reached X's hands. He clung to the pirate's wrists, further upsetting the man's grip and sending Kitto plummeting another foot.

"My legs, Kitto!" Akin said. "Take hold of me!" Kitto reached up with his right hand and grabbed Akin's ankle. He let go of the rope and the two of them swung out over the sandy embankment, Kitto's only foot just a few inches over the sand.

"Pull me, woman! Van! Pull me up!" X croaked. Sarah and Van grabbed X about the shoulders and armpits, the soles of their boots scratching and rooting to find a solid purchase. The boys rose.

Pippin, feeling no tension now on the rope, released her grip and instead clawed her way back up the sandy rise. She lifted her snout up at the swinging legs just above. Kitto reared back and dispatched a savage kick to the crocodile's chin. Pippin's head recoiled, and then she simply grinned up at them as they slowly rose ever higher and out of reach.

Within a moment Akin and Kitto each had managed to shinny through the crack, and the five combatants sank with exhaustion onto the rocks, Sarah clutching a fistful of Kitto's shirt. It was several seconds before any of them had the breath to speak.

"Pippin," X said. "You must forgive her. She is usually better behaved."

Kitto scowled at the captain. "Indeed you are a madman," he said, and then they all were laughing, none more than X, who remembered all over again the comedy he had witnessed out on the open water.

"Pippin would have had a nice meal of the two of you *jongens*, but her appetite was a bit satisfied." X giggled his high-pitched giggle. The others turned on him.

"What do you mean?"

"That vile turd, the one who took my hand from me. 'Spider,' they call him?"

"Is he dead?"

"Perhaps. This I don't know. Morris pulled him from the water, but the blood—it was beautiful!—and it was everywhere." X's giggling stopped and his face went grim.

"What is it?" Sarah said.

"He heard my voice," X said. "*Oui, oui.* He did. We hope that he dies and quickly, or Morris will know."

"Know what?"

"He will know he is not alone on this island."

Fortunately for the pirates and their new allies, Spider was in no condition to relay important information. He managed to mumble something about "X" and "The Hand" to Morris before slipping into unconsciousness in the rowboat, but this was lost on Morris, who strained at the oars to get Spider to shore. He doubted that Spider would survive, but he had seen men overcome such wounds. It could be done if one acted swiftly.

When he came around the bend in the cliff side he saw the small gathering of the crew at the beach.

"Fire! Prepare a fire, immediately!"

Spider would need to be burned.

CHAPTER 17:

Missing Duck

Dusk lay heavily over the jungle. Kitto and Van and Akin stood shoulder to shoulder in the huddle of men.

Sarah and Ontoquas stood a few steps off, Bucket in Sarah's arms. Akin had broken the news to Sarah—that he and Duck had been separated, and that Duck had continued on toward Jamaica after being hidden in the *Blessed William*, accompanied by a naval frigate. Sarah's frustration and worry grew so acute at this information that she found no other consolation but in holding the tiny baby. Bucket's eyes were closed, but he rooted about with a beckoning mouth, and Sarah bent her pinky finger to let him suck on a knuckle. Bucket gummed her finger and went still.

"You are certain, Roger, that the barrels are well hidden?" Fowler raised his chin.

"They could walk right by them and not see, in broad daylight even."

"And the winds, they will not blow the brush off?"

"I told you it was done, din't I?"

"*Ja, ja.*" X surveyed the faces around him. He felt

an odd surge of pride. "Then it is nearly time, *mes amis.* Tonight we take the ship, and if all goes well, we are sea dogs again by dawn."

"Let's hope the worms haven't had their way with this one," said Coop, a usually silent sailor with a tangle of teeth.

Kitto felt his stomach churn. It would be the second time he had taken part in a night raid of a ship at anchor. The first time was just a month ago in Cape Verde, when he had scaled the anchor cable of a ship in order to get on board and free Duck from slavery. Now again here he was. He and Van exchanged grim looks.

"You all right?" Van said. Kitto nodded.

"Butterflies."

"Me too."

"Akin, tell it again. I need to hear it again."

"About Duck?" Akin asked. Sarah nodded.

The sun had set nearly an hour ago. The band of pirates had scattered among the undergrowth of the northeast end of the island, hidden in deep shadow. Each found a place to lay his head before the attack, excepting the three who stood guard in case Spider had been in a condition to inform Morris they were not alone on the island.

Sarah reclined against the trunk of a leaning palm tree, Bucket in the crook of her arm. Ontoquas sat beside her, pressed to her side, watching Bucket sleep in Sarah's embrace. It occurred to Ontoquas that she should feel resentful, or jealous. This *wompey*, she had nearly taken over the task of caring for her little brother Bucket. But Ontonquas realized she did not feel these things: only relief, and the recognition that she, too, wanted to be mothered.

Ontoquas leaned her head into Sarah's shoulder, and Sarah unwound one hand from Bucket to run it lovingly over Ontoquas's cheek. Kitto and Van lay at their feet, staring up at a sky that was faintly studded with stars.

Akin cleared his throat and spoke in his high-pitched and clear voice.

"We sailed ten days. Ten days after the attack. And that whole time Duck kept himself hidden! With Julius the monkey."

"My monkey," added Van proudly, a blade of grass pinched between his teeth. Akin wagged a finger.

"Maybe not your monkey! He loves that little boy."

"Then I love that monkey. Go on."

"We caught sight of a navy ship, a frigate. Morris sailed for it and hailed it. He wanted to get the prisoners onto the frigate."

"Why? Why would he do that?" said Kitto.

Akin shrugged. "William Quick, he had told Morris what Morris needed to know."

Kitto propped himself up on one elbow. "That part is hard for me to believe," he said. "For seven years he kept it a secret. Why tell Morris now?"

Akin tucked his fingers into the dense curls of his hair. "After the battle was lost," he said, "Captain

Quick was a changed man. It frightened me."

"Was he wounded?" said Sarah. Akin shook his head vigorously.

"Perfect health. But like he was dead inside all the same."

"He still had his mates," Kitto said. "And his life. I would have thought his greed would have been strong enough to survive anything." Van looked at him.

"Maybe he lost something in that battle closer to his heart than his greed," Van said. Kitto knew what he meant. He stole a look at Sarah, and their eyes locked a moment, but then Sarah looked away and said nothing.

"Morris had what he needed," Akin continued. "But with Quick on board, there was still a danger of escape. He wanted Quick on board the frigate. It was heading straight for Port Royal."

"But Duck?" Sarah said. Akin nodded vigorously.

"Yes, Duck." Akin scratched at the crow's nest of hair atop his head. "I had just brought him some bacon— they had killed a hog two days before. Duck loves the bacon!

"He and Julius were in the barrel, quiet as mice. The *Blessed William* was to follow the frigate and head for Port Royal, while Morris's ship turned into the wind and sailed here."

Akin cast his eyes down. "I tried to stay with Duck, but I had volunteered to be cabin boy for Morris. I thought I could help Duck that way. And I had Morris fooled! He believed me. Too well, I fear. That day he had me moved over to the *Port Royal* just before we left the other two ships." Akin's eyes darted to Sarah. "I am so sorry, madam."

Sarah attempted an encouraging smile. "It is all right, son," she said. "You did your best. It is more than any of us were able to do for him." She blinked her eyes a few times to quell her tears and began to rock Bucket slowly.

Akin perked up. "He was very good in the barrel, Duck was! Very good. We had made it a game of how long he could be in there before I could hear him or Julius move around. At first they were not good at the game. But then they were better."

"Hard to believe," quipped Van. "Of Julius, I mean."

"The monkey, he loves Duck. He never left the boy. Not ever," Akin said. Van felt a lump in his throat. Good old Julius. He swallowed.

"I hope Julius keeps quiet too," Van said. They all thought solemnly for a moment.

"How will he eat?" Sarah whispered. None of them had an answer for her. Ontoquas rubbed her hand along the woman's arm.

Bucket and Van and Akin were able to sleep, but the others lay awake in edgy anticipation. They did not speak, but closed their eyes and waited for the signal.

Sometime well into nightfall Kitto sat up. He could hear someone thrashing through the underbrush, making no attempt to move stealthily. X swept aside the wide leaves of a large tropical shrub to look down on them. His white and gold teeth flashed a grin in the moonlight.

"*Vous vous réveillez,* my little pigeons," he whispered. He gave Van a lighthearted kick, and Van shot up from the ground with glazed eyes.

"Take hands, all of us," Sarah said. She reached out and took Ontoquas's hand. Ontoquas reached for Kitto. Kitto, in turn, looked up to Exquemelin, the hardened pirate. X rolled his eyes but took a knee and reached a hand out to Kitto and to Van. Akin made a space for himself between Van and the pinky toe of Bucket's chubby foot.

It was dark. Kitto lowered his head and closed his eyes and spoke to himself during the silent prayer.

I have done this before, haven't I? And alone, then. And I can do it again.

We shall succeed in getting to the Port Royal *unobserved.* Kitto imagined a dark and lifeless ship, pictured himself and Van scaling up the anchor cable. *We climb up and lower lines for the others to follow. No one will hear us.* Despite his silent words, Kitto's imagination ran from him a moment, and he saw in his mind a sailor on watch seeing them and calling out.

No! We will not be seen. And even if we are, then . . . He did not want to imagine that. It was too horrible. *If need be, then I can do it. I will do anything to see us safe again.*

Kitto opened his eyes and turned to Sarah. Her eyes were squeezed tight and she gnawed her lip. He wondered what she prayed for. Was it Duck? Bucket? Himself? All of them together? He took a deep breath and told himself once more that he would be brave.

"Let us go," he said aloud. Sarah opened her eyes and nodded. Together they rose and made for the jolly boats that the pirates had dragged from hiding down onto the beach.

CHAPTER 18:

Night Moves

Kitto and Van and Ontoquas rode in the first boat with X and Quid and a handful of the other men, each crowded shoulder to shoulder, four men at the oars. The surf was light and the wind easy, and it had taken little effort to get the boats out into the rolling waves and make for the southeast end of the island. Kitto and Van each carried two loaded pistols in their belts, although they knew they could only be used as a last resort, as the idea was to take the ship without alerting Morris and the others on shore that the ship was under attack. Van also had Kitto's dagger at his back. He needed it for the task he had volunteered to do. Ontoquas perched in the prow of the boat. A clutch of her crude arrows was tucked beneath her sash belt, and her bow leaned against her side.

"This must bring back memories," Van whispered to Kitto, but before Kitto answered Quid grunted behind them and shook his head slowly. They rode the rest of the way in silence.

Kitto reached down to caress his stump. Quid had

fashioned him another wooden leg just that day from a tree branch and fastened it skillfully to a split coconut. It served the purpose, but it would be some time before Kitto's wound had desensitized enough to make walking on the wooden leg painless.

He hoped they could take the ship without killing. His dreams still haunted him, dreams of the day in his father's workshop when his entire world crashed around him, when he witnessed a murder and committed one himself. *Was it murder?* he wondered. He was defending himself, was he not? Did that matter? For that he had no answer. Surely in the eyes of the law he would be found guilty.

What about in the eyes of God?

It seemed like they had been rowing a long time before Kitto could look out and see they were about to round the narrow end of the island and begin their approach. Ontoquas saw it too, and she and Kitto locked eyes. To Kitto she did not seem afraid. He wished the same of himself. Perhaps Ontoquas had seen enough horror not to fear it any longer.

Kitto chanced a look backward, and between the two rows of men laboring at the oars behind him he could make out the other jolly boat, Sarah and Bucket a blanketed huddle in the stern.

It was not long before the boat was passing the entrance to the cave. It lay in deep shadow some hundred yards off. X would have liked to steer even wider, knowing that it would be a likely place for Morris to leave a watchman, but any farther out and the jolly boats would be caught up in the wash of the reefs.

Van hunkered down and scanned the horizon. He tapped Kitto and pointed. Kitto could see nothing until he, too, leaned down to the line of the gunwales and could make out in the distance the silhouetted figure of the ship, a darker shade of black set against the faint glow of the horizon. Less than a half mile away it lay, swung out on the ebbing tide so that the he could make out each of its three bare masts.

At X's signal three of the rowers stopped and repositioned themselves so that Quid could take an oar in each hand and continue as the only rower. The first set of oarlocks had already been muffled with rags. Quid's tattooed scalp glowed in the moonlight, the checkerboard pattern glimmering.

Quid steered the jolly boat toward the bow of the *Port Royal,* its anchor end, the cable drawn tight as the ebbing tide tried its best to pull the ship farther out to sea. Kitto stole a quick look behind him and saw that all the men but X had drawn pistols and rifles. Pelota and the pirate named Coop bit down on dagger blades. X held up the spyglass, scanning the deck as best he could for sign of a watch.

"Sleep, you lazy dog," X whispered aloud. "There is nothing on the island to notice. And if you look out, it is to the sea you must look. *Oui, oui, oui.* Seaward, and not to starboard."

They drew closer. Kitto chewed the inside of his lip,

his stomach doing flips now, and assessed the grim faces of the men around him. Van shook a fist to him, as if to bolster him. Ontoquas withdrew from her sash her straightest arrow and nocked it on the string. X motioned to the ship behind them to stay toward the bows.

X must have seen someone! Kitto swallowed back his fear and tried to read X's face for some indication, but the pirate's pinched eyes revealed nothing. *Dear Lord, I will do anything. Anything.* Kitto wondered if God would still listen to him after what Kitto had done.

Know my heart, dear Lord. Please know my heart.

The hulking shadow of the ship loomed before them with a suddenness that made Kitto catch his breath. It seemed to glower down at them. Quid had steered expertly between the ship's hull and the taut anchor cable, so that the jolly boat lay in deep shadow from the moon that now hovered in the northwestern sky.

Van stood and took the cable in his hands, holding the boat steady. Kitto reached toward the hull on the opposite side, making sure to keep the jolly boat clear from banging up against the oak planks.

From the stern Pelota rose and made his way soundlessly past X and Quid, the spine of a large dagger still clenched in his teeth. A coil of rope wrapped about his shoulders. Kitto recognized the black metal contraptions attached to the ends—grappling hooks. Pelota maneuvered around Van and took the cable in his hands. Kitto watched Pelota look back to X. The captain scanned the towering ship above them. He nodded to the young man.

Kitto remembered how difficult it had been for him to scale the anchor cable in Cape Verde. Pelota made it look as easy as climbing the ratlines. In just a few seconds he had reached the hawsehole. Setting the point of one hook against the wood, Pelota managed to flip himself upward so that he straddled the line, riding it like a horse. He set the hook higher up into the wood, taking the time to embed it well. Kitto blinked in astonishment to see that Pelota had managed to stand up on the cable, and just a few seconds later he had disappeared over the rail.

They waited, all of them, shrouded in shadow.

Ontoquas stood. The arrow she had nocked she removed and put between her teeth. She slipped her bow over her head and turned toward Van, who gave her a questioning look. X pointed with authority back at her seat, but Ontoquas paid him no heed. Then, without any signal and in blatant disregard of the plan that X had set out for them back on the island, Ontoquas sprang up and took hold of the cable.

No! Kitto thought. *Let them do it. Do not take the risk!*

Ontoquas did not pause to consider her actions, but climbed up with even greater agility than had Pelota, dodging a weak attempt by X to lay hands on her. She scaled the cable, and in a moment she was over the rail.

Morris slipped out of the hammock his men had strung for him between two palm trees overlooking the beach. He gave a perfunctory check on Spider huddled in the hammock nearby, seeing only that the movements of his chest indicated he still lived. The cauterization had been messy work. It took three men to hold Spider down when the surgeon took the blazing iron to him. Spider had raved madly, talking all sorts of gibberish.

And why had he mentioned Exquemelin? Morris wondered. *A guilty conscience perhaps?* he thought. *No, not from Spider. Just made insensible from the pain.* Morris had seen others do no less.

But it was not concern for Spider's health that roused Morris from a restless sleep. He was there, on the island, and yet he did not have either treasure: neither the barrels of nutmeg, nor the fabulous riches from the *Santa Tristima*. Ah, the gold, the jewels, the handcrafted gold crucifixes. An incredible haul he had stumbled upon that day in the jungle while secreting off the nutmeg, only to have it and the nutmeg—and nearly his life—stolen from him by William Quick.

Had Quick time to peruse the treasure? Morris was sure he had, although Quick had not mentioned it when he had taken him and what remained of his crew into his custody. Would Quick know that Henry Morgan himself did not know about the second treasure?

William Quick must hang. Quickly. Before he comes out of his dazed stupor of loss and reveals all to Morgan. Morris knew that if Morgan found out about his attempted treachery, his life would be in peril.

Morris stepped down onto the loose sand of the beach, noting his uneven shadow cast upon the rippling sands.

Would both treasures truly be in the cave, as William Quick had attested? Surely the man could not have been lying. He had nothing left for treachery. Morris allowed himself a small smile and sigh of pleasure as he made his way down to the beach. Seeing Quick so miserable was a pleasure he thought he might never enjoy.

But still his hands were empty, and until they cupped the riches he sensed must be tantalizingly close, sleep would not come.

"Anything I can get you, Captain?" Morris glared at the man who approached him. Hardly was he a man in fact, having just enjoyed his nineteenth birthday before he set sail with Morris back in New York. "Flop," they called him, a scant figure, lanky, who moved with the unease of a teenager. Morris knew nothing about him except that he was an excellent shot, better even than Spider.

"No. You are the watch this hour, ah . . . ?"

"Flop, sir. Aye, sir. On watch until Simpson relieves me." Morris pointed away from him down the beach.

"Go that way," he said. Flop recoiled in obvious fear, realizing he had erred by approaching the man.

"Aye, aye, Captain."

Morris watched the young man go, mildly disgusted. A captain should not be disturbed. The boy was too green to know even that. Morris had been too kind to these men; he would be sure not to spare the cat-o'-nine-tails on the final leg back to Jamaica. He turned to his left where the cliffs rose that hid the cave.

My fortune is hidden inside that rock with some demon guarding it, he thought. *No matter. I, too, can be a demon.* Morris turned to face the sea and produced a spyglass from his coat pocket. He lifted it to his eye and picked out the *Port Royal,* its three masts nearly aligned from his vantage. The bow of the ship faced him.

Morris snatched the spyglass away for a moment. He squeezed his eyes shut, rubbed them, and lifted the instrument again. He squatted down on his haunches and stared some more. He stood again.

For the first time in years, John Morris broke into a run.

CHAPTER 19:

Boarding

Ontoquas set her feet against the smooth planks of the ship's fo'c'sle deck, her arrow again nocked. Pelota saw her the moment she came over the rail, and if he was unhappy to see her there, he did not show it. He walked from the midship, bent at the waist, staying in the deepest shadows possible.

When he reached the girl, he said nothing, but held up two fingers. Ontoquas nodded. *Two men at the watch.*

Pelota left Ontoquas and moved to the rail she had come over. The coils of rope and hooks lay in a pile on the deck. Pelota worked at unwrapping the first rope while Ontoquas made her stance. She shot best kneeling, so she bent onto her right knee and set her left foot firmly. She stared down the dark ship.

Yes, she could hear it now: two men talking in low voices. A faint yellow light shone toward the stern and then was gone. *Lighting a pipe.*

Pelota had set the first hook and tossed its line over the rail when they both heard the sound of approaching footsteps. Pelota scrambled for the shadows, and

Ontoquas slipped behind the black pillar of the foremast.

The fo'c'sle deck of the ship was reached by a set of stairs leading from the main deck. The heavy scrape of boots on the stairs told them all they needed to know. Pelota crouched low, the dagger in his hands. He reached out and grabbed Ontoquas by the arm to pull her back. She was closer to the approaching figure than was Pelota, but Ontoquas shrugged him off.

The man wore a black tricorne hat. It was the first detail of him she saw as it came into view with each step he made up the stairs. Two more steps and she could see he was slight of build, probably tall, and that he wore a white shirt. She could see nothing of his shadowed face.

Ontoquas pulled back farther on the string and sent a prayer up to the ancestors looking down on her. She could feel the brush of her thumb knuckle against her cheek, and her mind flashed to the first deer she had taken. Hunting with her father.

Three steps before the fo'c'sle deck the man stopped. He bent forward slightly. He had seen something, but Ontoquas was nearly certain that he had not picked her out of the shadows. A grunting sounded behind her, and she knew without turning that the first of the pirates had scaled the line, and had come up over the rail at the worst possible moment.

The man took one step closer, still uncertain of what he was seeing, but now Quid was throwing a leg over the rail, his tattooed scalp clear in the moonlight. The man gave out a startled cry, then turned and bolted down the stairs before Ontoquas could release her arrow.

She ran forward and reached the top of the stairs just as the man was stepping off them, running madly toward the stern. Ontoquas raised her bow and released her grip on the string. The arrow whiffled through the dim glow of moonlight.

There was a muffled thump as the arrow struck, and then the man collapsed into dark shadow. Before Ontoquas even had time to consider what she had done, Pelota darted past her, bounding down the stairs in two strides. The steel of Pelota's dagger glimmered in the moonlight, and Ontoquas turned away, not wanting to see what he did with it.

So turning, she found that she was looking directly toward shore a few hundred yards away. Clearly outlined in the moonlight she could see the shape of three boats leaving the beach, just having cleared the breaking waves at shore.

Van and Kitto were the last two left in the jolly boat. All the others had either scaled the ropes that Pelota had dangled, or came up the rope ladder that Quid had tossed over the starboard rail once Pelota had subdued the second sentry. Sarah had strapped Bucket to her torso with a long cloth she wrapped about her, and she huddled now with Ontoquas and the baby in the stern. Exquemelin paced about the deck barking orders. Silence was no longer necessary. The element of surprise had been lost, and they must make sail.

Kitto jabbed the tarred hull of *Port Royal* with the oar blade to keep the boat clear.

"How close are they?" Van asked. With Kitto's dagger he had cut through the first strand of hemp, but there were at least 5 others, coiled together in a clump.

"Still a ways off as far as I can—" Kitto never finished his sentence, as the loud report of a musket reached them. The ball walloped into the hull just beyond them.

"They'll be shooting for us, Kitto," Van said, feverishly cutting away with the dagger. "If we cannot drop the anchor we cannot sail off."

"Yes." Kitto had seen enough ships make ready to sail from Falmouth to know that raising an anchor the proper way required grueling effort by at least a dozen men and more time than they had. The cable must be cut for the ship to sail.

X leaned over the fo'c'sle deck rail and hailed down to them. "Do I need to mention that we are in a hurry, lads?" he shouted. *"Allons-y!"* Another shot rang out, and X ducked for cover. Behind them, climbing the shrouds of the foremast, Coop cried out when the shot parted the line on which he clung. He fell a dozen feet to the deck, landing in a heap, cursing.

"They cannot shoot like that!" X screamed, and raised the glass to his eye.

Yes, three boats. He had seen that already. The sharpshooter was in the first boat. Two other men were madly loading rifles and muskets for him to fire. The shooter was the young man known as Flop.

"*Morte!*" X spat. "That man must die!"

X charged to the stern, hailing to the men climbing the ratlines.

"On my order, the foresail and spirit sail!" he called. "Where is the woman?" He scanned about and saw Sarah and Ontoquas huddled at the stern.

"Woman! Woman!" X rushed forward and seized Sarah by the wrist.

"What is it? Is it Kitto?" Sarah said, standing. Bucket was still swaddled to her chest, his shining black eyes staring at the play of moonlight in the folds of Sarah's dress.

"*Ja, ja.* About to be shot. Now come with me!" Sarah began to unbundle Bucket, but X reeled off a spout of Dutch and jerked her toward the bow.

"Little John! *Ja, ja.*" Amidships they met the gargantuan man. Little John handed a rifle to X, who in turn thrust it into Sarah's arms.

"I do not understand . . ." Sarah protested, but X cut her off with a raised hand.

"They have a marksman. On the first boat. The man is a devil." He pushed the rifle at her so that she had to step back. "Go now and kill him. Go!" X said, pointing to the fo'c'sle deck.

Sarah stared at X. Their eyes locked. Yes, she knew it might come to this, but now that the moment was upon her, she felt herself quaver.

"Another man. Get one of your men to do it!" She pushed the rifle back at X.

"They shoot like women. I saw you at the beach. You shoot like Artemis. Do it!" He nearly screamed the last line, shoving the rifle at her so that she stumbled backward.

Another shot rang out, and a cry came from the starboard bow. X rushed to the rail and looked down. Van was writhing on his back in the jolly boat, holding his arm. The ball had grazed him, and he had dropped Kitto's dagger into the boat. Kitto picked it up and set to the work that Van had nearly finished.

"Cut the rope or we are dead men!" X shouted down to them. Sarah was at his elbow. She watched Kitto beginning to cut with the dagger on the frayed cable.

Rifle in hand, Sarah ran headlong to the fo'c'sle deck. Quid stepped aside to let her pass, pointing in the direction of the oncoming boats. A small gun was mounted at the very prow of the ship, enough to splinter a jolly boat to pieces, but Fowler and Pelota had yet little luck in finding the keys to the gunpowder stores from the two dead watchmen. They could break their way in, but there was no time.

Sarah set her sidelong stance and lifted the rifle. Bucket cooed beneath her. He reached out a hand and batted lightly at the rifle stock. Sarah pushed his hand away, tucking it hurriedly in the folds of the sash. She dragged her palm against her face to clear away the tears.

"It's okay, sweetheart," Sarah said. But it was not okay. She would have to murder a man.

Sarah's eyes pierced through the gloom. She could see the boat in front, and the man in the bow. Others behind him handed him a weapon. The sharpshooter lifted it to his shoulder.

Our father who art in heaven, hallowed be thy name.

Sarah fired. The rifle bucked in her arms and lit the air around them. Bucket broke into a startled wail, and Sarah waved off the smoke to look again. The man named Flop had fallen back into the boat.

"*Ja, ja, ja!*" hailed X behind her, withdrawing his spyglass. He gave Sarah's shoulder a squeeze. "Now we will live! That boy of yours down there, too." He looked up at a dark figure high up on the foremast.

"Xavier! Drop a hint of sail, you little rabbit." He leaned over the bows to Kitto and Van.

"Wait to cut the last strand until the slack comes, or the cable will take your head off. Then up you come. *Allons-y!*"

Within minutes Kitto and Van were aboard the *Port Royal*, abandoning the jolly boat the moment Kitto finished the final cut on the cable. The ship made way on light sail, easily outpacing the pursuing rowers who fired not a single shot further. X manned the tiller arm, and when the ship had finally come about and the stern aimed in the direction of the island, he broke into his girlish giggle again.

"*Adieu,* John Morris, you pig!" X waved toward the dark boats, their oars now easy in the water. He saw a bright flash from one boat, but already they were out of range.

"Perhaps another time, we sit down for tea!" he said, cackling now. Kitto wrapped a bandage about Van's arm and looked in Exquemelin's direction.

"He is a madman, you know," Kitto said.

"Crazy like a fox."

CHAPTER 20:

Secret Manuscript

ABOARD THE *PORT ROYAL*

Exquemelin and his assorted crew sailed their new ship away from the island to windward until the wind died in the late afternoon. The plan had been to return to the island in the wee hours of the next night, but unless the wind picked up in the next few hours, they would not be able to cover the half dozen or so miles to the southeast they had covered earlier in the day.

X, however, was not particularly concerned about the wind. For starters he had a ship again, a bit worse for wear, perhaps, and in need of a good careening, but a ship nonetheless. And on top of it all he had set Akin hunting in the mess, and Akin had produced a large tin of roasted coffee beans. X perched happily atop the capstan and watched little Bucket, whom Ontoquas had laid out on the fo'c'sle deck on a blanket to wriggle about. Bucket kicked his feet energetically and emitted a comical chortle with every roll of the ship.

"It is good to be king, ah?" X said to Kitto, who leaned against the rail nearby and stared out to the open sea. Somewhere out there was a ship that carried his brother and his uncle. He did not answer.

Thinking of Duck brought Kitto's mind to Sarah. He had not seen his mum for a few hours. He nodded at X and set off to find her.

After searching several places Kitto ended up in the main berth below where the hammocks were stretched between beams. Near the back he saw that one of the hammocks was occupied. Kitto approached quietly, thinking Sarah must be taking a nap.

Then he heard the sniffling sounds of someone crying quietly.

"Mum." Silence. "Mum."

A throat cleared. "I am here, Kitto. Just resting a bit."

"I heard you, Mum. Crying."

"Yes. Come here, Kitto." Sarah sat up and let her legs dangle from the canvas cocoon. Kitto pulled himself up into the hammock next to her. Sarah reached a hand out to him. They held hands for several seconds. Kitto gave hers an extra squeeze before letting go.

"It had to be done, Mum," he said finally. Sarah nodded.

"You could have . . . you could have been shot," she said, and the way she said it, Kitto could tell that she was trying vainly to convince herself.

"That man had already shot Van. And they were

getting closer. If you hadn't, then . . ." His sentence trailed off.

Sarah nodded. She looked down at her hands, and turned the palms up to herself as if inspecting them.

"I am worried, Kitto."

"Yes, I know. About Duck. But . . ."

"Yes, about Duck. But more than that. I am worried about God, Kitto." Kitto took a deep breath. This he did not expect.

"About God?"

Sarah nodded. "That man. I shot him. I meant to shoot him. I sighted down that rifle, and I . . . And as you say, I needed to do it. I needed to murder him."

"'Tis not murder, Mum."

Sarah raised a hand up to silence him, a gesture of impatience Kitto had never seen from her. "However it shall be called," she said. "Certainly some will call it murder." She wiped away a tear. "What kind of God is it, Kitto, who would make such a world in which killing another human being is the right thing to do? The justified thing? How is *that* God one we can look to for comfort?" Sarah let out a frustrated sigh, and a long silence spread between them.

Kitto had long wrestled with a notion of God. What kind of God would give him a bent foot if—as Sarah had always counseled him—it was not a reflection of God's plan for Kitto? He remembered the tearful conversations he and Mum had had on this very subject. He felt both awful and awed that now she needed the very counsel that she had given him for so many years.

"You once told me, Mum, in one of our talks . . . God is not so much a puppeteer, but the bearer of a lantern. He does not control all actions, either good or bad, but he shines a light, and if we learn to see and follow the light, it leads to the surest path."

Sarah looked at Kitto a long time. She smiled, but then the smile faltered.

"I cannot see the path. I once saw it so clearly." Sarah pulled herself up and wiped her cheeks. "Come here, son," she said, and Kitto moved into her embrace.

"I am so very proud of you, Kitto. I could never have done all that you have done, to keep yourself and your brother—and your new friends—safe. You are becoming just the man I always knew you could become."

Kitto awoke late that night. He could tell by the lack of motion in the ship that the wind had not yet risen. He slipped from his hammock to drop quietly to the deck, careful not to let his stump resound against the deck planks. Van snored nearby, and as far as he could tell, Ontoquas and Bucket, as well as Akin and Sarah, all slept soundly.

Stepping delicately, Kitto made his way up to the main deck. A few men were about, Fowler smoking a pipe at the bow and glaring out to sea. A lantern was lit on the stern quarterdeck, and Kitto made for it, recognizing X's rumpled tricorne.

Kitto thumped his way up the stairs, surprised at how

well he could walk without his crutch. He approached X, who hunched over a small table he must have had brought up from below, the lantern balanced on one corner. He sat in a chair with his back toward Kitto. An untidy stack of papers was piled on a corner of the table, secured by X's newly filled satchel of coffee beans. Kitto stepped closer.

X was writing, furiously scribbling away with quill and ink as if his very life depended upon it. His pen flew so fast that tiny spatters of ink flew off and scattered across his page like a sprinkling of black dust. Kitto stepped closer still and peered over the captain's shoulder. Instantly the quill came to a halt. X twisted about and fixed a beady eye up at Kitto.

"You cannot read the Dutch, can you?"

"No."

"Good." He motioned with the quill. "None of these sea dogs can either, or any language for that matter."

"You are writing something you want no one to read?"

X motioned for Kitto to come closer. He blew hurriedly on the paper he had been working on—further smearing the fresh ink—and laid it aside. He drew the sheaf of papers closer, and Kitto could see that at the bottom of the stack was a fine leather folder, the kind that might hold official papers of some kind. X set the bag of beans aside.

"Let me show you," he said, and dug through the papers with manic intensity for several seconds. "Ah! *Ja, ja, ja,* this is it." He pulled out a single sheet and held it to Kitto.

"Read this." Kitto took the browned paper and bent over the table to make use of the lantern light. He scanned down the page.

"This is not English," Kitto said.

"Ah, *ja,* I forget." He pointed to a paragraph halfway down the page. "What you cannot read, here is what it says. I like this part."

"'But Captain Morgan . . . who always communicated vigor with his words, infused such spirits into his men as to put them all in agreement with his designs; they were all persuaded that executing his orders would be a certain means of obtaining great riches.'" X wagged his eyebrows. "Good, ah?"

Kitto felt a rush of blood in his cheeks at the name of the famous buccaneer. "Henry Morgan? Why are you writing about Henry Morgan?"

"Who knows him better than one who has fought side by side with him, ah?" X said. Kitto shrugged.

"No one, I suppose. But why should anyone care?"

X plucked at his beaded beard. "Hmm. You do not think people want to read of buccaneers?" Kitto shrugged again. "I spoke with a merchant once in Barbados. He is Dutch, and there are not so many of us in these parts today. We began to talk of home. I told him how I had spent much of my time. He told me I should write a book, being a learned man. Such a book, he said, would be wildly popular in Europe. All those fat geese who sit at home and live out their boring little lives, they love to read about pirates and battles and adventures in the far corners of the world."

"So why Morgan?"

"He is but one part of the book, but I know that part the best myself. Some pieces I have gathered from others, too. But you see, with Morgan, not only do I get a good tale to tell, I get my revenge." X's eyebrows jounced.

"How so?" said Kitto.

"Morgan is now the lieutenant governor of Jamaica. He is one of the largest landholders on the island." X caressed the page lovingly. "He wants the world to forget his humble beginnings, his violent beginnings. And there is nothing that will stick in his craw more than to have a book come out in Europe that reminds the whole world that he is not nearly so respectable as he would make himself out to be today."

Kitto nodded. "And this is to get your revenge on Morgan? For your hand?"

X smiled and nodded. "*Très belle,* no? And not just for the hand, but for Panama, too, and all of us who fought there for him." X giggled and poked a finger at Kitto's ribs, his eyes a swirl of dancing lantern light. "But I think *that* revenge we will be collecting tomorrow, no?"

Kitto smiled. "If the wind will blow again." He reached out for the fine leather folio at the bottom of the stack. "And what is inside this one? It looks special." Kitto drew it out a few inches, but X slapped a hand down on it and pulled it to him, with a look devoid of his former glee.

"What made you do that?" X said. "Why you reach for this?"

Kitto raised his hands in the air. "I am sorry. I did not mean to . . ."

X stared at the boy solemnly for a moment, as if trying to read Kitto's deepest intentions. Finally he tucked the leather folder back beneath the pile.

"That is my *tour de force*. My rabbit in the hat. The straw that will break Morgan's back."

"And what is it?" Kitto found himself very curious to know what could possibly be contained in that slim folder that had the power to do so much.

X glared at him again. "You are not ready to know what it is yet."

"*I* am not ready?"

X's eyes darted down to the pile. He cleared his throat. "What I mean is, *I* am not ready to share that with anyone. Now if you do not mind, I have work to finish." X turned away to show Kitto his shoulder and dipped his quill into the ink.

Kitto felt the sting of rebuke. There was much to this strange man, and Kitto could not help feeling that more notions spun in the pirate's swirling brain than he would ever tell.

CHAPTER 21:

Spanish Galley

"Sail ho!"

The call brought Van and Kitto springing from their hammocks. Sarah sat up in her own next to Kitto.

"What is wrong?"

"Someone has spotted a sail. Could be nothing." Kitto thumped off to catch up to Van. When they reached the main deck, X was calling up to Pickle from the quarterdeck.

"Do not just call 'sail ho' and then just sit there mute like a giraffe, *idiot*! You were shot in the leg, not in your head!" Flecks of coffee beans sprayed from Exquemelin's mouth. Kitto could see the table loaded with papers behind him, and judging from the redness of the captain's eyes, he had not slept. "Tell me 'square rigger,' or 'lateen,' or 'frigate,' or 'big purple sea monster.' Tell me, Pickle!"

"Galley, captain!"

X stiffened. "You are certain?"

"The oars are in the water, sir. They be turning our way."

"Quid! Quid! Where is the wind, man?" Quid stood at the tiller arm, shaking his head.

"What is a galley?" Kitto whispered to Van.

"A ship with oars as well as sails. Huge ones, able to move an entire ship. In a calm like this they can still maneuver, while we are stuck to this spot until the wind picks up."

"Is it the navy that uses galley ships? English?" Kitto said.

"Not that I have ever heard. The only ones I have heard of in use are by the Spanish."

Kitto issued a sigh, a disturbing mixture of relief and disappointment: relief at not having to fear another ship of Morgan's, disappointment that the ship could not be the one holding Duck.

Van shook his head. "No breathing easy yet."

"We're not at war with the Spanish, are we?"

"No, but we are in a pirated ship. The Spanish are happy to hang pirates too."

X madly gathered up his papers, clutching them and the leather satchel to his chest. "Everyone get below! Everyone! Let the sails go slack! Quid, leave the tiller to flap about. We have no time to lose! And someone get below and find the signal flags."

They all gathered below in the fo'c'sle, not a soul out on the upper decks where they might be seen by spyglass.

"Did you find them?" X said. Pelota and Black Dog had burst into the room, knocking Pickle aside to lay a small chest on the deck.

"Aye, Captain. Signal flags." Black Dog snapped the latches at the front of the wooden chest and swung back its lid. X leaped upon the neatly folded contents, lifting one toward the lamp that Quid held, then tossing it behind his shoulder when it did not please him.

"No. Not this one. No." Flag after flag was tossed to the floor behind him, a jumble of bright color. "Ah!" X ripped a flag from the chest and held it up. "The quarantine flag!" he said. It was a yellow and black square flag, two small yellow squares at opposite corners, and two black squares at the other corners.

"Quarantine?" Fowler said. "You mean to act like we are carrying disease?"

X giggled. "Brilliant, no?"

"Me, I'd rather fight if I am to die."

X threw Fowler a withering look. "I am trying to save your neck, idiot! We cannot fight a ship like that. At least a hundred men aboard." He looked about the room, standing tall, taking the time to meet them all eye to eye. "You are all sick. We all are. Believe that or you will die by the rope."

"Shall I put the flag up?" Fowler said, pointing the way to the deck.

X scowled at him. "Do you look sick? You are too fat to be sick. Fat people do not look sick." X inspected the crew, his eyes coming to rest on Akin and Kitto.

"The two of you, ah? A strong wind could knock *you* down," he said, pointing to Akin. "And with that stump, it looks like the strong wind already had its way with you," he said to Kitto, who glared back at him. "Take the flag and put it up."

Kitto stepped forward and snatched it from X's

hands. He and Akin had just stepped from the fo'c'sle when X shouted out again.

"Wait! Come back here!" Akin and Kitto shared a look, then walked back into the fo'c'sle where the men still huddled about X. The captain had produced another flag from the chest, a large red X in a field of white.

Fowler made a face at X. "That one means we need help. What we want to hang that for?"

X smiled. He turned to Fowler. "If you are dying of sickness, you want help, *oui*?" Fowler nodded. "If you need help and are sick, would you ever hang the quarantine flag? No! If you did, you might risk that no one would help you."

Little John piped up. "But suppose we hang the help flag and they come to help?"

X stood up and walked to Kitto. He yanked the yellow and black flag from his hands and thrust the white and red one at him.

"A ship like that is coming either way. But! If they believe we are truly ill—terribly ill—they might well leave us alone." Kitto spun on his stump. Akin followed him.

"Remember! You must look *très* sick!"

While the rest of the crew skulked about below, Kitto and Akin and X lingered on the upper deck watching as the galley made slow but steady progress toward them. The red and white flag they had hung drooped slack from a line at the foremast. Whether it had communicated anything to the approaching ship Kitto could not tell. The sea separating the two ships lay nearly as unrippled as glass, eerily still, as Kitto had never seen it before.

X had demonstrated his theatrical flair by running below to fetch a few handfuls of flour that he rubbed through his hair and beard. Kitto thought the effect more ghostlike than sickly, but he chose not to criticize. The pirate complemented his appearance by hobbling about using Kitto's crutch—impossibly small for a man of his height—but it did make him look, if not diseased in body, then in mind.

Kitto and X stood side by side, looking over the port rail. X held the spyglass. He lifted a beaded strand of his beard to his mouth and nibbled on the bead, then spit it out vigorously, rattling the remaining beads and sending a dusty cascade of flour onto the breast of his coat.

"I hate people from Spain," he said. "They are so . . . *Spanish!*" Kitto threw him a quizzical look. Exquemelin raised a hand and waved it slowly at the oncoming ship, a gesture that might possibly have been visible to someone looking through a glass. The beads on his beard clattered.

The galley was now no more than a mile off. The swing and rhythm of the huge oars were impressive indeed. Kitto wondered how many men it took to operate a single oar.

What will happen to us? he wondered. He found it hard to fear the Spanish any more than he feared meeting up with an English naval ship, but the reaction of X's crew seemed nearly the opposite. The looks and murmurs below were somber.

There was little to do while they waited. X nibbled coffee beans until the galley was only a half mile off, at which point he tucked the sack away out of concern that snacking roasted beans might not be something a sick person would do.

"Leave the talking to me," X said unnecessarily.

"Have you done this sort of thing before?" Kitto said.

X giggled and had to wipe the smile away with a bony hand. "Of course not. This is madness."

The tension of the moment forced its way through Kitto into a smirk of his own. He turned away. "Madness or brilliance," he said.

"*Ja, ja!* Always they are so close to each other, no?" X said.

The Spanish captain was dressed in fine red wool and wore a hat with gallant sweeps of felt and adorned with a large crimson feather. The ship had drawn close enough for Kitto to pick out the details of the hat without the spyglass. He decided that such a hat would surely get a man shot in Falmouth. Another officer stood at his side, and the two of them bent toward each other to speak privately. About them a few dozen sailors stood by their stations, and a uniformed line of six soldiers stood rigid with muskets affixed to their sides. The galley's giant oars were still in the water, and through the galley portholes Kitto caught occasional glimpses of faces looking across the water at them. He counted twenty oars on the side facing them, which happened to be the galley's port side, the two ships lying bow to stern of each other.

The officers parted and the captain lifted a cone-shaped instrument to his mouth. Kitto had never seen one before, but its purpose was immediately obvious when the man's accented English rang out clearly over the water.

"Are you an English ship?"

X nodded. "Aye, English," he called weakly, not sounding very English at all as far as Kitto was concerned.

The Spanish captain pointed to the flag. "You require assistance?"

X cupped his hands around his mouth. "Have you a surgeon? Have you a good supply of medicines?"

The captain took his time in responding, huddling first with his mate. Finally, "Is there someone sick on your ship?"

X leaned toward Kitto. "Pretend I am telling you something secretive," he said.

"What?" Kitto said, shaking his head in confusion. X nodded at Kitto, as if the boy had said something wise. He turned back to the Spanish captain.

"Fever! There are only a dozen of us left alive, out of forty."

"That's a wee bit excessive, don't you think?" Kitto said out of the side of his mouth.

"Shut up," X said, patting him on the shoulder.

The Spanish captain exchanged alarmed looks with his mate. He lifted the horn to his mouth.

"Greatest apologies. We have no surgeon. Very sorry for your loss. When the wind comes again, head due west. Barbados is only a few days' sail. Should we see another ship, we will make inquiries on your behalf. But we must sail."

"Wait! Please do not leave us!" Exquemelin wailed.

"What are you doing!" Kitto hissed behind his hand.

X mumbled back, "Realism, boy. Harrowing circumstances require the finest of the dramatic arts."

It seemed to Kitto that the first mate and the captain were having some sort of disagreement about leaving the ship in its "forlorn" condition. The two ships were close enough that Kitto could see the captain's jaw muscles clench in frustration.

Into the midst of this argument a third man appeared, quite small in stature, and without the military uniform. He wore a fine jacket and a black felt hat sporting a showy peacock feather. He stood between the captain and first mate, his eyebrows puckering as he inspected the *Port Royal* across the water.

"*Ezel drol!*" Exquemelin wheezed, turning his back quickly on the other ship.

"What is wrong?" Kitto said.

"The man who just came up, he is looking over here, *oui?*" X tugged at his beard absently, his fingers searching for the beads.

Kitto narrowed his eyes. "He seems to be looking at you, mostly, more than the ship. And now he's pointing, and saying something to the other men. They are looking now too." For the first time since he had heard the call of the sighted sail, Kitto felt a hollow pang in the pit of his stomach.

"You know that man, don't you?" The little man in black was stomping his foot on the deck and pointing across the water at them.

"You remember I tell you we . . . helped ourselves to a ship? And then the worms sank the ship?" X said, his back still to the galley.

"That man is the captain of the ship you stole?" Kitto's voice quavered.

"In the flesh."

The Spanish captain was hailing them again. "Captain! Captain, have you perhaps heard of a ship, the *Santa Rosa Alegra*? It was taken by pirates a few weeks ago in these waters."

"And that was the name of the ship," Kitto said. X grunted in agreement. An idea struck Kitto. "Captain, you do not look well, sir." Kitto placed a hand on X's arm. "It would be terrible if the fever caused you to fall to the deck at this precise moment."

Exquemelin raised a finger as if to tell the Spanish captain to wait just one moment, his back still to the galley. He removed his hat and allowed his head to loll loosely on his neck. He reached out to grab Kitto by the shoulder.

"I will get below," X said. "The men must vote on whether to fight or surrender." With that X wilted and fell to the deck and out of sight of the galley behind the solid ship's rail. Kitto pretended to tend to him where he had fallen, though X scampered like a crab along the port rail, trying to get to the stern hatch where he could get below without being seen by any of the Spanish sailors.

Kitto turned to the galley. He pointed down at the spot of deck where X had fallen and contrived a distressed look.

"He is very sick!" Kitto called out. "He needs a doctor! Have you a doctor?" The little merchant captain had gone purple in the face now, spouting a veritable fire of Spanish to the two officers. The captain held up his hand to the merchant, then lifted the speaking horn toward Kitto.

"We will send over assistance! Please prepare to be boarded!" The Spanish captain turned from the rail, speaking quickly to the first mate, who turned to bark the orders to the men.

"But I fear you might catch the fever!" Kitto shouted, suddenly frantic. But no one was listening to him.

In perfect unison every oar quickly withdrew into the ship, and the hatch doors were slammed shut. Just above these hatches, a row of twelve doorways swung open, and the rumble of cannons being rolled out on their trucks carried clearly over the water. Kitto now stared at the gaping mouths of a dozen cannons. He gulped.

He forced himself to step slowly over to the rope ladder and toss it over the side. It occurred to him that he could choose not to do so, but that would only fuel the Spanish captain's fury.

Is there any way out of this?

Kitto turned and walked to the hatch leading down to the fo'c'sle.

There the entire company hovered in silence about X, who peered out a port hatch, his left eye twitching with nerves.

"A hundred men. Easily. *Ezel drol!* We cannot fight," he said.

"Bollocks! We've fought before against these Spanish, ain't we?" Fowler said, pushing his way to the middle of the men.

"Not this many, you ass!"

"Please!" Sarah said. She stepped forward. "Please." The men, surprised to hear a woman's voice among them, fell into silence. Sarah was a picture of contrast, Bucket tucked in the crook of one arm, the other arm resting on the pistol hilt at her hip. "Fighting would be suicide. Surely you all can see that. Surrender at least gives you all a chance at life!"

Now Pickle stepped forward. "I know the Spanish," he said. "Have you forgotten, Pelota?" he said. Pelota shook his head slowly. "We surrender, and many of us find ourselves on a Spanish plantation again. Slaves! I will fight."

"You will bloody well do as told!" X snapped. "I am the captain."

"That's not the articles we live by," Fowler said. "We vote, X. We put it to a vote."

Exquemelin thrust a finger out the open hatch. "They are lowering boats with armed marines, you pigeon-head! The men must be told. Perhaps I am the death of us all!"

"We vote," said Fowler. Enough nods about the room silenced any further protests by Exquemelin.

"How many say 'fight'?" Pickle called out, his own

hand raised. Pelota's hand shot up, as did Fowler's, Xavier's, and several more. Kitto counted the hands, and he couldn't help noticing that nearly every one of the dark-skinned seamen chose a nearly certain death rather than face the consequences of surrender.

"I count eight," X said. "Agreed?" Fowler pointed a chubby finger at each of the hands around the fo'c'sle, checking the count. He grunted approval.

"And how many risk surrender?" X said. Hands raised. Van lifted his own, but X swept past him.

"You are not one of us," he said. He counted on, and Van lowered his hand with a scowl.

"Eight again," X said. "A stalemate, ah? In such a case the captain should be the one to decide."

"There ain't nothing in them articles about that!" barked Fowler. He stepped roughly to grab X by the lapel of his frock coat. X did not flinch as Fowler dug about in X's coat pocket and came out with the oilskin pouch. He thrust it before Exquemelin's nose.

"Fine," X said, his voice eerily calm. "What, then, do you propose?"

Kitto pushed his way forward, elbowing Quid aside. He snatched the pouch from Fowler who glared dangerously down at him. Kitto withdrew the parchment and let the oilskin fall to the deck. He unfolded the document.

"Van is not one of you and does not get a vote," he said. "But there is one name missing from this document." Kitto glared about the room. "Mine!"

Fowler threw a nervous look toward Pickle, then

back at Kitto. "No time for any of that now," he said.

"The boy is right," X said. He reached out to pat Kitto's cheek, but Kitto pushed his hand away.

"Don't insult me!" he said. "A boy doesn't have to choose between life and death. I do." He pointed a finger at Fowler. "We made a deal. Here you are on the ship I promised you. Is that not true?"

"Still just a boy," Fowler grumbled, his brow hooded in shadow.

"Perhaps," Kitto said. "But I have not acted like one. 'Tis more than anyone could say of you if you deny me my due here and now."

Fowler's hand slowly raised and came to rest on the butt end of the knife at his belt. "You would best watch your tongue," he said.

"I will not," Kitto said. "You are not a coward, nor is any of these men. You agreed to sign me on if I made good, and you will not back down now out of fear." Fowler's head dropped a touch, and his hand slipped from the hilt of the blade.

X giggled. He dug in his coat pockets and produced a bedraggled quill and a vial of ink.

"Come, come, you smelly animal," he said, speaking to Fowler. "Make yourself useful. We must obey the articles, as you have reminded us so handsomely." Fowler scowled but turned and bent over so that Kitto could lay the document flat on his back. X dabbed the quill tip into the vial and handed it to Kitto, who took it and placed his palm on the document.

Alexandre Exquemelin

"Kitto, wait," Sarah said. Kitto turned to look at her. Sarah's piercing blue eyes seemed to glow in the uncertain light of the fo'c'sle. "If you sign that . . ."

"Aye," Little John said, speaking for the first time from the back of the crowd. "Sign that and you're one of us, lad. Whatever them Spanish do to our necks, they'll do to yours as well."

Kitto and Sarah locked eyes, and in that instant Kitto felt something he did not remember feeling ever before: compassion for his father, sympathy for the choices he had been compelled to make.

He never told me my true name. He never told me about my mother. He kept so much from me. But perhaps he did the best that he could with what life dealt him. I must do the same. Kitto turned away and lowered the quill to the page.

"Our lots are cast together then," he said. The quill tip scratched against the parchment.

Christopher Quick.

He looked up from the paper.

"I vote that we surrender without fight and look for our first opportunity to escape."

X slapped Kitto hard on the shoulder.

"Huzzah, boy! You are a pirate now. May your years stretch longer than your neck ever will!"

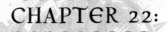

CHAPTER 22:

DUCK

EIGHT DAYS EARLIER, IN THE CARIBBEAN SEA

"Now keep quiet again, Julius!" Duck said, clutching at the hungry monkey in his lap. They were both hungry, and both uncomfortably cooped up inside a barrel. It had been more than a full day since Akin had come running into the hold to announce his depature. Akin was to be transferred to the *Port Royal*, and a naval frigate they had come upon was to escort the *Blessed William* the rest of the way to Jamaica.

"I hear somebody," Duck whispered. Julius let out a low growl. "Hush now, Julie." Whoever was poking around through the barrels, he was making quite a row of it, whistling a tune Duck had heard many times before. The barrel in which they hid was not tightly sealed, and the hazy golden light of a lantern glowed about the edges of the lid just above them.

"That can't be Kitto," Duck told himself. The

whistling was so loud it seemed almost the effort of someone who was trying to chase off the dark. Duck listened as the notes grew increasingly louder and more distinct. Suddenly unseen hands shifted his barrel with a jerk. Duck shot out a hand to brace himself against the inside staves, but when the barrel was tilted forward, he was thrown off balance. He knocked his head on the staves of the barrel's side.

"Oww!" he cried.

A long moment of silence followed, and then the barrel was lowered back to the deck.

"Now, Ethan," a man's voice said, muffled, "I loved you, lad, but you cannot keep doing this to me." The man made a sniffling sound. Inside the barrel Duck's brow furrowed.

"What?" Duck hissed to Julius. "Is that fellow crying?" The voice continued.

"Nearly a year gone you are, my boy. And I won't say I don't wish you weren't still with us. I do. Every day. But you've got to leave this world for the next, son."

Duck lifted his head up, his eyes wide, his lips curling into a grin. Fearing the dark as he did, Duck was quick to make sense of the man's words. "He thinks I am a ghost!" Duck whispered, and the notion struck him as terribly funny. He broke into a snicker that reverberated loudly in the barrel. Julius squirmed in his grip.

There was a long moment of silence before the man spoke again.

"Ain't funny for the living, Ethan, seeing your spirit,"

the voice said. "Now, hear me, and mind me like you did so well when you was living. I am opening up this here barrel, and your little soul needs to float off to heaven, boy. Please. Please." The man sniffled some more, and then Duck heard a scraping noise at the lid above his head.

The lantern light blazed through the barrel the moment the lid lifted. Duck cowered and covered his eyes.

"Ethan?" The man leaned over the barrel top. Before he could determine as to whether the barrel held the ghostly remains of his dead son—a spirit that had plagued him at sea since the day the boy died—Julius, recoiling from the light, broke from Duck's grip, let out a scream, and leaped straight out at the source of the light. The man let out a startled howl and stumbled backward. The lantern fell from his hands, smashing against the deck in a spray of glass and oil.

"Dear God!" the man cried, scrambling to his feet. Spirit or no, he must put out the fire. He leaped about the barrels, stomping at the burning splatters of oil on the deck. Thankfully the lantern had been nearly exhausted of its fuel, and the man was able to extinguish the patchwork of flames before they could spread.

Utter darkness descended, and silence too, but for the man's heaving breath.

"Ethan? That ain't you, is it?"

Duck, still hunched in the barrel, did not know what to say. He knew with the strange intuition that children sometimes possess that the man was asking after his son. He could sense the man's longing. Duck knew that pain. It had been just a matter of weeks since he had lost his own father, and now too, the absence of his mother and brother left a hole in him that he dared not dwell on long else tears came.

"Da?" Duck said, and reached for the barrel lip to pull himself to his feet. Scuffled footsteps drew closer, and then Duck felt strong hands grasp his shoulders. Before he knew what to do, Duck reached out for the man and they fell into a fierce embrace. Duck squeezed his eyes shut, but the tears leaked out nonetheless.

It is Da. It is Da. Come back from the dead to be here with me.

The little boy knew the fancy was not true, but if wishing could possibly bring back the dead, then Frederick Quick would have been the man holding him.

After a full minute the man cleared his throat. "You're not my Ethan, are you lad?" He had a gentle voice, scratchy like boot heels on unswept floorboards.

"And you're not my da," Duck said. "But I wish you was." Duck sniffled and wiped his cheeks against the man's shirt. It smelled of pipe smoke and old sweat.

"I can't say I wish you was Ethan," the man said. "His spirit been hauntin' me fierce."

"I wish my da's ghost would come to me."

"Don't you wish it, lad. Ain't what you think it would be like." The man pulled back from the embrace as if he could look down and see the boy he held, but the darkness was deep. "How are you called?"

"I'm Duck," he said. "Well, not really. Mum says to tell people my real name is Elias, but I would rather be called Horse Poop."

"'Elias' ain't a bad name. You should listen to your mum."

Duck let his hands fall back to the barrel lip. "She ain't here neither." He sighed deeply. "And besides, I like 'Duck' better. I'm from Cornwall, and there people say I'm 'happy as a duck.' That's how I got me nickname."

"Happy is good to be. How you can be that down here in the dark I'll never know. And what was that devil spirit that attacked me?"

Duck broke into a grin. "That's Julius. He's my friend. He's a monkey."

The man stepped back from Duck and grew silent a moment before speaking.

"What you doing down here, son? Have you stowed away?"

Duck explained as best he could, which was not very well. Tom—as the man was called—gathered enough to know that the boy had been hiding from the captain of the other ship that had now sailed back to the east. When Duck was through, Tom stepped forward and lifted Duck by his armpits out of the barrel to stand next to him.

"I need to take you to Fitch," Tom said, and the way he said the name filled Duck with foreboding.

"Who is Fitch?"

"First mate of the HMS *Portsmouth*, and now head

officer of this ship until we reach Jamaica."

Duck pulled away from the man. "Please don't, Tom! Captains and officers are nothing but trouble!" He pressed his palms together in a prayerful gesture. "I won't trouble a soul. Promise! Cross me heart even."

Tom muttered his misgivings. "But what if you get caught?" he said at last.

"I won't tell them I saw you!" Duck said. "And they'll never catch me. I'm too quiet. And I can be special quiet if now and then you find your way down here with a fistful of bacon?" Tom chuckled and ran thick fingers through Duck's hair. He sighed again.

"My Ethan was about your age when he got sick."

"I been down here awhile, and I ain't never seen your Ethan," Duck said, glad that it was true. His mother had told him that all spirits travel off to heaven, but the idea that one might be down in the hold with him was not comforting.

"Sometimes in dark places I see him," Tom said. "He never does say nothing to me, and I don't know if he really is there or if it's all in me mind."

"You won't tell old Fitch on me, will you?" Duck reached out and took Tom's thick index finger. He squeezed it tight. "I promise me and Julius will keep hidden."

Tom groaned. "Well, I ain't no officer, am I?"

"So you won't tell?"

"Neh." Tom patted Duck's cheek. "Now you must be a-hungry. I'll see to that bacon, young Duck."

* * *

And so it was that with Tom's help, Duck survived the
passage across seven hundred nautical miles to Port
Royal, Jamaica. Tom was no cooper, but he knew his
way about a hold. Most of the errands requiring a visit
there were conducted by him alone. He even set up
a hidden niche toward one end of the hold, stacking
barrels in an arch against the curving hull and string-
ing an unused hammock between them so that Duck
and Julius had a more comfortable place to sleep. The
bacon did not arrive as regularly as Duck would have
liked, but Tom brought enough biscuit and beans to
keep Duck quiet.

Over three weeks passed in this manner. He and
Tom shared bits and pieces of their lives together. Duck
spoke mostly of his brother Kitto, how brave he was, how
Duck wanted to grow up to be just like him, and Tom
spoke of Ethan and the mischief the boy got into even as
a wee lad. By the time the harbor master at Port Royal
first spotted the topgallant sails of the *Blessed William* as
she sailed for the bay in the wake of the mighty frigate
Portsmouth, Duck and Tom had formed a friendship that
each would miss when it was gone.

That morning Duck awoke with a start at the sound
of cannon fire. He had been sleeping in the hammock
with Julius, though it was late in the morning. Down
in the hold no sunlight ever penetrated, and Duck and
Julius sometimes kept odd hours playing games of hide
and seek. Julius seemed to comprehend the game so

thoroughly that it would have astonished anyone but his six-year-old companion.

Duck shot to his feet, upending the hammock and Julius, who squealed as he tumbled to the deck. Duck's mouth went dry and his heart hammered in his little chest. Another shot sounded—was it from the *Blessed William*? The little boy panted, a full panic coming on.

A lantern appeared at the top of the stairs, lighting the silhouette of a ragged set of boots.

"Tom! Tom, are they firing on us?" Duck said.

The lantern swung in Duck's direction. Tom waited until he was close enough to speak softly and still be heard.

"'Tis why I came. Thought it might put the fear of God in you. Come here, lad." Duck vaulted himself over the barrel stack and into Tom's arms. Tom held the little boy tight, feeling a great pang of sadness.

"When a great ship like the *Portsmouth* comes in, all the lesser ships around give a salute," he said. "That's all it is."

"That's what the cannon fire is?" Tom nodded. Duck released his embrace and pulled away from Tom to look him in the face. "So we've reached Jamaica?"

Tom felt a tightness in his throat. He sighed. "Aye. Your sea journey has nearly come to an end." Duck looked up into the thick lines of Tom's face, and the sailor put on a smile he did not feel.

"I can't wait to get dirty again," Duck said. "Not ship messy, but dirt dirty. I miss dirt." Tom rolled back his head and laughed, showing the gaps between his uneven teeth.

"I miss you, lad. Already. You been a sight for sore eyes these last weeks. But listen, your sea adventure might just be over, but your land adventure just be about to begin." Another round of cannon fire sounded off in the distance. Tom looked back to confirm that no one else approached the stairs.

"The unloading. I will try to be the one to lift your barrel and bring it topside, but after that you'll have to keep yourself and that monkey quiet as cockroaches. They'll lower the barrels down into several boats, and row these over to Custom Quay. You don't want to be found out until after you reach land."

"I can wait," Duck said. "Julius, too. But . . ." Duck's brow puckered. Duck's temperament and age did not yield itself to much in the way of contemplation of the future, but at that moment the depth of his predicament began to occur to him. Tom saw worry written on the boy's features for the first time.

"Now, now." He tousled Duck's hair. Julius, who had climbed his way atop the barrel next to Duck, stepped off to balance on the boy's head. Duck smiled again. "You made it this far; you got spirit."

"Where do you think I should head? I don't want to run into that Henry Morgan bloke."

"Port Royal is a big town, lad. Little chance of that. What you do is head for Saint Peter's Church. Some good people there will help you. I know it."

"And where is that?"

"Head straight away from the water on any street. Most of the roads head in the right direction. And then keep your eyes out for the steeple."

"Or I could just ask somebody," Duck said.

Tom's brow furrowed. "Not just anybody you ask," he said. "Trust your wits, Duck. There are some people best avoided in Port Royal." Duck understood. His mother had cautioned both him and Kitto in similar fashion when she knew they would be down at the wharf where the newly docked ships spilled batches of sailors from all the world's corners.

"God be with you, son," Tom said. He rose and cleared his throat.

"Your Ethan was lucky," Duck said.

Tom looked down at the boy, running his hand through straggles of sun-bleached hair. "Now why would say that, he being dead at six years?"

Duck smiled. "Well, he had you. As a da, I mean. I think that makes him lucky."

Tom turned away and stepped toward the stairs, bewildered with emotion. "You know, Duck. Since I known you now, these last weeks, Ethan ain't been back to haunt me," he said. It was true, though Tom could not explain why it was so. "God speed you on your way, Elias Quick. And know wherever you land you've got yourself a friend in Tom Peet."

CHAPTER 23:

Arriving in Jamaica

It was some hours later when Tom brought Duck his last supply of bacon wrapped up in a cloth. The *Blessed William* had dropped its anchor in the bay and had finally been granted space along the quay for the unloading of boats.

"Here's the last I can give you now. Save some of it."

"But it tastes best when it's fresh," Duck said.

Tom gathered up the hammock to erase any sign of the hidden encampment he had made for the boy and his monkey.

"Get yourself to the barrel, boy. It ain't but a few minutes now." Duck did as told. He and Julius scowled in the darkness.

Tom was right. They had squatted in the barrel just long enough to settle into a midafternoon nap when Duck was awakened by the sound of boots tromping down the stairs into the hold.

"These 'uns over here first," an unfamiliar voice said.

"Aye, aye, sir," came the answer. Duck recognized the second voice as Tom's.

A moment later he and Julius were being lifted into the air. Duck had braced an arm on the opposite side of the barrel so as not to be tossed about, but Julius was startled by the movement and gave out a small shriek.

Duck heard a man coughing loudly just inches above their head.

"That's a devil of a cold you have there, Tom," said a new voice off to the side. "Sounds like something crawled down your throat and died."

"Aye, a strangled monkey. Feels that way as well," Tom's voice said. "Some fresh vittles will do me right before we set sail again."

Duck stifled a giggle. "Good ol' Tom," he whispered to Julius.

In a moment they were on the upper deck. Duck knew it from the tiny tendrils of light that poked through the edges of the lid above him. He reached up to tug at the block Kitto had attached to the lid to help him secure it from the inside.

Soon the barrel was gently set upon the deck. A hand slapped twice on the lid.

"Good-bye, barrel," Tom said. Duck heard his footsteps recede.

"Good-bye, Tom," Duck said. He patted at Julius's head, and the monkey curled into his lap. "Really quiet now, okay?" In a few moments the voices of two men were above them, neither of them Tom's.

"Room enough for this one."

"Aye, lend a hand then." Duck braced himself in

time, and then he and Julius were being lifted again.

"Hardly nothing in this one!"

"True enough." The barrel was set down sharply and Duck rapped the back of his head on the stave behind him.

"Ow!" he said, then clamped down on Julius's head as if the monkey's mouth were the guilty party.

"What's that then, Jim?"

"What's what?

"What you said?"

"Din't say nothing, you madman."

A voice from far off rang out. It was Tom. "Might you ladies speed things up a bit, eh? Plenty more barrels down here to clear out, ain't there."

Good ol' Tom.

There was more movement that Duck could not discern, and then he could feel a rising sensation again as the pallet of barrels was hoisted by block and tackle over the port rail and lowered to the awaiting jolly boat below.

"Soon, Julius," Duck said. "Soon we're on land again, and then we make for that church." Duck bit his lip. "What *was* the name of that church again?" Julius did not tell him the answer.

There was some more heaving and jostling at the boat. Duck and Julius were turned on their sides so that Julius rested on Duck's belly, and Duck lay on his back.

"Right comfy," Duck said. "Must be in the boat now." He could tell by the rolling sensation.

Shortly thereafter the sound of oars creaking in their

locks reached their ears. "Can't wait to be on land."

There were no voices this time, but after a few minutes Duck could hear a great commotion off in the distance: the bustle and chaos of Custom Quay, Port Royal, the busiest English port in the New World.

Thunk! The rowboat suddenly struck something hard. Duck and Julius were pitched to the far side of the barrel, only now the barrel was spinning, rolling. Duck gasped at the sudden feeling of weightlessness.

Splash!

"Oh! Oh, Julius! Oh!"

Duck and Julius's barrel had fallen into the sea. Water streamed inside, seeping in through the lid. Julius let out a high-pitched scream. Duck reached up for the block at the lid to hold it tighter, but they were still spinning, and the two of them were tossed about. More water rushed in. Duck could barely hear over his own panic the sound of many voices, a great harangue of angry oaths.

"Well, get it then, you blackguard!"

"Shut your hole, you!"

"Come and shut it then!"

Something hard thumped down on the spinning barrel once, twice. Now they were spinning faster. Julius screeched again, so loud inside the barrel that Duck thought his head might explode.

"Shut it, Julius! Shut your bloody monkey mouth!" Duck screamed back. There were now several inches of water in the barrel, and with the next revolution of the churning cylinder, Duck got a mouthful of seawater. He choked and sputtered. Julius caterwauled, infuriated by the dousing.

"What the devil is inside that thing, man!" yelled one man.

"Something alive, for God's sake!" said another, and then the spinning stopped and Duck and Julius were heaved up and out of the water.

"Get it up there and off my boat!" Again they were pitched in the barrel and Duck gulped a fresh mouthful. Julius squealed in torment and scratched his monkey claws against the lid.

Duck felt himself being lifted through the air, and then there was a tremendous crash as the barrel was dropped down onto the pier. He landed on his back, knocking the wind from him. Julius got the better end of the transaction and was laid out across Duck's face, his bared claws digging into Duck's ears and chin. At the same moment the barrel lid jettisoned off and rolled down the wooden pier several feet before dropping off the far edge. Seawater gushed out, staining dark the planks of the pier.

For a moment there was a deathly quiet all around them. Duck disentangled Julius from his face and was instantly blinded, so bright the light did seem. Were he able to look out he would have seen—several feet away—a small crowd of sailors hunched over and peering intently, trying to see into the dark barrel.

"What the devil is that?" one man said.

"You imbeciles!" A voice shouted from a distance down the pier. "Clear that barrel or I'll have your backs striped!"

"Begging your pardon, sir, but there's something in it," one of the gathered men said.

"Of course there is something in it, you dolt! Why do you think it's being transferred ashore. Now clear that barrel!"

"Something alive, sir," another man said. Duck craned his head back and covered his eyes with his hands, allowing just a sliver of a crack between fingers through which to peer. He looked—upside down from his vantage—at the assorted sailors several feet away. In the distance behind them, he could see the familiar commotion of a busy quay.

"Alive! What in the name of God . . . ," said the imperious voice farther up the pier. Heavy boot-heeled steps rang out.

"Have it to light, then!"

Suddenly the barrel was hoisted again, tipped toward its open end. Duck and Julius came tumbling out, Duck landing squarely on his head. He let out a howl, and Julius screamed anew.

A huge eruption of laughter resounded all around them. Duck righted to a squatting position, Julius on the planks next to him. Duck clamped one hand over his eyes, the other atop his aching head.

"Why you little urchin!" fumed a voice—quite close now—and Duck screamed out when the officer snatched him by his ear and yanked him to his feet.

CHAPTER 24:

Flight

"Ow! That hurts! It hurts! Stop it!" Duck swung out with his fists, eyes still closed. The infuriated officer boxed at Duck's ears viciously and Duck cried out in pain. The gathered men grumbled in disapproval.

"Leave the boy alone!" a distant voice yelled. Others joined in agreement, but still the man clung to Duck, and still the boy swung away.

"I'll teach you to strike an officer of the marines, young man!" the voice hissed. Duck opened his eyes now despite the glare. He saw a sea of red that was the man's jacket, adorned with shiny brass buttons, and white trousers.

Now, Duck was no stranger to a fight, particularly with those who outweighed him, and he knew what every young boy learns at some point about the weaknesses of older boys and men. Duck reared back with his foot and delivered a sharp kick to the man's groin.

Instantly the man stepped back with a grunt, hunched over slightly at the midsection. Guffaws and chuckles sang out from the onlookers down the pier.

"That'll teach you!" Duck shouted—much to the delight of the onlookers—and he snatched Julius from the planks. Duck turned away and ran in the only direction he could, which was directly at the gathering of stunned and laughing seamen.

"Stop him!" hissed the officer.

Duck barreled straight for the middle of the pack, where stood a large man, his stance wide and his arms at the ready. When the man reached out his huge hands at Duck and Julius, Duck dove straight through his legs. He scrambled up again, but hands were upon him, grabbing him by either arm. Julius was launched through the air.

Duck felt hands lift him off the ground. He kicked and wiggled wildly.

"Easy, lad! Simmer down!"

Julius let out his most blood-curdling screech yet and threw himself at one of the men holding Duck. The sailor let out an anguished howl when Julius sank his teeth into the flesh of his hand, allowing Duck to wiggle free for a moment, only to be seized anew by another sailor. Julius leaped to this man now, gouging at his eyes, then leaping to another nearby to do the same.

The sailors—stunned by the monkey's violent ferocity—stepped back for a moment. Duck shot through a gap between two of them, Julius hot on his heels.

"Don't let him get away!" shouted the marine. "Stop that boy!"

Duck turned back.

"Come on!" he said, and Julius leaped from the planks and into his arms. Just behind him the group of sailors had regained their courage and began to give chase. One of them wielded a nasty looking cudgel in one hand.

Duck ran. He ran for his life, his eyes blinded by both sunlight and tears. The thunder of the men's footsteps rang out behind him.

The Custom House was located just beyond the end of the pier, but the typical bustle of activity seemed to stop for a moment. Hundreds of eyes had turned to watch the little monkey-bearing boy sprint down the pier, pursued hotly by a motley mob of angry sailors, a few of them streaming blood. Bemused merchantmen stopped their negotiations to watch; stock clerks pushed one another aside for a better view; and every naval officer barked out commands that no one seemed to hear.

"Belay that little piker!"

"Leave him be. He's just a boy!"

Duck was a fast one, but not so fast as a grown man, and it looked to the crowd as if the boy would be snatched up just as he reached the cobblestone quay. The only visitor to the quay at that moment who was entirely oblivious to Duck's flight was a porter who hurried his horse along the cobbled roadway. The wagon trailing behind him was empty; he had made his delivery late and he knew he had to hurry back to his handler or face withering contempt. Pleasantly surprised to see the roadway clear, the porter lashed at the horse to hurry through.

Duck's feet hit the cobblestones the moment the wagon passed in front of him. He could not wait; the men would be upon him in an instant. Tucking Julius into the crook of one arm, Duck launched himself into the air. Julius screamed.

The sidewall of the wagon caught Duck across the ribs, but his momentum threw him up and over its lip and into the wagon in a heap. The men were shouting behind him, hailing the porter to stop his wagon, but the porter ignored them, whipping his horse to a gallop. Duck wrestled his way to his feet. He stood upon the pile of barrel staves—of all things—and looked back toward the retreating quay. A cheer rang up from the assembled crowd there, curiously thrilled to see a little boy outrace a handful of grown seamen.

Julius took that moment to voice his protest once again with a terrible caterwaul. The wagon's driver turned and saw the boy standing behind him.

"Whoa!" He pulled back hard on the reins. The horse's hooves clopped unevenly on the cobblestones, and the wagon slowed. "Get off my wagon, you little waif!" shouted the man. Julius twisted from Duck's grip and leaped for the ground.

"Julius!" Duck jumped too. His feet shot out to one side as he hit the moving ground, and he tumbled along the cobbles several feet. He rose to see Julius scrambling down a tiny alleyway between two buildings.

"Julius, come back!" Duck shouted and ran after him, glancing over his shoulder to the pursuing sailors—red-faced, hair streaming behind as they ran at full tilt—the cudgel-bearer in front and not twenty paces away.

The alley was barely wide enough to fit a man, narrowly separating the fishmonger's shop and the victualler, who provided outgoing ships with all manner of supplies. It was wide enough for Duck, though, to hit at full stride. He ran pell-mell, Julius lurching ahead of him. Suddenly Julius stopped and whirled around, for he had seen what Duck had not yet. Duck scooped the monkey up into his arms, and then he saw.

"Aw, crumb!"

The alley was a dead end. It ran itself directly into a windowless stone wall that rose two stories.

"Now you keep that beast in your 'ands, boy, or I crush his cursed skull right here and now." Duck turned to see the large man with the cudgel stepping along sideways so as to fit in the narrow passage. He edged toward Duck and Julius, still near to the alley's opening. Instinctively Duck stepped back, retreating until he bumped up against the stone wall.

He looked up. Above him, on the second floor, a shuttered window to the victualler's shop was open. Inspiration struck.

Back in Falmouth—when both his parents were occupied and not paying Duck any mind—he would occasionally entertain himself by what he called "flying." He would bridge his palms and the soles of his bare feet against either wall of a narrow hallway leading to the back door overlooking the garden. So doing, he would lift himself all the way up the wall—setting his feet and reaching higher with his hands and vice versa—until the crown of his head touched the dusty ceiling planks.

The alleyway in which Duck now stood was precisely the same width as that hallway. Duck set Julius up onto his shoulder and planted his palms against either wall, fingers down. He lifted himself up several inches, then braced his feet.

"What the devil you doing?" the man said, sidestepping closer.

In seconds Duck had reached a height of four feet. Then five.

"No, you don't!" the man barked. Duck's elevation allowed him now to see over the man's head at the four other sailors behind him in the alley.

By the time the man with the cudgel stood under him, Duck was nearly to the open window. The man jumped, swinging the cudgel at Duck's lowest foot. Duck snatched it away and hoisted himself up another six inches.

"Get back here!" The man swung again. Again Duck lifted his foot out of the cudgel's range. When they reached the open window, Julius jumped from Duck's shoulder and into the room beyond. Duck looked down at the man below him. He stuck out his tongue and blew his best raspberry.

"You meanie!" he said. The man replied in vulgar terms as Duck shoved off the far wall to flop gracelessly onto the windowsill. He twisted and thrashed until he'd swung a leg up and over. He tumbled to the second story of the victualler's shop.

Barrels. The entire floor was filled with them: all sizes imaginable, stacked three high in some places, others flopped onto their sides. Toward the windows overlooking the street was a large table littered with papers, and at that table sat a man as thin as the quill he used to write. The man perched at the end of his chair in shocked disbelief at the boy picking himself off the floor and the monkey who had vaulted up to the top of a stack of barrels and was glowering at him dubiously.

"What? What?"

"How do I get out of here, sir, if you please?"

"What? What?"

The sound of raised voices rang out below as the pursuing sailors burst through the front door of the victualler's shop.

"Please!" Duck whimpered. Toward the middle of the room was the flight of stairs leading straight down to the shop. Duck ran over to it in time to see one of the sailors starting up.

A stack of three barrels stood just to the far side of the railing. Duck ran over to them and pushed at the top barrel. It teetered, overbalanced, then fell silently over the rail and out of sight until it smashed into the stairs and bounced into the man charging up them, knocking him backward into the cudgel-bearer two steps behind.

"Please!" Duck said again to the lanky clerk. He

yanked a second barrel down and wrestled it over to the top of the stairwell. He lay it on its side, and the moment another set of boots came into view below, Duck kicked at the barrel. The empty cylinder bounded downward, greeted by a chorus of howls and angry shouts.

"Ain't there another way out of here?" Duck said to the man, who had now raised himself half out of his chair, his back straight as a board, the quill in his hand dripping ink.

"What?"

"Another way out of here!" Duck said. The man pointed. At the front corner of the room a wooden ladder was fixed to the wall, leading up to the ceiling where a hinged door allowed access to the roof.

"Oh, yes! *Thank* you, sir, and God bless!" Duck tossed one more barrel down the stairwell for good measure, whistled for Julius, and ran for the ladder. When the first sailor reached the top of the stairs, Julius emitted another caterwauling scream—stopping the man momentarily in his tracks—giving Duck time to work the hasp and flip open the doorway to the tiled roof.

In a moment Duck and Julius were standing atop the victualler's roof. Duck slapped the door closed and stood upon it, thinking his weight might stop his pursuers.

"Which way, you think?" he said. He and Julius turned about. The choice was clear. To one side, leading away from the quay, there was nothing but open air to greet them beyond the roof's end of the victualler's shop. Back in the direction they had come, however, there was the small gap between this roof and the one of the fishmonger next door, followed by a row of several buildings built smack upon the other, stretching nearly fifty yards.

Duck felt a pounding on the tar-papered hatch beneath his feet, followed by a stream of muffled curses.

"How do we get back down, do you think?" he asked Julius, who glared at the door on which Duck stood. Duck wobbled as someone pushed from beneath, nearly upsetting his balance and throwing him off the tiled roof and into the lane far below. Quickly he stepped aside, and a second later the door whacked open.

Duck retreated several steps, then turned to face the gap between roofs. A man's head appeared at the hatch. Again it was the man with the cudgel, one eye clenched shut from where a hurtling barrel had struck him.

"Aye, you better run!" the man said. And so Duck did, Julius right behind him.

"Don't look down!" Duck shouted to Julius just before he jumped. An indistinct blur that was the alley below passed beneath him, but Duck easily cleared the gap and landed, running along the tiles of the fishmonger's shop. He dodged a chimney and ran on, risking a look back to see that three of the men had emerged now and were giving chase.

On they ran. Thankfully the roof levels were on a rough par with one another, requiring no great drops or climbs to go from one to the next. But it was not long before Duck—Julius on his heels—had reached the last rooftop. Duck peered over the tiled edge. His foot struck a loose piece of slate and sent it spinning out into space to smash against the cobblestones below. A few passersby looked up and pointed. Duck retreated from the edge and took refuge behind a large chimney that protruded from the last roof high enough to conceal him.

The men were nearly upon him now, three of them, with two more in the distance. The three had stopped running, seeing that Duck had nowhere to go. The cudgel-man whispered something to the other two, and they spread out along the width of the roof to create a human net.

"You best stop right there!" Duck said, his voice trembling. "I ain't done nothing to you!"

"You stowed away is what you did," the cudgel-man said. "And you done injured me."

"That's 'cuz you chased me. I didn't mean to."

"Nowhere to go, lad, but down," another man said, dark-haired but with a friendly enough face. "You come take your medicine. It's not nearly so bad as falling to the lane from this height." The men drew another step closer.

Duck clung to the corners of the chimney. And then he looked up, inspiration striking again. The chimney was a fairly large construction, boxy, built simply, and open to the elements at the top with a square aperture roughly ten inches on a side. Duck leaped up to perch on the chimney's lip. He lowered one foot down into the blackness.

"You'll never fit, lad," the friendly man said. "You'll get stuck and die in there." Duck inserted the other foot.

And then the cudgel-man charged for him.

"Run, Julius!" Duck called. He pushed his hips off the lip of the chimney, thrust off his arms and let himself go, taking a deep breath as he went as if diving underwater.

The air in his lungs came out with a scream, though. The cudgel-man had thrust a hand into the chimney just in time to grab Duck by a handful of his hair, holding him in midair. Duck cried out and twisted his head about, unable to bring up his arms to fend the man off. The pain brought tears to his eyes. Duck thrashed and thrashed, felt something give, thrashed some more, and suddenly he was weightless.

CHAPTER 25:

Excrement

He was falling. Above him the man with the cudgel withdrew a fistful of hair from the chimney opening.

Fortunately for Duck the rains had not yet arrived in Port Royal, and the owner of the Royal Coffee House had not yet resumed his habit of starting an early fire to drive off the morning chill for his customers. Nor had he employed the use of a chimney sweep in at least three seasons. When Duck tumbled out onto the large brick hearth, sputtering and momentarily blinded, a cloud of black dust billowed out into the parlor with him.

It was Sunday, a day for religious observation in many parts of the world, but in Port Royal it was a high time for trade. The coffeehouse was packed full of men and a few women, exchanging news and haggling over the finer points of their trades. It was a loud place that afternoon, each group raising its voices to be heard above the din.

When the blackened boy appeared so dramatically at the hearth—haloed in a blooming cloud of soot dust—and got to his feet, not a single silver spoon stirred in a porcelain cup. Duck stared out at the adults with their open mouths and arched eyebrows, expecting at any moment for someone to grab at him. The crowded room offered no escape.

"It's the boy on the run!" yelled a man over at the bar. He lifted his teacup toward Duck. "Give 'em hell, lad!" he said, flashing an uneven assortment of teeth.

"Huzzah!" called another. And to Duck's astonishment the crowd was smiling and cheering him. Duck's teeth shone bright against his sooted features. He took a step forward and the crowd parted, revealing a path to the door.

Duck ran. "Thank you and God bless!" he shouted as he ran, and the crowd erupted into cheers, spilling out into the lane just behind him to watch the chase.

Out in the lane again Duck turned to his right in the direction he had come. He locked eyes with the red-coated marine from the pier who pointed and snapped orders to the men behind him. In the distance beyond, Duck caught a glimpse of the sailors who had pursued him on the rooftop, having found another way down.

Duck stepped farther into the lane, forcing a wagon-cart driver to pull back on his leads and slow his horse.

"Julius! Julius, where are you?" Duck shouted up at the roof edge high above him. Two scores of onlookers had spilled out of the coffeehouse, and they too looked up to see what it was this fleeing boy hailed.

Sure enough, the monkey appeared at the edge of

the roof, just where Duck had left him. Duck held out his arms.

"Come on, boy!" He made a kissing noise with his lips. "Come on, Julius!"

"Naw," said a man in a fine suit, elbowing his mate.

"Bet you two pounds," his friend said.

"Done."

"Julius! Come on now!" Duck dared another sidelong glance at the approaching sailors, the marine at their lead. They had nearly reached the crowd milling outside the coffeehouse.

"Jump, you bloody monkey!" called the man who had placed the wager. And sure enough, Julius did. He gave a terrific shriek and leaped out into open space, all four limbs outstretched, his tail curving up behind him, his mouth wide with terror.

Duck caught him neatly and held him fast to his chest. The crowd erupted, hot coffee spilling from cups and staining the cobbles.

"There it was! That's a fine lad, there!"

"Out of the way, please! Disperse at once!" barked the marine.

Poor Julius, ever confused and enraged by the mob of people all looking at him, did something Duck had never seen him do. Julius reached toward his backside, defecated, and with a whip of his bony hand, he hurled his excrement at the grinning crowd.

The effect was instantaneous and horrifying. Stricken men and women recoiled in disgust. Cheers turned into howls. Jackets, dresses, and several cups of coffee were ruined.

Duck turned and ran. He reached the corner of the coffeehouse and veered down the lane.

"What did you do that for?" he said, but Julius just growled ominously in his arms.

Run!

Duck had a lead of just thirty yards when the marine officer and sailors rounded onto the lane in time to see the boy's heels disappear around the next corner. The chase was on.

Duck, of course, had no idea which way to turn. But he was no stranger to a sprint, and what he lacked in speed he made up for in quickness, darting down the lanes without losing a single step. Once he doubled back on his path by traveling the entire perimeter of one building, thinking it might throw off his pursuers, but a stolen glance over his shoulder told him that he had neither gained nor lost ground.

Duck knew now it was only a matter of time. They would catch him. What would they do to him? Tears filled Duck's eyes anew, and he careened around another corner and into a wide lane. Toward him walked a woman, an older woman judging by her wrinkles and the wisps of gray that peeked out beneath her bonnet. She wore an elaborate white and gray dress that billowed out wide at the bottom, and she held up a white parasol to ward off the sun.

She turned surprised eyes upon Duck.

"What's the hurry, little man?" she said. Duck ran straight for her.

"Oh, please, Gran," he said. "Please don't let 'em take me away to that awful Henry Morgan!" he said, and with that, Duck reached down to the woman's feet and grabbed a handful of the hem of her dress. Before the woman had even the time to respond, Duck had tossed the many layers up and over his and Julius's heads and hunkered down behind her legs.

"Now hush, Julius!" the woman heard the boy say. Then she felt a strange, tiny set of hands clutching at the soft flesh behind her knees.

"Oh, my," she said, bemused. She looked up to see the handful of men round the corner, led by the officer.

"Ma'am!" the man said to her. "A boy, running this way," he panted. "Which way did he go, if you please?"

"A little boy, you say?" the woman said, a slight smile on her lips. "With some sort of creature in his hands, perhaps?"

"Which way, madam!"

The woman turned behind her, careful not to move her feet. She shifted the parasol to her right hand so as to point with her left.

"Down that lane, I believe, although the habits of young children are hardly my concern. Good day, offi-cer." These last words were thrown to the backs of the men now sprinting past her. They rounded the corner and the woman now stood alone, so to speak.

"A nefarious brigand you must be, young man, to

attract such powerful enemies," she said. Beneath her she heard a sniffle. The woman bent at the waist and pulled up her dress high enough to have a peek. Fresh tears carved clean lines down the boy's soot-covered cheeks.

"Now, now, lad, all is well. You are in safe hands. Or something like that."

A movement ahead caught the woman's eye, and she let go her dress. She stood still, pretending to admire the flowers of a mahoe tree that towered nearby. Two men, well dressed, walked the lane in the opposite direction.

"Dame Bethany," one of the men said as they passed. Each tipped his hat.

When they had moved beyond earshot the woman said, "Can you scoot yourself along with me, then?"

"Yes, Gran. I'll just stay hidden right here."

"Very well. We have not far to go. Keep your little friend from tearing my stockings."

Duck found the going rather difficult, trying to walk and squat at the same time while keeping Julius tucked in one arm and pulling down at the folds of fabric concealing him with the other. Any keen observer would not have failed to notice the bulge at the back of Dame Bethany's dress, but the lane was empty, and soon they had turned from it to one even less traveled.

Duck kept his eyes trained on the black boots in front of him. When they climbed a set of wooden stairs, he climbed with them. Now they stood on what appeared to be a porch of some sort. A door opened.

"Richard, is the upstairs parlor occupied, perchance?" the woman said.

"No, ma'am, all occupants are out and about at the moment," said a man.

"Very well." The woman swept back her dress to reveal the boy clutching her leg.

"Ma'am?" said Richard.

"Stand up, young man," Dame Bethany said. Duck stood. Julius climbed up to his shoulder. The man standing before Duck had the very dark skin denoting African descent, and watery black eyes.

"This is Richard," the woman said. "He takes care of things for me. Tell him your name."

Duck pointed up. "Well, Richard, this one here is Julius, and he's usually very well behaved, but he did just throw his business at some decent people, and I am sorry for that. My name is Elias, but everyone calls me Duck."

"Have you no surname, Duck?" asked Dame Bethany.

"I do, ma'am, or I think maybe I have two. I am not so sure." This was a point Duck had not fully sorted out from Kitto's explanation back on the *Blessed William*. "It was Wheale—and maybe it still is, but I know it is also Quick. That's what my brother Kitto told me anyways, but I will believe it for sure when my mum—"

"What did you say? That name?" Dame Bethany had gone rigid. Duck looked up at her. There was some sort of fearful look in the old woman's pale blue eyes.

Duck began again. "Well, my name was always Wheale, but then—"

"No." The woman cut him off again. "Your brother. 'Kitto,' you said."

"Yes, ma'am. It stands for—"

"Christopher. 'Christopher Quick' is his name?"

"Yes, ma'am." Duck turned to Richard, but the aging man gave no sign of recognition. The woman clutched Duck by the wrist.

"We must go up. At once!"

CHAPTER 26:

The Grand Dame

Duck lay back on the sofa in the parlor, his mouth and cheeks smeared with powdered sugar and the juices of unfamiliar fruits. Dame Bethany had blanketed her chair with an old tablecloth in the hopes of protecting it from the ashes that clung to Duck's clothing. His every movement left smudges on the worn fabric. He had been offered a wet rag as well to make himself more presentable, so his face was clean enough of soot, but for two dark marks at his nostrils and the corners of his eyes. Richard had brought up a tray loaded with pastries and cut melons, and with no mother there to tell him he had eaten enough, Duck ate until he felt his stomach would surely burst. Julius hunched in a corner of the room, nibbling at a white chunk of coconut.

"Your appetite has not suffered from your journey, I see," Bethany observed. She sat on a chair opposite the low-slung table that held the diminished tray of sweets.

"But, Duck, you have kept me in suspense too long. I said after your treats you would have to tell me your story and spare no details. Please, lad."

Duck looked over at her through drooping eyes. "I think I could nap," he said.

Bethany poured him a cup of tea. "Sit up." Duck did as told. The woman tilted the cup to his lips and he took a sip.

"I don't like tea," he said.

"Now don't be rude. Did not your mother teach you better?"

It was the wrong thing to say. She could tell it by the hangdog look that overtook the boy's face.

"I don't know where Mum is, or if ever I'll see her again."

Dame Bethany moved from her seat and came around the table to sit next to the boy. She put her arm around his shoulders and did not protest when Julius hopped up onto the sofa and curled into Duck's lap.

"Have it out, son."

And Duck did. He told it all, or at least so much as he understood, and not necessarily in the order that it happened. Duck told her about the uncle named William who had arrived in Falmouth, how bad men named Morris and Spider were following him. He told Bethany about the dagger, and his ship journey, and how he was nearly sold off into slavery. He told her about his father's fate, or at least what Kitto had told him. He told her about Kitto saving him and about the battle during which he cowered in the barrel as Kitto and Van had told him to.

At one point Richard knocked softly on the door

and peeped his head in. Bethany went to him, and the old man whispered in her ear for a few minutes, then closed the door again. Duck resumed his tale.

The little boy was not one for excessive speeches, and this one might well have been his longest. As he neared the end of it he reached out for a jam-filled pastry to give him the support he needed to finish.

"Your father was a cooper?"

"Yes, Gran. Did I say that part?"

"And your brother. His foot?"

"I didn't tell you that! Do you know him?" Duck brightened. "Yes, it's all crooked like, but he's the best brother. You haven't seen him here, have you?"

Dame Bethany stood. She nearly pinched herself. *Can it even be possible? That dear boy . . . I lost Mercy, but is it possible that Kitto I have not lost?* Bethany walked to the window overlooking the lane. She lifted a hand to pull back the curtain and noted that it shook.

"I did know your brother, some years ago, when he was about your age and he lived in Jamaica."

Dame Bethany watched a horse-drawn carriage roll past on the paved road. It did not seem so many years ago to her now. The depth of her loss felt raw, and more than that, the ache of her own guilt gnawing away at her as it had these last seven years felt as fresh as it ever had.

Her beloved Mercy. Like a daughter to her, the daughter that she had never had, the daughter who wanted to leave her and take away little Kitto, too.

Dame Bethany had suffered before. She was married once as a young woman and lost her husband to war. She had carried a child, but that child had not survived. She had endured long nights alone in the strange and sometimes ugly city that was Port Royal. But there was never any pain that stung like the rejection of when Mercy had told her she would leave Jamaica forever, following the cooper and taking young Kitto with her.

I should have let them go. I should never have informed Morgan, she told herself for the thousandth time. Bethany turned around to look at the little boy who was trying to lick the end of his nose with his tongue. Her heart quickened for a moment.

Could it be that into her lap had fallen the opportunity to redeem herself for her crimes? Her sins?

"Morris knows you to see you, Duck? He would recognize you?"

Duck nodded. "I'd recognize him first. And Spider, too, and the whole crew."

Bethany sat down next to the boy. She removed the remainder of the pastry from his hands and set it back on the tray. She took Duck's hands in hers. The feel of such small fingers startled her memory. How long had it been . . . ?

"Look at me, lad." Duck lifted his chin. "I was a dear friend to Kitto's mother. She was . . . I thought of her as my daughter. But I did her a great wrong, and your being here might just allow me to right that wrong."

"Yes, Gran. Can I call you that?" Duck said. "If it

don't bother you, I mean. I don't mean as if you was really old."

Bethany grinned. "Of course you can. But hear me, Duck. Port Royal is not safe for you, not if all that you tell me is true."

"I swear it is true."

"Then you are going to have to trust me."

"Already do," Duck said. And that was true as well.

"I shall try to visit your uncle," she said. "You must stay here, not even go outside. Not until I come back. You made a bit of a scene, I hear, when you arrived."

Duck hung his head. "Am I in trouble bad?"

"If they find you, yes. And worse, if all of Port Royal knows of your arrival, then surely Henry Morgan will too, and it will not take him long to connect you with William Quick."

CHAPTER 27:

Prison

"Wait here for me, Richard," Dame Bethany said, stepping from the carriage and into the dirt lane. "They shan't allow me but a moment."

Bethany approached the iron bars of the doorway. It was a suitably grim-looking place, the prison. Its walls were composed of gray stone, and it was set into a steep hillside as if the earth might have thought to swallow it but wisely reconsidered. Only along the second story were there any windows at all, where the constable would bring inmates for questioning or to prepare them in the event of a trial.

Bethany put a hand to one of the bars and peered in toward the alcove inside. The floor was covered in straw, and on that straw lay a man of titan proportions, sleeping on his side with his back to the locked door.

"Gibbs, my dear! Come and see me." The body stirred and pushed up onto an elbow. "'Tis Dame Bethany, Gibbs, and I have brought something for you." The man was slow to stand, and when he finally found his feet, he did not bother to brush the straw from his rumpled clothes. Gibbs towered well over six feet, and when he walked through the alcove door to the main hall, he had to duck low. He had big droopy eyes and a bulbous nose, hair the same color as the straw that clung to his shirt.

"Mmmmm," he said, rubbing his stomach. He was looking at the basket hanging at the crook of Dame Bethany's arm.

"Yes, Gibbs. Something for you. My Janie just made it." Bethany withdrew from the basket a meat pie wrapped in a white cloth. Gibbs reached out a grubby hand for it. He rotated it to draw it through the bars and then lifted it to his nose. His mouth opened wide in a smile that consisted of a single brown tooth. Bethany smiled back at him.

"Gibbs, I need you to fetch Mr. Sims for me. Will you do that for Dame Bethany?" Gibbs turned doleful brown eyes on Bethany. He looked down at the warm bundle in his hands. Bethany could see that he was considering giving the pie back rather than fetching the jailer.

"Shepherd's pie, Gibbs! Fresh meat, too. Now run get Mr. Sims and be a good boy." Gibbs brought the bundle to his chest and cradled it between his two massive hands. He nodded slowly, then turned to shuffle back to his alcove. He covered the pie beneath a bundle of straw, then exited the room again and turned to walk down the dark corridor out of sight.

After a few minutes a man emerged from the utter darkness of the passageway—as from the depths of hell itself—the musical jangling of keys accompanying him. Bethany stepped back from the bars. Vernon Sims sauntered up the dark hall, the perpetual smudge of a sneer spread across his face. Sims spent his days doing what he could to pique the torment of those unfortunate enough to find themselves in his prison. He was never short of work and never tired of it.

"You must have bought old Gibbs off." Sims flashed a tangle of teeth. "I hope it was worth it to the dumb ape."

"I have brought you more than a meat pie, Mr. Sims," Bethany said.

"Better have. I don't like being interrupted when I am tending to my inmates."

"I have no doubt your heart is in your work. I know, too, that you love a few coins in your pocket."

"If they be silver, then you're right."

"They are." Dame Bethany pulled herself up straighter. "You have a prisoner, a new one?"

"The Pirate Quick!" Sims rubbed the knuckles of his right hand. "I was just teaching him some manners."

Bethany's jaw clenched, but she choked back her anger. That would have to wait.

"He is an old friend of mine," she said.

"And he's gonna die with a rope about his neck soon enough."

Bethany nodded. "This I do not doubt. Which is why I am here now. I would like to pay my respects."

"Constable says no visitors for that one."

"Of course he did." Bethany reached into her basket

and withdrew a small bundle wrapped in burlap and tied with twine. "But you are not a man who takes orders from such an oaf lightly. After all, you are the jailer and not he. Is not that right, Mr. Sims?"

Vernon Sims reached a hand out through the bars to take the bundle from her, but Bethany withdrew it from his reach.

"William Quick," she said.

Sims led Bethany through a maze of dank corridors and past countless dreary cells, many of them occupied. Most jailers kept petty criminals—pickpockets, thugs, cheats—in large holding cells, but not Sims. He found that separating inmates into solitary units added to their torment.

After what seemed like a long walk, Sims set down the stool he carried in one hand and pointed into a dark hole. He handed Dame Bethany the lantern.

"There's your pirate," he said. "Don't bother trying to walk out alone. I'll come fetch you." Sims slunk off into the darkness, unbothered without the lantern.

Bethany dared not look into the cell until she heard Sims's echoing boot heels fade away.

"William!" she whispered. Bethany peered into the gloom. The chamber was only a few feet wide but several feet deep. It was made fast by thick bars that reached floor to ceiling, interrupted only by a narrow barred door set in the middle, from which hung a large padlock. Matted black straw clung to the stone floor and piled up at the rear.

Bethany lifted the lantern and squinted her eyes. Yes, she could make out a dark form at the back, a man lying down.

"William! We have little time! It is I, Dame Bethany. The Grand Dame." The dark form stirred. It gave out a moan. "I have fresh water," she said. "Come and get it, William."

It took William Quick nearly an entire minute to find his feet. Without the wall to lean upon, he would not have been able to do it. Slowly he rose, looking as if at any moment his knees might buckle. He shuffled toward the barred door, grimacing with each step.

Bethany set her basket on the floor and withdrew from it the flagon of water. She plucked the cork out and lifted it to William, whose grimy fingers curled around the thick bars. The flagon was too wide at the base to pass through, but it had a narrow neck, and with Bethany's help the two of them were able to lift the container to his lips.

William took a long drink, sputtering once or twice. Finally Bethany withdrew it. "More shortly," she said. She set the flagon down and brought the lantern closer. "Let's have a look at you."

What she saw gave her a start. One of William's eyes was entirely swollen shut and his face was smeared with some combination of blood and dirt. His cheeks were sunken and his skin pale, giving him a cadaverous look that chilled Bethany. The mustache he once wore with such flair drooped lifelessly and lost itself into tangles of matted beard. Had she not looked closely, she never would have recognized him.

"Time has not spared you, William. You look terrible."

A slight smirk curled beneath the mustache. "Hello, Grand Dame," he said thickly. His eye adjusted enough to the light to allow him to squint. "Though you are not changed at all."

"Yes. I remain an old and wrinkled woman." She reached out and wrapped a hand over his on the bar. She sighed. "What have they done to you? What has *he* done?"

William gave a grunt that was intended to be a laugh. "The usual things on the ship," he said. "Nothing so surprising. The jailer, though, he has paid me a visit I did not expect." Bethany felt her face flush with anger. She would deal with Sims.

"I shall take care of him," she said. William grunted again.

"Pardon me, but I must sit," he said, and leaning his back against the wall, he slowly slid to the floor with a chorus of moans and grunts. Bethany pulled the stool close. She reached into the basket and withdrew another bundle.

"Have some meat pie," she said, and placed it in his lap. William unwrapped the cloth and dove into the small pie with shaking fingers. He dug at it ravenously, bits of pastry crust and gravy clinging to his beard. Bethany was quiet until he was finished, then reached through the bars to wipe his beard clean for him with the cloth.

"Do you need anything else?" she said.

William's smirk had recovered a bit more of its former sauciness. "Not unless you happen to have a set of keys like the jailer's."

"Do not think I have not given thought already as to how to spring you from this hellhole."

William turned his good eye upon her. "Not just me. My men are here too. I would never leave without them."

"Yes, yes. You and your men," Bethany said. "I remember when Henry Morgan was one of them. Or rather you one of his." She reached out and took William's right hand, turning the back of it toward the golden light. She saw on his hand a blackened square.

"I see you have covered over the skeleton hand tattoo," she said.

"Aye. Couldn't stand the remembrance. I had that done in prison in Cuba."

"Is that where you have been then? All these years? I figured Morgan had caught up to you after all and made you to disappear."

"No such luck. The Spanish were ahead in the line."

"And yet you escaped? Certainly they would never have let you go."

William attempted to wink, but with only one eye working, the effect was lost. "My charm finally won them over."

"Oh, please." Bethany looked down into the blackened hallway, hoping that the occasional stirrings she could hear were those of other prisoners and not Sims trying to eavesdrop. "Your charm was never as impressive as you thought it was." Bethany leaned closer to the bars.

"William, we must speak in earnest. Do you know of a boy who goes by the nickname of 'Duck'?" William's head came up from the wall where it leaned.

"Yes. Of course. He is her son."

"Whose son?"

"The woman I have fallen in love with, and the one who is either already dead or will be so at any moment from exposure to the elements."

"Duck did mention something to me about her."

"Wait." William touched his hand to his head. "Say again, now. 'Duck mentioned' . . . You have spoken to this boy? How? Last I knew Kitto and Van had hidden him somewhere aboard the *William*, but that was weeks ago!"

It was Bethany's turn to smile. "He is your nephew, William. I think he got more than his fair share of your charm, and possibly all the luck you never had."

"Explain, woman!"

"Don't get irascible with an elderly wench who brings you hot meat pie! Somehow the boy stayed hidden. Apparently there was a sailor who helped him, and then he came to land in a barrel—with a monkey of all things!"

"I hate that monkey."

"Julius seems quite harmless to me. He is in my parlor now back at the rooming house."

"Duck is at your house too?"

Bethany explained how it had come to pass.

"Hid beneath your dress? I shall have to try that sometime. . . ." William smirked.

"You will get the heel of my boot if you do. But his mother?" Bethany said.

William explained what he had heard, that Duck's mother had last been seen adrift in a rowboat with Kitto during the battle.

"And Frederick, too, is dead?" she said.

William grunted in assent. "I am a plague of disasters for that family."

"Not such a plague as I have been, William," Bethany said softly.

"Whatever do you mean? You took Kitto's mother Mercy in, made her like a daughter to you. You risked Morgan's contempt, did you not? And you treated her boy like your own grandson despite his clubfoot."

"I killed her, William," Bethany whispered. William grew quiet. "I killed her." William waited for her to elaborate, but she did not.

"Old age has addled your brain, woman." He patted her hand. You were her faithful friend."

"I am the one who told Morgan."

William's hand froze. "Told him what?"

"I told him that Mercy and Frederick intended to leave. I told him that she knew about the nutmeg."

"I don't understand. Henry Morgan is the one who told Mercy about the nutmeg," William said.

"Morgan told Mercy to convince her to stay. He said

he would share the treasure with her and Kitto if she would just stay in Jamaica."

"But she was married by then! The fool! He never stopped loving her, did he?" William said.

"I do not know if *that* is the best word for his attachment. He was both obsessed and repulsed by her. But he would never allow her to leave Jamaica for good."

William grasped Bethany about the wrist. "Then why did you tell him she intended to leave!"

Bethany snatched away her arm and covered her face with her hands in shame. "I, too, I could never allow her to leave. Her and my sweet Kitto both? No. I was sure that if I told Morgan, he would convince her somehow. That together we could keep them near us."

William scoffed. "Morgan's convincing was a bit on the deadly side."

"Yes." Bethany puzzled. "I have never understood that part. Poison her? Why?"

"Because she was going to leave him. Makes perfect sense."

Bethany shook her head. "You did not see him after he returned from Panama—or rather, returned from chasing you. For months he was like a walking dead man through the streets of Port Royal. He neither ate nor slept; he spurned everyone who was close to him, even Morris. Why would he have seemed so distraught if he was the one who murdered Mercy?"

William reached to twist the ends of his mustache. It pleased Bethany to see some of his old habits again.

"Maybe he did not then. But who did? Frederick?"

"Never. Frederick was a lamb with her. No one but Morgan makes any sense."

William patted Bethany's hand anew. "A curse to the whole family line, we are. A matched pair of killers."

"Yes. But now we have an opportunity for not so small a penance."

William's eye glinted in the lantern light. "Duck, you mean?"

"We're all he has left in the world, you and I."

"He's my nephew. He is nothing to you."

"When he smiles I remember the look on his father's face when Mercy was in the room. It is not much, but that boy's smile might be as close to Mercy as I will ever get."

The meat pie had renewed William's spirits, and his wits, too. He leaned against the bars to peer into the darkness. Paranoia is a hard habit to break, especially when it has proven useful for many years.

"Duck is not safe in Port Royal," William said. "Perhaps you are still involved in that other business?" His eyebrows arched.

"Business? That is not a business. Businesses make money. That is only an expense."

"So you still help the caged birds to freedom?" he said slowly.

Bethany nodded. "Now and then. Not enough as I should, but yes. I remember you and I were of like minds in this regard."

"In Jamaica even the priests bless slavery," William

answered. "That is proof enough to me it is an evil thing."

It was Bethany's turn to caress William's hand. "I can get Duck to Nanny. But I am not a woman of means. We'll need you, too."

"My personal worth is at a bit of a low, madam. The pie in my stomach is all I have left in the world."

"Where is all your treasure, Pirate Quick?"

William shook his head. "By now it is all in Morris's greedy hands."

Bethany turned. Sims's footfalls approached gradually from the abyss of darkness. "Perhaps. Perhaps not. Life has set upon me more times than all the times you have ever known, young man. Remember the Greek proverb: 'There is many a slip twixt a cup and a lip.'" Bethany rose. "Stay alive for now, and leave the rest to me."

"My men, too," William said. "My men, too."

Bethany scowled. "As stubborn as ever."

"Pigheaded," William agreed.

Bethany walked with the lantern toward Vernon Sims, who had come to a stop several yards away. She handed him the lantern, the yellow light distorting the man's features into the mask of some kind of demon.

"Mr. Sims," she said. "I will be taking care of Mr. Quick's food and drink for the remainder of his stay here."

"That's all fine and good, ma'am, but . . ."

"Shut your mouth, Mr. Sims, if you please," Bethany whispered. "Hold the lantern up a bit higher, man."

Sims raised it. "I would like you to see the look in my eye when I say these words to you."

"Now wait, Dame."

"I will not wait. You may kill me now, here, in the dark, Mr. Sims, and discard of my body. If that is your intention—"

"Of course it ain't!"

"If it is not, sir, then you had best hear *my* intention. Should Mr. Quick or any of his compatriots in this cursed gaol meet with any further torments at your hands, I can assure you that I will arrange to have your head stove in. I would wager that even Gibbs would do it for an extra meat pie, and if not him, then I have plenty more who owe me a favor or two who would do it gleefully. Am I understood, Mr. Sims?"

"You threatening me?"

"I am. And not idly."

Sims grunted.

"The words, if you please."

"Good enough," Sims said, scowling. "But I don't like it."

CHAPTER 28:

Dumaka

"I am sorry, Gran-B, but Julius could not hold it. He made his business over there in the corner."

Bethany had just reentered the parlor after unlocking it with the key that Richard had given her for the task. She rested her collapsed parasol against the leg of an upholstered chair and looked to where Duck indicated.

"As tidy as a cat," she said, impressed.

"Even cleaner!" Duck said. "Cats lick themselves with their tongues all the time. Everybody knows that ain't clean."

"*Isn't* clean," Bethany said, arching an eyebrow.

"Aw, Gran!"

Outside the sun had just set, and the shadows stretched long.

"I need you and Julius to come with me. There is someone you must meet."

Duck gathered Julius up onto his shoulder and followed as Bethany led him to a door at the far side of the room. She opened it to reveal a back stair leading down to the kitchen.

"Very quiet now," she said. "Two of the boarders have returned. It is best that no one knows you are here."

Duck knew how to be quiet. He hoped that Julius remembered as well. They stepped gingerly down the painted planks and reached a kitchen in which a slim and very dark woman poked a wooden spoon at a boiling chicken on the stove. The woman turned to greet them but froze when she saw Duck. Duck smiled and waved at her. The woman pointed the spoon at the boy.

"Miss B, is this one of them things I am not really seeing?" she asked in a low voice.

"That is correct, Janie. Two of them, actually. You neither saw a boy nor a monkey in my home."

"Seems I would remember if I had seen such strange sights."

Duck looked down at himself, then up at Bethany. He leaned a cupped hand toward the old woman. "Is she blind?" he said. Bethany winked at him and pushed him toward a narrow door at the back of the kitchen. She undid the bolt at the top and turned the knob. Janie brought over to her a candle she lit from the fire in the oven.

Behind the door was a set of rough steps leading down into darkness.

"Go on, Duck," she said, but the little boy hesitated.

"Oh, not again!" Duck lamented. "Can't whoever it is come up here instead?"

Bethany held her hand out to him and Duck took it. "Fear not," she said, and together they made their way down the creaky stairs. Behind them Janie closed the door and turned the deadbolt. Duck squeezed tight Bethany's hand.

"I think she just locked us in, Gran-B," Duck said. Bethany tucked the boy's arm under hers. "All is well, Duck. Trust me." The stairwell was not long, and ran itself out against a hard-packed dirt floor. Duck looked around at the stacks of old vegetable crates and cob-webbed jars. The cellar was larger than a typical root cellar, occupying most of the rooming house's footprint.

"Dumaka!" Bethany said. The dirt walls and floor seemed to swallow up her voice. Duck looked up at her questioningly, but then recoiled in fear as he saw some-thing move off in the recesses of shadow. The shadow approached them, and the first that Duck could make out of the darkness were the whites of two eyes. A young man stepped forward into the candle's glow.

"Dumaka," Bethany said. She pointed at the young boy clutching her dress. "This is Duck. Duck," she said again slowly, and Duck looked across the candlelit space suspiciously, thinking this other fellow must be a bit hard in the head to have to be spoken to so simply. He cast a wary look at the man. He seemed barely old enough to call himself a man, really, but he stood tall enough and had the darkest skin that Duck had ever seen. He wore no shirt, simply a pair of ragged trousers that ran to the knee.

"And Julius," Duck said, pointing at the monkey on his shoulder, who gave Dumaka a leery appraisal.

Dumaka held an open hand out to Julius to show the animal he meant it no harm, and Duck was curious to see that the skin on the palm of Dumaka's hand was much lighter than on the rest of his body.

"Duck," Bethany looked down at him. "This is Dumaka. He is a slave who has run away."

"Oh!" Duck had very little sense of what it meant to be a slave. Before his journey across the ocean he knew the term only from hearing it when little kids complained after being ordered around by the bigger ones down at the wharf in Falmouth. They would say things like, "It ain't like I'm your slave!" Now he knew slavery mostly by smell, a visceral memory of the slave ship on which he had spent a single night some weeks before, an odor that etched an indelible mark in his memory.

"I am a slave who ran away too!" he said to the young man. He held out his hand to shake as his mother had taught him. Dumaka looked at the boy's hand, then back up at Bethany. She nodded at him, and slowly Dumaka extended his own. Duck lifted the man's arm in two dramatic shakes, then released his hand. Dumaka's lips lifted into a slight smile. "Who did *you* run away from?" Duck asked. The man looked up at Bethany expectantly.

"Henry Morgan," she said.

"Same!" Duck said aloud, grinning broadly. "Well, sort of." He grinned. Dumaka smiled broadly now, deep dimples puckering his cheeks. He reached out and patted Duck atop the head. Julius growled softly and shoved Dumaka's hand away.

"Julius, be nice! He ain't hurting me or nothing." Duck tilted his head.

"Isn't," Bethany corrected.

"Aw, Gran."

"Listen to me, Duck," Bethany said. "This is important. Dumaka was very lucky. He happened to hide in a shed owned by a Quaker man opposed to slavery. That man knew to bring him to me."

"Why you, Gran-B?"

"Because from time to time I help slaves to make it to the maroon colonies, something for which I could be severely punished by the law."

"What's a manure colony?"

"*Maroon.* It is a place on this island where runaway slaves live. It is far from here, deep in the mountains, hard enough to get to that no one ever tries to bring them back."

"Oh. Is that where he is going?"

"Yes. And you are going with him."

Duck looked up at Bethany with wounded eyes. "But, Gran, I thought I would stay with you!"

Bethany brushed her thumb against the boy's cheek. "It is only for a time. Until I can get my affairs in order, and then I shall fetch you and we shall go far from here to live."

"Will my mum and Kitto be able to find me there?"

"We can hold out hope, can we not?"

"Right," Duck said. "More of that hoping stuff." He breathed a heavy sigh.

"So when are Dumaka and me leaving for the manure?"

Duck slept atop a fresh pile of straw, a bundled wool blanket tucked under his head for a pillow. Julius curled in his customary place—in the crook between Duck's legs—while Dumaka made his bed farther along the dirt wall of the cellar. A rickety stack of crates on the floor provided a makeshift wall to hide them should one of the boarders happen to venture down, but the likelihood of that was small. Janie could be quite cross when her kitchen was invaded during the day, and her nights she spent on the sleeping porch adjacent to the kitchen.

"Wake up, son. Wake up!"

Duck stirred but did not open his eyes. He had not slept in safety for weeks, and for the first time in so long his dreams were untroubled and deep.

"Rise up. It is time," Bethany said. Her efforts were helped along by Julius, who scampered up Duck's prostrate body and inserted a furry monkey finger into the boy's left nostril, and then—when Julius received little reaction—a second finger into the other. Duck sat up sneezing and swatted at his pet.

"That's rude!" Duck said, scowling up at the lantern Bethany held. The boy's eyes came into focus, and he saw that Dumaka had already risen and was standing behind Bethany, his eyes wide with fear.

"Is it time?"

"It is. Sit up now and be alert. I have important

things to tell you. Dumaka will not understand it all, so you must be able to hear and to remember for the both of you. If you do not, then neither of you will survive."

"Oi!" Duck rubbed his eyes with the heels of his palms, then gave his head a savage shake. Blades of straw slipped from his head onto his shoulders. Bethany brushed them away.

"A man will come to take you on a wagon ride. Get in the back of the wagon and cover yourselves with straw."

"To stay hidden?"

"Yes. He will ride you well out of town, to a creek. Follow the creek upstream and just keep going. It will take you several days before you get there."

"To where the other runaways live."

"Yes. They will see you before you see them. And they have guns."

"Do they know we are coming?" Duck said.

Bethany shook her head. "Stay with Dumaka and they will understand that you are runaways. Find a woman named Nanny. She is the leader of the colonies. And tell her that I sent you." Bethany produced a small leather pouch with a thong that she looped about Duck's neck. She tucked the pouch beneath his shirt.

"What's that?" he asked, patting the pouch under his shirt.

"It is some money for Nanny, and a note of explanation."

"When will you be coming, Gran-B?" Duck said. He hated the thought of having to leave the kindly woman.

"You're . . . well . . . you and my uncle, you're like the only family I have got in Jamaica." Bethany pulled Duck in for a hug. She held him long and tried to squeeze all her love into the little boy. How could he have found his way into her heart almost instantly? But she knew how. She knew that her heart had been waiting for just such a moment for the last seven years.

"Your uncle and I will come fetch you, just as soon as we can."

"How long?"

"Soon."

Duck accepted the answer with a scowl. At least he had action to look forward to. After having spent weeks in the hold of a ship—much of it cowering in a barrel, never knowing when Julius might screech out his frustrations and land both of them in shackles—the idea of a long hike into unknown mountains sounded appealing.

And he wouldn't be alone. Julius was always good company, and maybe Duck could teach Dumaka how to speak the King's English.

"Take my hand, now," Bethany said. "It is this way." Bethany led them to the far corner of the cellar where some old boards leaned against the dirt wall. Bethany handed the candleholder to Duck and motioned for Dumaka to lend a hand. Together they lifted away the boards one by one from where they leaned. There were several layers of wide planks, but after they had removed a few, Duck lifted high the light.

"'Tis a door back there!" he said.

"Yes. A secret door, too." Bethany slid the iron bolt aside, then pulled hard on the handle. The hinges groaned as the heavy wooden door swung open. Duck held out the candle and peered into the black passage beyond.

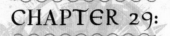

CHAPTER 29:

Flight by Night

"Where's it go?" Duck said, a tremor of fear in his voice. He squinted suspiciously into the dark passage.

"Not far at all," said Bethany. "The shaft passes just below the lane out front and comes out in the midst of a stone hedge at the far side."

"Do we have to go in there?" Duck said. He had spent enough time in dark places for them to populate a lifetime of nightmares. "Can't we just go out the back door of the kitchen?"

"If you were seen, my dear," Bethany said, "you and Dumaka would be the last two ever to be helped along to freedom from my house. That hardly seems fair to me. Does it to you?"

Duck made a face. "Oh, fine," he said. "And what we do once we pop out the hedge?"

"Travel along it, keeping the hedge between you and the lane. Keep your monkey quiet."

"He don't always listen to me."

"Keep the hedge on your right side. You do know which one is your right, don't you?"

"Sure. This one." Duck lifted up his left, then grinned.

"Do not be cheeky," Bethany said. Duck raised his other hand. "Yes, that one. Do not forget, or you shall end up back at the wharf."

"I know which way *that* is, don't worry." Bethany put her palm atop Duck's head and wagged it side to side.

"Little scamp you are," she said. "Now listen. Go along the hedge until you reach an intersection. Wait there out of sight. The man in the wagon will arrive. If it is the right man, he will stop his wagon to tend to his horses. When he does that, the two of you get in the back and cover yourselves."

Duck looked up at Dame Bethany with doleful eyes. "You quite sure I can't just stay with you here? I'd stay right here in this basement!"

"I promise I'll send for you, boy, or arrive myself when the time is right. Until then Nanny will care for you."

Duck patted the pouch Bethany had put round his neck. "And if my mum or Kitto should come looking for me?" he said.

"Then I will deliver them to you just this same way."

With a few more reassurances and a hurried embrace, Bethany shooed them into the dark passage. Dumaka went first, taking the candleholder and waving it in front of him to part the thick cobwebs.

It was a low-slung passage they entered, so Dumaka had to bend at the waist to walk. Duck clung to the back of his trousers and shrank from the eerily wavering cobweb strands. The spider silk crackled in the candle's flame. Julius rode atop Duck's shoulder until he became entangled in filaments of web. He swatted them away frantically, then dropped to the ground behind Duck with a screech.

"Julius, shut it!" Duck said. The monkey leaped up and dug his claws into Duck's pants, clinging to his backside so as to avoid both the darkness of the floor and the disconcerting stickiness of the cobwebs.

"I don't like the dark, Dumaka," Duck said. "What about you?" Dumaka said nothing but grunted at the effort of walking in such an awkward position.

The earthen walls of the shaft were punctuated by wooden posts that connected to a network of crisscrossing joists at the dirt ceiling. The path was clear excepting the cobwebs, and the two moved quickly. It was not long before Duck bumped into Dumaka, who had come to an abrupt stop.

"Here," the man said, and it was the first word that Duck had heard him say. Dumaka moved aside so that Duck could see an iron ladder against a wall, leading up into blackness.

"Let me go first," Duck said, not interested in being left alone in the shaft. He pushed his way past Dumaka and scrambled up the rungs, Julius still clinging to his trousers, swinging this way and that as Duck climbed. Together they entered into a narrow vertical tunnel of dirt and rock.

Quickly Duck noted a dull brightness above him. A

few more steps up and he saw stars overhead, somewhat obscured by overgrowth. The rough tunnel opened up into the neatly stacked stones of the hedge. He pushed his way past the vines and climbed out and over the stones. On the far side he could make out the strip of pavement that was the lane. Julius propped himself onto a stone and looked down into the blackness for Dumaka.

The man arrived moments later without the candle, one hand clutching the bundle of food Bethany had given them. He too clambered out over the rocks and onto the carpet of overgrown grasses beyond the hedge. This side of the stone wall bordered a cleared field that held no crop and looked as if it had been left to lie fallow.

Duck turned to look either way up and down the stone wall, determining which was the correct direction. Dumaka seemed to know. He took Duck's hand and led them so that the hedge and lane were on the their right side. Julius scampered along behind them.

"Is this the right way?" Duck hissed. Dumaka turned around and tapped his fingers against his own mouth, a gesture Duck had never seen before but knew its meaning nonetheless. They walked on, the silence of the night heavy and the lane thoroughly deserted.

After just a few minutes of walking along the dew-moistened grasses, they reached another stone hedge, meeting their own at a right angle.

"This is it," Duck said as softly as he could. Dumaka nodded to him, and they sat on the ground. Dumaka leaned back and rested his head on a rock. Duck spread himself out on the grass and closed his eyes, and Julius nestled into a warm spot atop the boy's chest.

Duck awoke sometime later to the feel of Dumaka's rough fingers pressed against his lips. Duck sat up. In the distance he could hear the clomp of horse hooves and the jangle of harness and leads. The two of them huddled up against the wall and waited.

By the time the wagon drew alongside their hedge the sounds of the horses and the creaks of the wagon seemed impossibly loud to Duck. But then a voice called to the horses and the wagon stopped just at the intersection.

"Well, Athena and Apollo," a low voice said, "seems only fair to give you some oats for carrying me at such an odd hour." Duck heard the driver's boot heels scrape the gravel as he hopped down to the lane.

Duck pulled himself up and peered at the wagon in the lane standing in dappled starlight. One of the horses neighed contentedly and tossed his head.

Duck found Dumaka's hand.

"Come on!" he said. "Now is when Gran said we go." Duck scooped Julius up into his arms, and the monkey did not resist. Dumaka watched the boy scamper over the stone hedge and climb into the open wagon. The driver remained rigidly facing forward even though Duck's complaints about Julius's sharp claws would have been audible to any passerby.

Dumaka gathered his courage and vaulted over the hedge.

CHAPTER 30:

Captives

SEVERAL DAYS LATER, IN CUBA

Exquemelin was the first to be called in for questioning. Hours earlier a barred wagon had transported the alleged English pirates from the Spanish galley at Havana Harbor to the prison not far from the wharf. The ride in the wagon through the tidy lanes of the town had not been a long one, but a gathering of curious townspeople trailed the vehicle as it made its way through the lanes. It had been Van who had pointed out the gibbet to Kitto and Akin at the wharf. It was a large pole standing in the water, and hanging from a hook at its top was a metal frame encasing the skeletal remains of some poor victim of the Spanish justice system. Kitto did not need to ask what it was. When the marines unloaded them in shackles and led them through the stone archway and into the prison, Kitto knew that the gawkers were eagerly anticipating the entertainment that was soon to come to them.

Hangings always drew a crowd.

Two marines had led Exquemelin away, leaving the rest of the gloomy company to ponder its dire predicament. They were kept in a single cell. The ceiling was quite high—twelve feet at least—and up at the top of one wall a barred window admitted the glow of daylight.

The massive stones surrounding them threw echoes of their hushed voices.

"What you think they be doing to him?"

"You know it already."

"They sure to hang us, you think?"

"Of course they will! It's what they do to English."

"They don't know nothing about us."

"They got a witness, ain't they? That is more than they need."

Kitto and Sarah and Ontoquas sat at one corner of the cell. Bucket, having just eaten a bowlful of corn mush that Sarah had goaded from the jailer, slept peacefully in the woman's arms. Kitto leaned his head back against the stones.

He hardly dared admitting aloud what he knew was true.

"I signed the articles," he said in a whisper. Sarah shook her head.

"You are a boy! You could not have known the import of what you were doing. They surely do not hang boys!" The men, overhearing them, threw long looks in Kitto's direction. They knew otherwise.

"I would not change what I did, Mum," Kitto said. It was true. *How can it be true?* he wondered. But it was.

Signing the articles had been their only chance, but it seemed they had no chance after all.

Perhaps only a handful of days I have bought all of us, he thought. *But still I would change nothing. If I have saved the lives of sixteen men for these several days, have I not done something?*

"We cannot give up hope," Sarah said. Kitto lowered his head and stared down at the sewn pant leg that covered his stump.

I, who was destined to do nothing . . .

Ontoquas reached to her chest and felt for the small amulet hanging there. When she was sure no one watched her, she slipped the necklace over her head and gathered it into the palm of one hand. She nudged Kitto with an elbow, and he turned to see her extending a clenched fist out to him beneath their folded legs.

Their hands met, and Ontoquas dropped the chain and cross into Kitto's upturned palm.

Why? he wanted to ask, but could only manage a questioning look.

"To protect," Ontoquas said. Whether she meant to protect Kitto or to protect the necklace, Kitto did not know. In fact, she meant both. Ontoquas had not been granted a vote ten days earlier when Exquemelin and his sworn pirates had decided whether or not to fight the Spanish out at sea. She would have voted to fight.

Ontoquas's name may not have appeared on the paper, true, but she knew in the pit of her stomach what would happen. With her skin, her hair, her age? The

Spanish would see her as all the *wompey* did—a menace to be dealt with. They would make her a slave again, a fate she swore she would never revisit. Death would be better.

And Bucket? Would they even let him live? Ontoquas let her long hair fall over her eyes so that Kitto could not see the tears that had begun to gather. She had failed Bucket. She had not saved him.

Kitto slipped the necklace over his own head and tucked the cross beneath his shirt. Next to him Sarah had closed her eyes, and her lips were mouthing a silent prayer. Kitto tried to do the same, but fear knotted his stomach and he found it hard to shape the words.

At that moment from beyond their cell came the sound of voices. A door clanged shut and footfalls approached, along with the sound of something being dragged along the stone floor.

Little John stood and peered as best he could through the bars set into the massive oak door of the cell.

"It's him! It's X," he said. "They be carrying him." Little John withdrew when the guard reached the door and barked something at him in Spanish.

A key grated in the lock, and the door opened. One guard stood at the entrance, and two others behind held X between them by his arms. X's bare head hung low and swayed as the men struggled forward.

"*Lo pongan ahí, el cerdo,*" the guard at the door said. He stepped aside so that the two men could enter. They heaved X inward, hurling him without a care into the cell. He would have struck the stone floor but for Quid, who leaped forward and snatched X from the air.

"Spanish pigs!" said Little John, struggling to stand.

The pirates rose to their feet in anger and surged toward the open door, but the first guard produced a pistol. He pressed it against Little John's cheek, puckering the skin.

At the rear of the cell Sarah thrust Bucket over to Ontoquas and pushed past Akin.

"Gentleman, please!" she said. "Let us not worsen our situation. Step back and allow me to attend to the captain's wounds."

The sound of a woman's voice subdued their anger. The guard with the pistol sneered.

"*Cobardes,*" he said as Little John backed away from the muzzle of his pistol. "*Piratas, cobardes, cerdos!*" His eyes swept over the assorted gathering with undisguised hatred.

For a moment Kitto thought he might fire the pistol regardless, but then an agitated voice sounded from behind him.

"*Perdón! A un lado!*" the voice said, and the guards stepped aside. A thin man dressed in black stepped into the doorway, the wide corners of his hat brushing against the iron doorframe. He had a pointed nose and long fingers with manicured nails that looked strikingly unfit in such a filthy room. He withdrew a scap of paper from a pocket.

"Which of you is known as 'Sarah, Van, Ontok . . .

Ontoquas, Akin, Bucket'?" he read in clear, but accented English. Sarah raised her hand and indicated the others.

"We are they," she said. "What news do you have for us?"

The man eyed her coldly before continuing. "The following words do not pertain to you," he said. He tossed the scrap aside and withdrew from a different pocket a folded piece of parchment that he opened before him. Kitto recognized it as the articles he had signed, and he felt a tight knot in his throat.

The man's eyes swept over the pirates. He coughed neatly to clear his voice. "'The Honorable Ernesto Delgado has ordered that by the evidence gathered against the following men'"—the man stopped himself—"meaning, the rest of you—'that they shall be hanged by the neck until death at precisely nine o'clock tomorrow morning for the crime of piracy.'"

Kitto had stood when X had been brought in, but now his knees buckled and he sagged against the wall behind him.

"No! No, this cannot be! What evidence?" Sarah protested, stepping forward. But the man did not regard her.

"Alexandre Exquemelin, John Phillip, Simon Xavier . . ." The man's voice droned on through all the names of the doomed men in the cell.

Kitto's thoughts swam circles. *How? How could this be? Is this to be my punishment? Am I to die?*

The man read the final name, snapping Kitto from his tortured thoughts.

"Christopher Quick!"

CHAPTER 31:

Hanging

After the man had spoken the sentence and left, a pall fell over the pirates that lasted into the evening. X sat with his head in his hands, the dangling beads of his beard utterly still. Even Sarah seemed lost, staring unblinking and pale at the stony floor, giving no notice when Ontoquas tried to pass Bucket into her arms to draw her from the black depths of her despair.

Only Van and Akin seemed to have any life left in them. They each moved to be closer to Kitto. Van draped an arm around his shoulders.

"It ain't over yet," Van said. "Perhaps that God you love is not yet done with you." Outside the prison the sun had set, and the cell was draped in a cloak of dusk.

"I want to be brave," Kitto said.

"You are very brave," Akin said.

"At the moment, I mean. When the rope . . . I want to die as a man should die."

"None of that matters," Van said.

"It does matter. It matters to me," Kitto said. He wondered if he had that kind of strength. "How you leave the world matters." Van and Akin had no answer for Kitto, and for a long time the three sat quietly. From a distant corner of the cell they heard a faint sniffling.

Van leaned closer so that he could whisper in Kitto's ear.

"I want you to know," Van said, and he had to stop to swallow hard. "You are not done with me, Kitto Quick, not even if you quit that body. I will take care of your mum. Akin and I both. And I will find Duck and bring them together. I swear it. On my worthless soul, I swear it, Kitto."

Kitto lifted his head and looked over at Van. Their hands came together in something of a shake.

"Yes," Kitto said. "But that is not the last you owe me, Van. One more thing."

"Say it."

"Once you have done those things, seen to the safety of Duck and my mum, I want you to go back to the island, Van."

"To the devil with that island!"

"Promise me. You will go back there and fetch the nutmeg. You will need to share it with the men you bring, and with Sarah, too, for my share. But then make off with a fine haul, Van. Go find your sister!"

Tears filled Van's eyes. He started to speak, but a sob broke through and it was some minutes before he could do so.

"How can you think of that now?" Van said.

"My dreams are shattering. I want you to see yours

fulfilled," Kitto told him. "And one more thing. When you go back to the island. Get inside the cave with someone small, perhaps Duck if you have found him. There is another treasure inside, Van. Fit for a king."

In the morning a detachment of Spanish soldiers dressed in dark blue uniforms entered the prison. The sharp cadence of their polished boot heels tore Exquemelin and his band from their last sleep, if such fitful nightmares could be called such.

At some point in the night Sarah had risen from her despair. She had nudged Akin aside and took Kitto into her arms as she sometimes did when he was a young boy. Kitto buried his head in the shelter of her soft neck. Together they had wept themselves into unconsciousness, but the sound of the approaching soldiers brought both to an instant and panicked attention.

Sarah tried. At the first glimpse of the brushed wool uniform and polished musket barrel, she rushed to the barred door.

"There has been a mistake. My son . . . he is just a boy! Please do not do this evil deed!" Sarah pleaded. None of the Spaniards would meet her gaze but attended instead to their duty of binding each of the men in shackles about the ankles and wrists, and leading them one by one down the stone hall and into the same wagon cage that had transported them from the ship the day before.

When it was Kitto's turn to go and the cell stood

empty but for Sarah, Akin, Van, Ontoquas, and Bucket, Sarah's pleas turned frantic.

"This is wrong! He is a boy! You must not do this thing!"

"Mum!" Kitto seized Sarah by the shoulders and turned her from the soldiers. "Let me go like a man," he said. "*You* must live. For Duck. He is your son!"

Sarah brought Kitto into her arms for a final crushing hug.

"You are my son," she said. She whispered in his ear, her voice catching. "It was you, Kitto. You have shown me how deep love goes. It was loving you that made me!"

The guards pulled Kitto away.

It was not a long ride in the wagon, but the driver kept the two horses in check so that the contingent of what must have been fifty soldiers in high uniform could flank the wagon on all sides as it rolled through the dusty lanes.

As they moved through the heart of the town and toward the wharf, people of all ages poured from the buildings and walked along with the procession. Some of them hurled insults, and a few even tossed rotten vegetables, which bounced harmlessly against the cage that held them and dropped into the lane.

Kitto watched a young girl who could not have been more than six bound out of a rickety doorway and skip along with the crowd. She wore a cheery red dress that billowed behind her as she skipped. She clutched some sort of stuffed doll in her arms which she tossed into the air and caught again. The dark curls of her hair bounced along with her as she ran, and Kitto allowed himself to be swept up for a moment in her joy. She did not seem to notice the wagon, only the excitement of the throng.

Look how happy she is! he marveled. *She is so very alive. . . .*

Finally the wagon rolled into an open cobblestone courtyard. The brilliant blue water of the harbor spread out to the north, dotted with dozens of anchored ships. At one end of the square stood the gallows, a massive construction erected of thick beams, wide enough to accommodate the entire party of seventeen at one time.

Kitto had kept his eye on the little girl as they traveled, but when the soldiers opened up the cage to lead them down in shackles to the stairs at the base of the gallows, the courtyard swelled with onlookers and he lost sight of her. Kitto was the last to leave the wagon. He had thought that perhaps X or Fowler or another of the men would try to fight or to run, but none of them did. They each stepped their way up the steep wooden stair to the elevated gallows platform and allowed themselves to be led by a soldier to one of the dangling nooses awaiting.

Kitto told himself he would do the same. He would die with dignity at least, if nothing else.

The chain between his ankles rattled as he stepped up the stairs. As he was last to reach the platform and the other men had been directed to either end first, Kitto found himself in the direct center of the long line of nooses, between Exquemelin and Quid. He looked down to his feet to see that he stood atop some sort of trap door. He knew that once the noose was placed around his neck, the doors would be released and there would be nothing but rope to hold him.

"I am sorry, lads!" X called out loud enough for all the men down the line to hear. One of the soldiers jabbed a musket into Exquemelin's spine and the crowd hooted.

"We knew what we was doing, old man!" called Fowler near the end.

"I don't want to die!" whimpered Coop.

"Shut your mouth and be a man for once," Fowler said, and received a sharp blow to the back of the head with a musket barrel for his continued outburst.

Three officials climbed the gallows stairs, all dressed in fine powdered wigs. One of them stepped near to Kitto and unrolled a parchment from which he began to read aloud in droning Spanish. Far to the back of the crowd Kitto spotted the little girl again, and he focused all his mind on her as the man continued to speak. Now and again cheers rose up from the masses as the man read, but the little girl seemed hardly to pay attention at all. She tossed her little doll into the air. Higher and higher she threw it, seeing how high she could throw it and still snatch it before it hit the cobblestones.

Kitto let his mind drift off with her, and it was not

until he heard Fowler speaking at the end of the column that he realized the men were being given the chance to speak final words before the nooses were fitted to their necks and their heads covered in white sacks.

"I ain't got a thing to say to you swine," were Fowler's words. Pickle crowed an apology to his mother. Little John said he wished he had married that sweet lass who loved him back in Devon.

Kitto turned back to the little girl. She seemed so important somehow. He remembered running on a beach when he was very young. It must have been Jamaica. The surf curled around his feet. He, too, clutched a little lovey doll, tight so that the water could not take it away from him. And there, just down the beach, was his mother—his first mother—smiling and opening her arms to him. For the first time in years Kitto could see her face, as clear and as memorable as anything he knew in this world.

She was beautiful. She loved him.

Why have I not seen you before? he wondered. *Maybe I will see you again. Yes. And soon.*

Next to Kitto, Pelota barked something in a native tongue that no one understood, and then it was Exquemelin's turn.

"Coffee beans and the love of a good woman! I shall miss them and little else!" he shouted out, and the crowd booed him. The guard reached forward to cover his head, but X wrenched to one side. He stuck his tongue out at the crowd and blew a spit-filled raspberry before the soldiers could slide the sack over his head and adjust the knot at his neck.

It was Kitto's turn.

"Your final words, sir," one of the officials behind him said.

My final words. My final words.

"I have a gift," Kitto said. "Not words." He turned around to face the man who had spoken to him, but the soldier behind him jabbed him with his musket and pushed Kitto's cheek to face forward.

"Do not deny a condemned man!" Kitto said. "About my neck there is a chain. That sweet girl in the back there, tossing her little doll. I would like her to have it." Murmurs arose behind him as the officials considered.

Apparently they agreed, because rough hands dug beneath his shirt and withdrew the chain. It was drawn over his head, and in a moment the thick noose had replaced it.

Kitto felt the scratchy fibers of the rope against his Adam's apple.

The little girl. Keep your eyes on her.

Down below him Kitto saw dozens of heads turn as the spectators tried to catch a glimpse of the girl who would be the recipient of the pirate's gift.

A gift. That is a way to end a life with dignity, Kitto told himself. The sack went over his head. The girl was gone.

"Viva las piratas!" X shouted, and laughed a loud and lusty laugh.

The crowd shouted back at X. Kitto's eyes were open

but all he could see was the glowing white of the sack. He could just hear above the din of the crowd the sound of the surf, the waves crashing against a seawall. It made him think of home.

Home.

"Mother and Father," he whispered. "Be there for me. Be there to greet me."

A Spanish voice called out an order. Kitto heard some sort of a thumping sound, and felt a vibration beneath his feet.

The trap door gave way.

CHAPTER 32:

Weeping Madonna

Kitto felt his shackled feet kick out. He felt the rope rip tight against his neck. He would have gasped, but he could draw no air.

And then there was the beach. Again. He was running on the beach, running to his mother's open arms. Closer he ran to her. Closer. He held out his arms toward her, the lovey in one hand. She would gather him up in her arms.

He was running. *Look at me run, Mum! Look at me!*

Caught in the noose, Kitto was dying.

The world reeled and went black, but then there was movement again, confusion, a jostling.

Kitto opened his eyes and blinked against the bright sun. The cloth sack was gone, the noose too. He was lying on his side on the wooden platform of the gallows. The crowd booed in bitter frustration.

A man behind him was screaming something at him. Kitto blinked and strained to suck in air. A sharp hand slapped him once across the face. Twice. Kitto's eyes spun but then took focus.

Inches before his nose was the small golden cross with the weeping figure at its base.

"That is for the girl!" he tried to say, but all that came out was a croak. Now a voice came clear.

"Where did you get this? Where did you get this, boy! Tell me now and perhaps you will not be hanged!" The voice came from the official who had told him to recite his last words.

"What?" Kitto groaned, his mind thick and muddled.

"Tell me!" the man screamed again, and struck Kitto harder.

"Cut them down," Kitto said. He felt his eyes drifting off of their own accord and knew that he could not fight off unconsciousness.

"Cut them all down!" Kitto said. "Only then will I ever tell you."

Blackness filled his vision, and Kitto let it carry him away.

When he came to, Kitto found himself lying on an upholstered sofa of some kind, covered in plush crimson fabric. He blinked a few times to get his eyes to focus. He heard voices speaking urgently in Spanish very nearby. The room was bright, painfully so, sunlight filtering through a breathtaking panel of stained glass. Bookshelves teeming with leather-bound volumes spread on either side of the window.

"You nearly caused a riot in Corona Square, Christopher Quick," said a mild voice in English. "The people came to witness a hanging and you spoiled it for them."

"Not for long," grumbled the other voice.

"That is not for you to decide, señor."

Kitto pushed himself to a seated position on the sofa. His head rang with a splitting ache, and his tongue felt two sizes too large for his mouth. The men sat across from him in high-backed chairs with claw-footed wooden arms and feet. The man on the left he recognized as the one who had read from the parchment at the gallows. His wig had slipped and dark hair peeked out beneath. The second man wore a deep purple robe, some sort of a flat red cap atop his head, and a large wooden crucifix hung down his chest along a beaded chain.

"I am not dead," Kitto said in a whisper.

"You are not dead," the robed man repeated.

"Yet," muttered the other.

"And my companions?" Kitto said.

"The other pirates are alive and well and have been returned to their cell. All but one."

Kitto felt his heart flip. "One?"

"A very large man, quite a giant. His neck broke when his body was dropped. He died instantly." The man in the robe made the sign of the cross along his body.

Little John. Kitto felt a terrible sadness hit him. His eyes filled with tears.

"He was a good man," Kitto said, his voice rough.

"He was a pirate!" said the official. The robed man held up a hand for silence, and Kitto knew instantly who was in charge.

"The Lord has his soul now," the man said. "Only he can judge." He turned to the official. "Please leave us, señor."

"But, Your Excellency . . ."

"That will be all, Señor Delgado." The wigged man glared at Kitto as he rose quickly from his chair and strode out of the room, letting the heavy wooden door slam behind him.

The robed man took a deep breath. He looked over at Kitto and smiled.

"Who are you?" Kitto said.

"You may call me Padre Alberto," he said. The man gestured toward a low table between them. Kitto looked down to see that it held a tray of silver serving bowls full of cut fruit and a pitcher of drink.

"Might you take a refreshment, Christopher?" the man said, pouring a bright yellow liquid into two ornate goblets. He held one out to Kitto. Kitto eyed it doubtfully. The padre set the vessel on the table and took a sip of his own.

"Without Señor Delgado here, we may speak more freely," Padre Alberto said. Kitto leaned over and picked up the goblet. He sipped the juice, and his eyes closed reflexively as the bright taste exploded on his tongue. He had not had fresh juice in what seemed like months. When he swallowed, though, the harsh pain in his throat made him gag. He sputtered several drops of pineapple nectar onto the sofa.

"The gallows have left their mark on you," Padre Alberto said, gesturing about his own neck but looking at Kitto's. "But time shall heal the wound."

Kitto reached for his neck. The skin felt chafed and tender.

"Why am I here?" he said when the burning sensation had passed.

The man eyed him quietly for a moment, then withdrew something from a pocket of his robe.

"Tell me about this artifact, Christopher," Padre Alberto said. Dangling from his hand was the gold chain and its cross. It rocked back and forth in the air.

Kitto felt his breath quicken. He knew where it came from, even knew where more like it lay at that very moment.

Think like your uncle William, he told himself. *Cunning.*

Kitto reached for the chain, and the padre did not protest when Kitto took it into his hands. He lay the cross along his palm to study it.

"Of course you have no reason to trust me," Alberto said. "Except for the fact that you are still alive, and that is somewhat due to my intervention."

"I am alive because I possessed this?" Kitto said, knowing the answer without having to wait for it.

Alberto nodded. He ran his palm across his thick jowls.

"It will be difficult to overcome the Honorable Delgado's ruling," Alberto said. "But it is within my power, as head of the Catholic Church in this part of the world." Alberto sipped at the goblet and set it on the table.

Kitto lifted the necklace so that the cross and the kneeling woman at its base rocked gently, washed in the green and gold light from the window. He looked up at the padre.

"It is beautiful," Kitto said. "But not so beautiful—is it?—to save the lives of seventeen pirates?"

The padre smiled slightly and shrugged. "To me it is a thing most moving. You are not aware of its history, then, or its name, 'The Weeping Madonna'?" he asked, eyeing Kitto shrewdly for signs of deception.

"All I know is that William Quick had it. He is my uncle."

Padre Alberto froze. "William Quick is your uncle? Truly?"

"Yes, Your Excellency."

"Did you know that he was a prisoner here, in Cuba, for many years?"

Kitto nodded. "He told me."

Padre Alberto leaned forward in his seat. "And did he confess to you that he murdered fourteen priests and nuns and peaceful citizens to obtain that piece of art in your hands?" The man's voice had gone cold.

"I . . . with all respect, sir, I believe you are mistaken. William Quick would not have done that. He was—he is—an imperfect man, perhaps not always a good man even, but he is not a murderer."

"Yet those men and women died."

"Who were they?" Kitto said.

The padre considered the question as he fingered the crucifix around his neck. "Panama, 1671. The great city, the crown jewel in Spain's New World Empire . . . attacked and destroyed by English pirates."

This history Kitto did know. "Yes, sir! William Quick was there. He was one of Henry Morgan's buccaneers."

Alberto set the goblet on the table. "Those men burned the city to the ground and stole everything they could get their hands on. But the inhabitants of Panama had gotten word from friendly natives that the English were coming."

It was Kitto's turn to lean forward. "My father told me of this! And my uncle. The treasure the buccaneers expected to find in Panama was not there."

"*Correcto.* It had been removed, mostly by ship, but not all. There was a great trove of very fine religious art in Panama as well, most of it kept in the church there in the heart of the colony. They were truly magnificent, these pieces, the work of an artist inspired by God. The artist's name was Ignacio Asalto."

"Were these works of art stolen during the raid, then?" Kitto said, looking down at the cross in his hands, realizing its presence already answered his question. The padre continued.

"The head priest of that church, a Cardinal Pérez, worried that a ship containing all of Asalto's great works would be too vulnerable—pirates, shipwreck, etcetera. So he ordered that a mule train travel ten miles into the jungle, far from the path of the buccaneers, and remain hidden there until they received word that the infidels had fled."

"And those were the men and women who . . ." Kitto began, then faltered.

"Who were found dead? Yes. I know this because I was one of the priests who was sent out to find them after the pirates had burned our fair city and left. I led the expedition."

"Why?" Kitto shook his head. "Why would someone have killed priests and nuns?"

"They were unarmed," Padre Alberto said. "A few of

the men had machetes for moving through the jungle, but otherwise nothing. So you tell me, Christopher Quick, nephew of William Quick, why would your uncle have killed fourteen men and women when all he had to do was take the treasure from them without violence?"

Kitto wrapped one hand around the cross and closed his eyes, thinking back to what William had told him of Panama.

"He told me," Kitto began slowly, "that he and his men had hiked off into the jungle, but it was not this treasure he was after. He was hunting down one of his fellow buccaneers, a John Morris, one of Henry Morgan's closest friends and partners."

Padre Alberto grimaced. "Yes. I know this name. He is a vile predator whose cruelty was once known widely among our people."

"Yes," Kitto said. "John Morris and Henry Morgan had stolen . . ." Kitto paused and chanced a glance at the padre. The man was watching him intently. Kitto decided that he must speak the truth, that the man would know otherwise. And the priest was likely all that kept him and his friends from the hangman's rope.

"Morgan and Morris had stolen nutmeg. The spice. Many barrels of it. It had belonged to the Dutch, but somehow ended up in Panama at the time of the attack."

Padre Alberto gave a slight smile of satisfaction, knowing honesty when he saw it. "Yes, I know of the nutmeg. You are correct about its origins. Continue."

Kitto let out a quiet sigh of relief. "William said that he came upon Morris in the jungle. Morris only had a few men with him. They fought, and Morris escaped into the jungle, but not before my uncle had . . . cut off a piece of the man's nose."

The padre's eyebrows arched. "That is where 'The Beak' received his wound? In Panama?"

Kitto nodded. "But this is the part that has always troubled me. When my uncle spoke to me of the nutmeg he took from Morris, he sometimes used the word 'treasure,' and then would correct himself. I believe there were two treasures, and that he was not ready to tell me of the second."

Padre Alberto folded his hands before him in a position that resembled prayer. "You believe your uncle found Morris after Morris had stolen the Asalto collection?"

"I do, sir! Truly I do," Kitto said. "Make no mistake, my uncle would have quite happily taken it from priests and nuns. But kill them? He is not that kind of man."

Padre Alberto shrugged. "If not, then you are saying John Morris is capable of such butchery. Why is this any more believable?"

Kitto gritted his teeth, and he could feel the heat rise in his cheeks.

"It is far more believable, sir. John Morris murdered my father. Right before my eyes!" Kitto stared balefully at the padre and did not turn away when his eyes filled with tears.

Padre Alberto stood and walked to the window. He let his eyes trace the leadwork on the stained glass. The silence grew long between them before he spoke.

"If you speak the truth, then your life was forever

altered by that man," he said. He cleared his throat. "I will share with you another truth.

"Before I became a man of God, I had a wife and a son. When my wife died during childbirth, I turned to God to aid me in my grief, and he saw me through. I returned this generosity in the way I felt I should, abandoning my profession as a tradesman and taking the orders of holy office. My son was raised with the help of church members, nuns, and myself, of course. God ran deep in my boy, but he and I . . ." The padre ran a hand across his clean-shaved chin. "We struggled. He left me when still a young man, left Spain, and traveled to Panama. Some years later I received orders to minister in Panama, and I discovered that my son was making a name for himself there as an artisan—an artist even."

Kitto understood. "And he worked in gold?" Kitto said. "Ignacio Asalto was your son?" The padre turned, and Kitto was surprised to see a single tear roll down the man's cheek. Padre Alberto seemed not to notice it.

"We had just begun to mend our relationship when the barbarians attacked Panama. My son insisted on traveling with his art into the jungle, accompanying the church officials."

Kitto's jaw dropped. "Your son was one of those who was murdered?"

Alberto nodded. "If what you say is true, Christopher, then John Morris has undone both of our lives."

Kitto looked down at the cross in his hands and felt a momentary loathing for it. He rose and hobbled over to the priest, holding the gold cross out in front of him.

"I . . . I should not even have this a moment, Padre," he said. Kitto held out the necklace, but Padre Alberto did not turn. "Please take it, sir."

Still the man did not move. "Wear it, Christopher. Many people have said that my Ignacio's hand was blessed by God himself. You need all the protection our Father can possibly provide you."

Kitto saw his moment. *Now, when the man's back is turned.*

"William Quick knows where the rest of your son's works are hidden," Kitto said, speaking quickly, hoping that the detail he was leaving out—that he too knew the location of the treasured art—would not be written on his face somehow for the padre to read were he to look now. "He could lead you to them. But, Your Excellency, we have little time! William Quick has been captured by John Morris and has by now reached Jamaica. He is sure to be tried and hanged, sir!"

The padre turned, a look of alarm on his face.

"Your uncle could return my son's works to me? To Spain?"

Kitto nodded. "Yes, sir."

"Then we must act with haste."

CHAPTER 33:

Jamaica's Secrets

Kitto stood at the starboard rail of the Spanish ship, looking out over the endless glister of blue that was the Caribbean Sea, lit with gold fire from the new sunrise. The Spanish crew had kept to themselves the last three days. Only Exquemelin, who seemed to know passable Spanish, could provoke them to speak at all. He informed Kitto that they would likely sight land that day.

A deal had been struck back in Havana. Padre Alberto—using his sway as the most powerful church official in the New World—arranged for a ship to take Exquemelin and Kitto to a remote section of northeastern Jamaica, along with Van, Sarah, Ontoquas, Bucket, and Akin. None of the other pirates were allowed to accompany them. Although Padre Alberto had not put it in such terms, Kitto understood that the remaining fourteen men were collateral to the deal. If Kitto and Exquemelin returned to Cuba with the Asalto treasure, the men would go free. If not . . .

Unconsciously Kitto traced his fingers along his neck. The abraded skin from his near hanging had grown scaly, but it was not so tender as it had been.

"You are thinking of it again," Sarah said. "That horror." She came up behind Kitto and wrapped her arms around him. Nearby, Ontoquas held Bucket up in outstretched arms, then would lower him slowly to rub noses together. Akin looked on, grinning broadly. Bucket's brown cheeks glowed, and his low chuckle was like music, but this time Kitto did not smile.

"I woke myself up dreaming of it last night, the moment when you were taken from the prison cell," Sarah said.

"All I could think about at first was that I had failed Father," Kitto said.

"How could you possibly have done that?"

"You. And Duck. I was going to die and not be around to see to you."

"Kitto," Sarah said, squeezing him tight. "It is not your role to care for me. It is no one's role but my own. Do I seem so fragile to you?"

Kitto lowered his head, his cheeks flushed. "I suppose I could not care for you, anyway," he said. "Without my foot I am even more useless than I used to be."

"Not true," Sarah said. "You are somewhat less able, yes. But the world will see you differently now, strange as that is."

"Yes, it is strange. Makes me . . . angry," he said.

"Do not bother with the anger, Monsieur Quick!" Exquemelin said, suddenly appearing beside them, a spyglass raised to his eye. His voice still rasped as it had since the near hanging. "Anger devours the soul."

"What do you do, then?"

"I laugh. Laughter is a balm, young pirate. Keep laughing and life's bitter arrows will never find their mark on you." X winked.

Kitto raised an eyebrow. "Good advice if it could be heeded," he said. "You have not been laughing so much since we were cut down. I would have thought that alone would give you plenty to laugh about."

X shrugged. He fished about in the brown sack at his belt, producing a small handful of roasted coffee beans, which he inspected with a scowl.

"It would be easier for me to laugh if the Spanish knew how to roast coffee like the Dutch," he said.

"You are worried for the men," Kitto said, then wished he had not.

X nodded, chewing thoughtfully. "Only Little John is beyond worry." They were quiet a moment, each thinking of the gentle giant of a man.

"But does that help me, this worrying?" X shook his head. "No. *Helemaal niet.* Worry makes a man think too much, and too much thought makes him dead."

"You love your men," Sarah said. "That is nothing to be ashamed of. Love is a blessing that sometimes has the weight of a burden."

"Easier not to love," X said.

"No. That is far more difficult indeed."

"Tierra a la vista!" hailed a voice from above them.

"Land!" said Exquemelin. "They have sighted it.

Dónde?" he called up to the sailor, but an officer had occupied the lookout's attention. The man above pointed straight ahead, a few points to port.

"*Ja, ja.* That will be Jamaica," X said. "Eh, *jongen,* lookee here." Kitto turned to see the comical grin spread across the captain's face. "I am feeling better already!"

Two hours later Kitto, Van, Sarah, Ontoquas, Bucket, and X were all piled into a small rowboat along with several satchels full of provisions and leather skins filled with fresh water. X skulled the oars to keep them a safe distance from the Spanish ship while he engaged in conversation with Captain Peña up on deck.

"Two weeks," the captain called down to them in a thick accent. "In two weeks time we return. We wait for one week, no more." Peña had a long mustache groomed to perfection and waxed so that the ends came to neat curling points. The mustache added to his haughty air.

"Perhaps I will need you here before then," X said.

"Two weeks, pirate. Be thankful I will do even that."

"Oh, but I am!" X put his hand to his heart. "Your generosity fills me, and my cup runneth over. I will be sure to commend you to His Excellency Padre Alberto." Peña sneered and turned away.

"Is it wise to irritate a captain we will need in a few weeks?" Van said, but X simply stuck his tongue out at Van and started rowing for shore.

The rolling waves tossed the rowboat, and Bucket opened his eyes to wail in protest. Sarah offered a finger in front of the infant. Bucket snatched it and popped it into his mouth.

"Is there a path to follow?" Kitto said. The island ahead was a mass of tropical forest stretching out as far as the eye could see in each direction. Were it not for Exquemelin's certainty that it was indeed Jamaica, Kitto would never have known it was an island at all. It seemed enormous. He searched the wooded shoreline for some sign of humanity, but there was none.

X wagged his head side to side. "There is a path. It might be a while before we find it." Kitto and Ontoquas exchanged a look.

"Oh, good," Kitto said. "I would hate for this to be too easy." X threw him a grin of teeth speckled with coffee bean shards.

They made shore without incident in light surf, Exquemelin gallantly offering his hand to Sarah, who held Bucket in her arms. Van and Exquemelin and Akin dragged the rowboat up the beach and then into the undergrowth at the edge of the wood so that it could not be seen should any ships happen by.

Kitto stood on the beach and surveyed the shoreline anew. All that could be seen was dense and uninterrupted forest. From the ship they could see that mountains rose in the distance, but here at the shore they were not able to make them out over the tree line.

After a brief meal of biscuit and a jug of cider passed between them, the party set forth. Van traveled at the front, swinging a cutlass to clear the way, while

Exquemelin followed closely on his heels, instructing him in infuriating detail which way they should go.

"A bit more to the east," he would say. "*Ja, ja, ja.* Ah! No! Too much!"

"Yes, Your Worship."

"Boy-man," X said. "Have I told you about the time I was with Henry Morgan and we attacked Maracaibo?" Without waiting for an answer the pirate launched into a long story that flowed straight into another. Van hacked at the greenery and let the words wash over him.

Kitto insisted on taking up the rear. He did not want Sarah to see how he struggled to keep up. The wooden leg that Quid had made him fit better than the first, but Kitto still found it hard to maintain his balance on the uneven ground. Every several steps would throw him to one side or the other, and were it not for the hacked ends of branches Van left behind to grab in desperation, he would have spent as much time on the ground as on his feet.

After several hours of effort Exquemelin came to an abrupt halt.

"Enough!" X straightened his back and put his hands on his hips, unbothered by the fact that he had been in the middle of telling a rambling tale. "That stand of trees, Van. *Oui, oui, oui.* Perfect for the hammocks."

Perhaps a half dozen miles they had covered and each one hard earned. Kitto had barely the energy to string his own hammock between two likely enough trees with Akin's help, then toss himself into it. Sarah deposited Bucket into his arms, and the two of them swung gently. Sarah worked with Van to clear a spot for a fire pit.

X held his nose aloft like a bloodhound and sniffed.

"West. *Ja, ja.* Tomorrow we head west; we will find the trail."

The meal of salt pork and biscuit left much to be desired, but the last of the cider washed it down and left their bellies full if not satisfied. By the time the sun had disappeared below the horizon, all were soundly asleep.

Kitto awoke in the middle of the night alone in his hammock. His stump throbbed, and he swung his legs off the hammock so that he could massage it and ease the pain. The unmistakable glow of a candle shone through the woods perhaps twenty yards away from where he slept. Kitto's heart leaped to his throat until he made out the slumped profile of Exquemelin amid the glow.

Kitto fumbled about along the dark forest floor for his false leg, and finding it, he attached himself to it with the belt mechanism Quid had devised, cinching it around his thigh. The throbbing increased, but not unbearably so, and Kitto stalked off toward the glow.

The crunch of leaves and sticks beneath him seemed obnoxiously loud, but none of the sleepers stirred in their hammocks. Kitto drew closer to the wide tree where X sat, his head tilted back at an impossible angle, the tricorne hat having fallen to the forest floor. X gave out a gentle snoring sound with an added snort at the end of each breath.

The single candle stood mounted on a rock. Spread out before X and along his lap were the very papers Kitto had seen him working with weeks ago on Morris's stolen ship. Either the Spanish had considered them worthless to confiscate, or they had been returned to X when he was freed. Kitto did not know which. A quill was still clutched in the captain's hand, and the vial of ink leaned dangerously on one of the tree's exposed roots. Kitto leaned over to right the vial and hunt for its cork.

There, partly under Exquemelin's right knee, was the leather folio. Kitto remembered the man's secretiveness when he had asked about its contents aboard the *Port Royal*.

Shall I look? he wondered. The notion went against his principles, but then Kitto told himself that he owed it to Sarah and Duck to know everything and anything that could be of help to them. He bent, careful not to lose his balance on his wooden leg, and slowly withdrew the leather folio from beneath the captain's knee. Ever so tentatively he stepped around X's outstretched legs to the far side of the candle and lowered himself to the forest floor.

Kitto opened the folio to find three sheets of parchment tucked behind a flap of leather. He drew them out and leaned toward the candle's glow.

The first two sheets were part of the same document, and they looked rather old. The black ink had faded to a dull brown over the years. The document was dated 8 January 1650. In large letters at the top were scratched the words AGREEMENT OF INDENTURE.

Some sort of a contract, Kitto thought. And then his eye snapped upon a name written halfway down the page: Henry Morgan. Kitto read on.

> *This document in the presence of witnesses notarized below does name one Henry Morgan of Abergavenny, Labourer, to be Bound to one Timothy Tounsend of Bristol, Cutler, for three years, to serve in Barbados on the like Conditions. Said Morgan shall complete said period in the service of said Tounsend and comply therewith according to the rules of land and the Tounsend household as said holder of indenture sees fit.*

Kitto understood. *This is the proof of Morgan's humble beginnings.* Kitto remembered the page about Morgan's life that X had read to him. He smiled. Somehow the wily pirate had obtained his proof. Morgan wanted to be a man of society now, wanted to buy his way into the gentry. No indentured servant could possibly do so. No doubt Morgan would kill to see this paper disappear. Kitto figured that it was likely the only such copy in existence. He wondered how Exquemelin had come by it.

The indenture contract ran onto the second page, mostly legal writing that seemed of little added import. Kitto tucked the two pages behind the third. Ornate cursive letters drew his eye.

License of Marriage, granted by powers
of the Governor of Jamaica as vested by
King Charles II , Monarch of England,
year 1665.

Kitto read on, letting his eye skim past the portions in Latin. And then he froze. His hands began to shake.

CHAPTER 34:

Maroon

TWO WEEKS EARLIER

They would not be called boys, but the lanky frames of the two youths indicated that they were not yet full grown. The first had skin the color of dark sand and straight black hair, a sure sign of his Arawak heritage. The other was much darker, his hair a kink of tight curls: the son of escaped slaves who had never himself known bondage. Each sat with a musket across the lap.

An exceedingly narrow gorge dropped away just inches beyond their reclined toes and fell a distance of sixty feet. So narrow was the gap to the other side of the gorge that some days on a dare, the two would each get a running start and leap across the opening, landing lightly among the greenery. But today was too hot for such tom-foolery. Like brothers, though, they each kept a sharp eye out for some way in which to compete with the other.

"Come lookee lookee."

"Don't want to."

"Scared is what."

"Who do you call scared? I make you scared!"

The darker boy pointed. "That leaf down there, you see it?" The other boy leaned forward toward the precipice, scowling. Far down the path at the bottom of the gorge a dark green plant clung to the rocky soil, its broad leaves spread wide in the gorge's shadows.

"I see it."

"Bet I can shoot it first."

"Nanny said not to be wasting the powder."

"Nanny, Nanny! You scared of a whipping?"

"And you ain't?"

"I am not scared. And she will not hear this little musket all the way out here."

"Then you shoot, big man. Go on."

Nelson—for that was the challenger's name—rolled over onto his belly and lay on the rocky dirt, his elbows propped at the very edge of the cliff face. He settled the butt of the musket into his shoulder and lowered his cheek to the stock. A bead of sweat ran down his forehead and hung from the tip of his nose. He blew at it, and the droplet flew off into the abyss.

"Anybody shoot that lying down," Chock-ti said, wishing now that he had taken up the challenge.

"You come and do it, then."

Chock-ti chose silence instead. He scooted forward off the tree on which he had been leaning so that his feet dangled out over the edge and he could look down the line of Nelson's musket. "Too high," he said.

"I push you off, you see how high you are," Nelson said. His finger eased back toward the trigger.

* * *

For three days Duck and Dumaka had been hiking. Or was it four? Duck had lost track. At least the worst part was over, the exhausting climb up into the mountains. They still gained altitude, but through various stretches the creek trickled along shady flat plateaus where birds of assorted colors flitted among the trees, chirping contentedly. Having seen no trace of humans for days, the worry that slave catchers might pursue them had lessened, and so had the blistering pace that Dumaka had set.

For lunch the three nibbled the last of the biscuits and drank from the cool stream. After a short rest they headed on. Dumaka scanned from side to side the thick forest. It was not pursuers that worried him now, but a dwindling supply of food. Soon the forest would have to provide them their meals. After a few miles of walking Duck complained of a pain in his leg and asked if he could ride on Dumaka's shoulders. The young man squatted down so that Duck could climb up, and on they went. Julius scampered off into a nearby tree and kept up with their pace easily by leaping from branch to branch. Duck cheered him along.

Soon the banks of the tiny creek rose up higher and higher, the sides growing steeper and composed more of rock than the black dirt at lower altitudes. This development Dumaka did not like. A rocky gorge would offer up little in the way of berries or coconut-bearing trees. Julius scrambled down the embankment and leaped straight up into Duck's arms.

"Let me walk now, Dumaka," Duck said. "I can make it a ways." Dumaka reached up and lifted Duck up and over his head. Julius growled faintly in Duck's arms until they were set upon the ground. Dumaka patted the little boy on the head.

"Strong Duck," he said. "Strong legs you have."

"Not so strong as yours. Do you think we'll be there soon?"

"Soon," Dumaka said, but in truth he wondered if they had taken the wrong fork in the creek two days earlier. He did not worry for himself; Dumaka would gladly die a free man in the mountains than exchange it for a life of work and whips. But the little boy? He could not let the boy be forced into such a choice.

The sides of the creek grew higher and higher still, and within a half mile they were walking in a steep gorge, the cliff walls curling up in bulges of brown rock. The creek had dwindled to a narrow dribble just a foot wide and a scant inch deep. The path the creek carved in the rock meandered lazily, sometimes heading straight forward, other times curling about like the groove a snake carved in the sand.

"Look at that bush!" Duck said, pointing ahead to where the creek bent off to the right. On the side of the cliff a plant had found an unlikely place to sink its roots, somehow clinging to the narrow crags of the cliff face. "If that bush can survive in this canyon, so can we!" Duck darted around Dumaka and ran ahead toward the greenery, Julius clinging to his shoulder.

* * *

Nelson tensed his finger against the trigger, his eye trained on the wide-leafed plant far down in the gorge. He did not want to miss. Likely Nanny would hear the shot, or someone who did hear would tell her about it, and Nelson would have to explain himself. He wanted the trouble to be worthwhile.

Nelson took a deep breath and let it out slowly, noting the beat of his heart and how it made the end of the muzzle pulse up and down. He would shoot between the beats, when the barrel settled to total stillness. He pressed the flesh of his finger against the trigger.

Suddenly the leaf rocked, as if by a gentle wind that reached down into the deep gorge.

Nelson squeezed.

An instant before he did so Chock-ti kicked out a foot and whacked the barrel of the musket. The shot careened against the cliff face just across the gorge, kicking up a cloud of dust and raining a shower of pebbles down into the gap.

"Are you a stupid man?" Nelson said, leaping to his feet, mad enough to throw fists. But Chock-ti stared down into the gorge, pointing. Nelson turned.

Standing under the broad leaf was a small boy with some sort of animal perched on his shoulder. The boy squinted up at them. A man—a black man—appeared suddenly too and pulled the boy to cover behind the bend of rock.

"Are you shooting at me?" the little voice called up at them, his voice barely loud enough to reach them.

"No, no!" Chock-ti shouted down. "This boy can't hit a mountain with his gun!"

"I shoot you next," Nelson muttered, but gave Chock-ti a playful punch. He sighed deeply, thankful for Chock-ti's keen eyes and quick reflexes. "Nanny been talking about a boy," he said.

Chock-ti nodded. Nanny conferred with her magic deck of cards each day, and for a week now she had been talking about a white boy who would come.

"That must be the boy," Chock-ti said.

The tiny voice from the gorge came again. "You sure you ain't shooting at me? Or my monkey or Dumaka, neither?" The little boy poked his head around the corner and back again quickly.

"We not going to shoot you! Any of you!" Nelson said. "I promise."

Duck stepped out into full view now, Julius in his arms.

"Are you the manure people?" the boy said. "We're looking for the manure people."

Nelson grinned. "Not me, but this one here," he said, pointing to Chock-ti, "he is manure all the way to his toes." Chock-ti glared.

"Is there somebody up there named Nanny?" the boy said. Nelson and Chock-ti looked at each other, shaking their heads in disbelief. The old lady was right!

"She is some kind of witch, that Nanny," said Nelson.

Chock-ti cupped a hand to his cheek.

"Keep walking!" he called down to them. "We meet you down there."

The little boy smiled, and the young man waved up at them.

CHAPTER 35:

Birthright

"What troubles you?" Van said. He had handed off the cutlass to Akin and lagged behind for the others to pass him until Kitto drew near. Van's shirt was soaked through, as was Kitto's, although the sun had yet to reach its zenith. Kitto stalked past Van, then whirled.

"Do you remember your parents, Van?" Kitto said. "Your mum or dad?" Van drew back in surprise.

"Not so much," he said warily.

"What if you could?" Kitto pressed. "Or what if you discovered they were people you could never respect? That they repulsed you, even."

"Why you asking a thing like that?" Van said. Their eyes locked, each pair afire with a touch of anger.

"Would it change you?"

Silence surrounded them for several seconds before Van answered.

"Would it *change* me?"

"How would it change you?"

Van considered. The anger drained from him as he

stared at the trodden leaves beneath his feet. *Could Kitto know what I know?*

At last he answered.

"I believe in what I am doing," he said. "I believe in you and your mum and Duck, wherever he is. And I believe that . . . just maybe . . . all this could help my sister someday. So, no . . ." He lifted his head and met Kitto's gaze. "Not a whit would it change me. My parents delivered me here, but what I do here on rests on my own shoulders."

Kitto nodded, and not it was his turn to stare down at the mat of hewn palm leaves below.

Does it not matter where I am from? he asked himself. *Can a boy—can a man—stand apart from those who brought him into the world?*

"Now, why you asking me all this?" Van snapped.

Kitto turned away and began to walk on.

"Nothing," he said. Van stepped in behind him.

"You are not any good at lying, Kitto," Van said. "You have hardly said two words since you awoke. What, are you jealous seeing your mum carrying Bucket?"

Twenty yards ahead they could see Sarah trudging along the rough-hewn path behind X, Bucket's little feet poking out to one side.

"Of course not." Kitto spoke the truth. Bucket was magical for Sarah. Kitto could see that. Somehow the pain of Sarah's anxiety over Duck was lessened when she cared for the baby. "Bucket is a blessing for her. I would never want it different."

"What then?"

"I do not want to speak of it."

"Perhaps that is why you should." Van knew what it was like to carry the burden of a secret.

"I saw something X has," Kitto said. "I . . ." He stopped, fearful of saying it aloud, that somehow when he did so it would become more real. "I keep learning things about myself, and they keep getting more and more nasty," Kitto said. Behind him the sounds of Van's footsteps ceased. Kitto turned.

"Did X tell you then?" Van said. Kitto felt a tingle of goose bumps rise up the back of his neck.

"Did X tell me what?" Kitto said. Van stared back at him, then looked down with something like guilt written on his face.

"Do you know about it?" Kitto said. "How could you know of it?"

Van dragged a toe against a root. "Before we reached Falmouth, I overheard the captain. Your uncle, I mean. He was speaking with Peterson. They did not know I was there."

"So my uncle knew too?" Kitto said, feeling his heat rise, and he welcomed it. Anger was easier to feel than fear. "Of course he did! He would had to have known!" Kitto turned back in the direction of the others, now some fifty yards ahead.

"Stop!" he shouted. From the sash belt about his waist he withdrew the dagger his father had given him. *His father?*

Kitto ran forward awkwardly, stumbling and shouting for Exquemelin to halt.

"Kitto, wait!" Van called from behind him, but Kitto charged blindly on. The ground went fuzzy on him, but he did not bother to wipe away the tears. He rushed toward Sarah and Ontoquas, who stood staring at him in shock and dismay.

"Kitto, what is wrong?" Sarah said. She thrust Bucket into Ontoquas's arms and reached to take him by the shoulders. Kitto reeled back from her touch.

"Did . . . did you know?" Kitto said to her.

Sarah shook her head, bewildered. "Whatever do you mean? Did I know what?"

"Did you know!" Kitto screamed. "All this time, did you know?" Sarah turned toward Exquemelin, who watched with grim aspect several yards ahead, sweat dripping from his nose. Akin looked on with the cutlass slung over his shoulder.

"Did you?" Kitto said again. Sarah raised her hands.

"I have kept nothing from you, Kitto! I keep nothing from you. What *is* it you are asking of me?" The acute pain in Sarah's face made Kitto feel a pang of shame. He turned to Exquemelin, and strode forward to him.

"You knew," Kitto said softly, holding out the dagger like an accusing finger.

X removed his hat and hung it on a cleaved branch. He wiped the arm of his shirt against his brow.

"If I knew, you will stab me with this thing?" He shrugged. "*Ja, ja,* I knew," he said. "Anyone close to

Morgan knew." He looked past Kitto's shoulder to send a menacing look to Van. "And it was not for you to tell him!"

"I didn't!" Van said.

"You fell asleep among your papers last night," Kitto said. "I looked through them." Kitto lowered the dagger and held out his other hand. "Give it to me. It belongs to me more than it does you."

Sarah stepped over to them. "What on earth is going on here? What is it that you have, sir?" she demanded.

Exquemelin wiped sweat away from his brow with the sleeve of his shirt and gave out a sigh. Draped over his shoulders were two leather satchels. He fumbled with the latches. In a moment he had transferred some of the materials from one to the other, then handed one satchel over to Kitto by its strap.

Kitto opened the hasp and withdrew the single sheet of paper inside. He held it out to Sarah, who snatched it up and began to pore over its contents.

"I do not understand," she said. "What is the import of this?" She looked up at Kitto, still mystified.

"Look at the date," Kitto said.

Sarah returned to the top of the page. "Twenty-two November, the year 1665. I still don't see . . ."

"What happened about ten months after that date?" Kitto waited until he saw the realization hit her. Sarah lowered the page, and turned a look of great empathy on Kitto.

"Oh, Kitto! Is this . . . is this your mother? I did

not know her name was Carter. Oh, Kitto." Sarah covered her mouth with her hand, aghast.

Kitto probed her expression, looking for the slightest hint of guile, while also knowing Sarah was never capable of such.

"You never knew? Father never told you?"

Sarah shook her head slowly. "Never." She reached forward and took Kitto's face in her hands. "You were *his* son, Kitto. That is the only way he ever thought of you."

Kitto pulled from her hand the piece of paper still pinched between her fingers.

"Apparently not," he said bitterly. "I am the son of Henry Morgan," he said. "Henry Morgan is my father. And my ruin. And now I am going to seek him out."

CHAPTER 36:

The Path

Eventually the party had continued to hike, at Kitto's insistence. There was little more to say. Exquemelin apologized to Kitto for keeping the information from him. He had not realized at first that Kitto did not already know. Surely William would have told him! When he came to realize that Kitto did not know the truth of his parentage, he did not believe he was the person to break such news.

Kitto's rage had quieted, but it was replaced by an unsettling fear. He trudged on through the jungle trying to grapple with it.

Henry Morgan is my father? And my mother married that villain? Who am I, then?

Who am I?

The party hiked on in stony silence a few miles until they stumbled across a pleasant creek from which they drank deeply. Kitto kept his distance from the others, his head a swirl of conflicting thoughts and uncertainties. X blundered off into the brush beyond the far bank of the creek after sniffing the air, and in a moment he was hailing them all jubilantly.

"*Ja, ja, ja!* This is it! I have found it!" He burst through a brace of thick leaves, the gold tooth shimmering in his grin.

"What's that?" Van said.

Exquemelin pointed with the machete. "The path!" he said. "We are not far now. If we hurry, we can make it to the camp before nightfall." He turned toward the wood and raised a hand to his cheek. "I am coming to you, my sweet Nanny!" X howled out into the jungle.

Onward they trudged, the way much easier now that they did not need to clear a path as they went. The trail itself was quite narrow and nearly swallowed up in undergrowth in places, but X practically galloped along it, never once concerned that he might lose his way. He rushed ahead and then waited impatiently at a turn or the top of a rise for the others, tugging savagely at the beads of his beard. The rest of the party struggled to keep up.

After several miles Sarah insisted that they take a break. Bucket needed to eat something and his undergarments needed cleaning. X relented, chewing on his finger as Sarah knelt in the stream that the path had crossed several times over the last few miles. Bucket gummed at a piece of biscuit soaked in water and some coconut, reaching out to the food Ontoquas held before him in cupped hands.

"The food is about to get much better, my boy!" X said, grinning. "My Nanny, she can cook."

"She is . . . she is your wife?" Sarah said, rising from the streambed.

"She is my love," X said. "My *raison d'être*. And the reason I will never be anything but a pirate."

"I would think most women would desire that you take a less dangerous line of work," Sarah said, wringing out the wet cloth.

"She does worry for me. But she needs me to continue. So much of what she does depends on my work," X said, stroking his beads. "If I could just convince her to give it up, then we could be together so much more."

"And what is this work that she does?" Sarah said.

X smiled at her. "We wait. Soon you will have your answer to that."

Kitto stepped forward. He said nothing, but stroked his hand lightly over the top of Bucket's head.

"His hair is getting longer," he said. It was true. The tight black curls that had hugged so close to the baby's scalp were thickening into an opaque fringe. Sarah smiled down at the baby in the crook of Ontoquas's arm. He looked up at Sarah with watery black eyes.

"Heh! Heh!" Bucket said, and grinned a wide, toothless smile.

"Bucket will never know who his parents were," Kitto said. Sarah looked up at him. "I suppose I should feel lucky."

"You have had two mothers who loved you, Kitto, and one father who loved you and who was there for you. That the man who sired you is fearful, evil even, does not reflect upon you."

X stroked his beads and nodded thoughtfully. "My own father, he was a demon. I would have been better raised by wolves." He rose to walk away, not feeling that such a discussion was welcome to him, but Kitto's words stopped him.

"I wonder if it was my clubfoot that drove him away."

X cleared his throat and turned. He made his way back over to Kitto, sitting down in the path next to Bucket, who he chucked under the chin.

"Your mother was common, Kitto. Low, even. Morgan married her in secret, perhaps because he was already troubled by her status. John Morris berated Morgan for it, told him he would regret the decision. So, by the time you were born, Morgan was already putting some distance between himself and Mercy."

"And then after?" Kitto said. X nodded.

"After you arrived, he took steps," X said. "He had me break into the clerk's office and steal the certificate of marriage. I did—along with some other documents I found." X winked. "I showed Morgan some blackened parchment and told him I had burned it."

"Why did you lie to him?" Sarah said. "Why not just do as he asked?"

X ran his fingers along the curves of his black hat. "I knew then," he said. "I knew that if Morgan were a man to turn his back on his love—on his own son, even—to improve his state in the world, he would not hesitate to turn his back on me someday as well."

Kitto was silent a moment. *So there it is. My father by birth abandoned me because of my twisted foot. And the father who raised me, the one I spent much of my life resenting, he took me in. Even with my clubfoot, even being the son of another man . . . he took me in and loved me.*

The knowledge was awful and unforgiving and true. He turned back to Exquemelin.

"So you kept the documents to use against Morgan someday?" Kitto said.

"If necessary, *oui*."

"I would like to see that happen."

Van and Akin wandered back to them from where they had dangled their feet in the cool water of the creek.

"About ready?" Van said. He smiled at Kitto, searching his face for some clue as to his mood, glad to see that Kitto seemed less dark of aspect.

Kitto looked to his friends, at this eccentric pirate before him, and at his mother—yes, she was his true mother, his parent, more so than either of his fathers.

"Thank you, Mother," he said softly.

Sarah searched his eyes questioningly, then she nodded in understanding.

"No. Thank you, son."

CHAPTER 37:

Reunion

Three hours later the party ascended slowly through a switchback pass when from far up the slope came the sound of two voices shouting.

"X is here! X! The pirate is returned!"

"What in the world?" Van said, holding up the cutlass in alarm.

Two dark-skinned young men clad in nothing but breeches came hurtling down the mountainside. They held weathered muskets over their heads as they ran headlong through the brush, ignoring the switchbacks of the path and instead launching themselves through the air with abandon.

"I hope those are friends," Van said.

X let out a whoop.

"We thought you dead! Huzzah!" one shouted.

"I am too pigheaded to die!" X shouted back at them, laughing and holding his arms wide. The first man broke through the brush near them, tossed his musket to the ground on his last step, and without slowing launched himself into Exquemelin. The two tumbled together off the trail, X swearing and laughing.

The second man caught up, fired his musket into the air, tossed it aside, and threw himself into the tumult. The embrace evolved into a wrestling match, the younger men pummeling Exquemelin while the captain attempted to put them each into headlocks.

"As odd as I would have expected," Kitto said.

Finally the three wrestlers collapsed in a heap of groans and giggles.

"I am too old!" X yelled up to the treetops from where he lay on his back. Akin stepped forward to retrieve the captain's hat, which had been knocked well down the slope. The two young men, all smiles, pulled X to his feet and helped him back up to the path where Kitto and Sarah and Ontoquas watched, wide-eyed.

"Introduce yourselves, you knaves," X said, sweeping out an arm. The one who had tackled Exquemelin stepped forward. He was the younger of the two, dimples set into his bright cheeks.

"I am Amos," he said. "And this one is Joseph," he said, thumbing to the other man, whose features seemed carved from a slice of onyx, lean and strong. He gave them something of a salute with his smile.

"We know the pirate," Joseph said, as if to explain their antics.

"Sadly, this is true." X introduced his companions, and Amos and Joseph hugged each of them in turn as if they were old friends. Akin they lifted up in their embrace and slapped his shoulders as if he were a brother, and Akin looked so happy he might burst. Then the young men crowded around the baby in Sarah's arms and cooed in wonder.

"Ooh, Nanny loves a baby!" Joseph said. "Where you get this baby, X? You steal him away?"

"Not me. That one." X pointed to Ontoquas, who stood her ground and held her head high.

"You Arawak?" Amos said, naming the tribes he knew. "Carib?"

Ontoquas shook her head. "Wampanoag," she said.

Amos shrugged. "You saved the baby?"

Ontoquas nodded. "We were on a slave ship," she said quietly. "We jumped."

Amos smiled wide and clapped his hands. "Then I love you!" he said. "*And* your baby! And Nanny, she going to love you too."

"How far are we, *mes frères*? These old legs grow tired," X said.

Without another word Joseph gathered up all their meager bundles into his hands and Amos reached to take Bucket from Sarah with a smile.

"No, you mustn't," she said, but Amos had already snatched him from her weary arms. He spun the little baby skillfully so that Bucket perched in the crook of his elbow looking out.

"I am good with the babies!" Amos said. "They love me!"

Seeing Bucket's dark skin against Amos's, nearly the same tone, Sarah felt a momentary pang of sadness that she did not quite understand. She forced herself to smile.

"Very well. Lead on."

Two hours later the path wound on over steep terrain. They trudged through massive fields of boulders that X explained provided excellent cover should the English ever be foolish enough to try to attack them.

"Ten men could hold off an army," he said. "And we are more than a hundred strong."

Kitto would not have been able to keep up were it not for Van and Akin. The boys stood astride Kitto so that he could drape an arm over each of their shoulders. Together they forged their way. Even so, the going was difficult, and just when Kitto thought he could endure no more, the rise of the hillside tapered off. Up ahead of them Joseph called out to someone farther up the trail.

"A village ahead," Akin said, catching a glimpse of some huts in the distance.

A few steps in front of them Sarah gave out a sharp cry. She stopped cold, her hand raised to her mouth. Kitto and Van caught up to her.

"Mum! What is it?" Kitto said. Sarah was looking farther up the trail.

"Is it . . . is it real?"

There in a grassy clearing, perched atop the shoulders of a very tall black man, was Duck, with the monkey Julius in his arms.

"Duck!" Kitto yelled.

"Julius!" Van said.

Duck turned and saw them: his mother and brother, walking out from the Jamaican jungle.

Duck shrieked and tossed Julius into the air before hurling himself from the man's shoulders. He hit the dirt belly first but bounced up grinning. Duck ran for them.

They were all running now, Sarah and Kitto and all of them.

Sarah was the first to reach Duck. The little boy leaped into her arms and would have knocked her over backward had Kitto not been there to throw himself into the embrace as well.

"Oh, Mum! I thought I might never . . ."

"Duck! Duck, can it be!" Together they hugged one another and wept.

"I am so sorry, Duck!" Kitto said. "I left you alone on the ship."

Duck pulled back from the embrace, grinning.

"I wasn't alone! I had Julius!" He turned and made a kissing noise. Julius ran forward, leaped up to Kitto's head, and walked over to Duck's shoulder.

"Hey! You're *my* monkey, remember?" Van said, snatching Julius away and nuzzling their foreheads together.

"Mum, don't cry," Duck said, but Sarah could not stop the tears. Duck wiped them from her cheeks.

"We thought we would never see you again," Kitto said. "We thought maybe Morris had hurt you." Duck reached out and gave Kitto's nose a tweak.

"I was too fancy for old Black Heart," Duck said. "And I knew you would come find me, Kitto. I always knew it."

Kitto felt his heart swell. If he could only live up to the person his brother knew him to be, what great things could he do with his life?

Farther ahead in the clearing X had snatched his hat away to plant a huge kiss on a tall, dark woman. She also wore a man's tricorne hat, but it was knocked to the ground by the kiss. X lifted the woman into the air and whooped.

"Nanny! I am home, *mon amour!*"

"Where you been, you mad pirate!" Nanny said, flashing a brilliant smile of white teeth.

Amos paraded Bucket on into the village.

"Feast!" he called. "Kill a pig, quick! We must have a great feast!"

Kitto stood. He pulled Sarah to her feet and tousled Duck's matted hair.

"Come on, family. Let us find a cool spot in the shade. We have many stories to tell."

Duck wrapped an arm around Kitto's waist, and so doing he felt the dagger at the small of his brother's back.

"What's this?" Duck said, and pulled the dagger out. The blade was sheathed in the reed covering that Ontoquas had made.

"You know it," Kitto said.

Duck smiled as he cast the reed sheath aside and

slashed the dagger through the air as if it were a sword.

"This is the one Da gave you!" he said. Kitto nodded. Splashes of sunlight played off the polished steel.

"There is a lot to that dagger, as it turns out," Kitto said.

It belonged to my birth father, my birth mother, my father who hardly thought me capable of wielding it . . . My mum used that dagger to save me from a certain death by the sharks, and it has put me in league with a notorious pirate who might have taken my life when I was just a lad. And still, I do not think that dagger's tale is yet told.

"Much indeed," Sarah agreed. The motion of Duck's arm ceased, the dagger poised in the air. He lowered it slowly.

"You know something, Kitto?" Duck said.

"What?"

"Da. He would be so proud. Of us, I mean," Duck said.

Kitto felt tears rising into his eyes. He reached out with each hand and gave his mother and his brother a squeeze.

"I am sure of it, Duck. Very proud indeed."

A NOTE ABOUT THIS BOOK

The world of 1678 was caught in the midst of a huge global shift. Since the late 1400s, Portugal and Spain had pretty much split the Western world between them (check out the Treaty of Tordesillas, 1494). Spain claimed all of the Americas except for Brazil—which Portugal had already staked out—and Portugal claimed all of Africa. This was a wonderful arrangement for the Spanish and Portuguese, but a horrifying one for Native Americans and the inhabitants of West Africa. Spain had hit it rich quick by conquering Native American kingdoms and stealing (as well as mining) the incredible quantities of gold and silver located there. Portugal, after being initially disappointed at discovering little gold or silver in Africa, had nonetheless found the continent teeming with an incredibly precious resource: humans. By trading goods they brought with them from home (often metal items like nails or pots and pans), the Portuguese found that African leaders they encountered were happy to give up members of enemy tribes who had been captured in battles. Portuguese traders took these people across the Atlantic Ocean and sold them to their countrymen in Brazil and to the Spanish in other areas of Central and South America. Humans were desperately needed for labor in the growing plantations both countries had established there for growing crops like sugarcane, which grew far better in places like Cuba and Brazil than it did in Europe.

The three geographical points (Europe, West Africa, the Americas) formed a triangle, and the trade that revolved clockwise around the Atlantic Ocean is often referred to today as the triangle trade. Manufactured goods (metal objects, cloth, tools, etc.) left Europe for Africa where they were exchanged for human captives; these prisoners were shipped west across the Atlantic Ocean (this gruesome leg of the journey is often called the Middle Passage today) and forced to work. The efforts of their work (chiefly sugar, after mining silver and gold became less profitable) headed on other ships back to Europe, where it was sold for a profit. Part of that profit was spent on more manufactured goods (metal objects, cloth, etc.), which were loaded onto ships bound for Africa. And so the cycle continued, over and over.

By Kitto's time, the rest of the countries of Europe had long grown tired of watching only Spain and Portugal get rich. They wanted part of the action. The Dutch were the first to find an avenue to another source of great wealth—spices— which they mostly got from islands in modern-day Indonesia. (It is odd to think that Spain, Portugal and the Netherlands— countries that no one would call huge global players today— were immensely wealthy and formidable in 1678.)

The people of the British Isles had not stood idly by either. By the time of this story, the people of today's United Kingdom had elbowed their way into this trade of slaves, sugar, and spices. Through its success in this trade, the UK would grow so large that by 1800 it was an empire "on which the sun never sets."

Ontoquas speaks several words in her native Massachusett language throughout the story. As a member of the Wampanoag tribe, she is a descendant of the Native Americans who first welcomed and provided critical aid to the "pilgrims" from Europe who arrived in Plymouth in 1620. By Ontoquas's time, however, tensions had built up between the native peoples and the new arrivals. When English settlers began taking over tribal lands without permission, the tribes of the area banded together and began to attack English settlements. The result was called King Philip's War, a catastrophe for the Wampanoag people. This conflict resulted in the death of roughly 40 percent of the tribe. Many of the surviving Wampanoag people were sold off by the settlers into slavery in the West Indies, explaining how Ontoquas (and Black Dog) might have ended up so far from home.

Massachusett Words

netchaw: brother

nippe: water

nitka: mother

noeshow: father

quog quosh: make haste, hurry

suckis suacke: a clam, clams

tunketappin: where you live

wawmauseu: an honest man

weneikinne: it is very handsome

wompey: white

Alexandre Exquemelin was a real person who is on his way in this tale to writing a bestselling book about pirate history that will be in print for centuries. Little is known about the man. He was likely French by birth but spent time in Amsterdam, and his famous book was first published in Dutch. Throughout the tale he sprinkles his speech with French and Dutch words and phrases.

Exquemelin's Garbled Tongue
allons-y (French): let's go
ezel drol (Dutch): donkey turd
helemaal niet (Dutch): no
jongen (Dutch): boy
krijgt die schoft (Dutch): get that child of unwed parents
mes amis (French): my friends
moeder (Dutch): mother
ongelooflijk (Dutch): incredible
venez, les petites filles (French): come, girls
vous vous réveillez (French): you wake up

Today's Caribbean islands were densely populated with African slaves by about the mid-1600s. In Jamaica, these captives were forced to work primarily on sugar plantations. Jamaica is a large and mountainous island, and throughout the seventeenth and eighteenth centuries, vast areas remained uninhabited and very difficult to access. Escaped slaves would make for these regions, banding together with other fugitives and forming colonies. Some of the colonies grew quite large. The people were called "maroons" from a Spanish word that means "living on a mountaintop." The character of Nanny in this story is based on a historical person who lived somewhat later. She was the leader of the most significant maroon colony in Jamaica's history. She organized attacks on plantations and is credited with freeing hundreds of slaves from bondage. Today Nanny is considered a national hero in Jamaica.

SUGGESTIONS FOR FURTHER READING

History of the Bouccaneers of America by Alexander Exquemelin was published originally in Dutch in 1678. This bestselling eyewitness account was translated into several languages and is still in print today. In the original version of the book, Exquemelin claimed that Henry Morgan had been an indentured servant as a young man. Outraged, Morgan sued the publisher for libel. He won the case, and the subsequent editions of the book made no mention of the claim. Other interesting books about pirates include *The Pirate Primer: Mastering the Language of Swashbucklers and Rogues* by George Choundas, *Pirates* by John Matthews, and *Under the Black Flag: The Romance and the Reality of Life Among the Pirates* by David Cordingly.

ACKNOWLEDGMENTS

I read this manuscript to Jack and Keyes when I was not yet through with it, and their excitement and suggestions helped me get it gritty. And some weekday mornings when they bicker at each other over the kitchen table, I like to think, "What would Spider do?" That has been . . . educational. Hayes continues to be a monkey, so there has been inspiration aplenty there. Jesica is my Sarah: my lantern, my optimist, the one whose glow keeps me from the rocks. Whenever I began to think #1 was a fluke, she was there to lighten me up.

My official readers aided me greatly. Chief among them is Natalie Bernstein, the librarian extraordinaire at the Paideia School. Among other things she helped me tone down from a PG-13 rating the scene where Ontoquas liberates Bucket. Then of course there are my kid readers. They are all turkeys, but I feel I should acknowledge them, either in alphabetical order, or in the order of how many Charms Blow Pops they begged me for throughout the year. They are: Linden H., Keb B., Erin M., Analla R., Sam B., Daywe M., David C., Grace H., Hector G., Sophia W., Nick V., Aiden O., Isabella C., Leo S., Alex W., Elijah H., Camille J., Aree P., Jack R.,

Sophie S., Jack P., Laney C., Liv C., Lucinda "Coop", Julian S., Hanna Z., Nora S., and Eliza G. Thanks as well to Jonny Poulton for putting up with my distractibility. Andy Sarvady and Gary Bannister each offered creativity and experience to assist me in marketing, and I am grateful to them both.

Neither this book nor its prequel would have been possible without my agent, Carolyn Jenks, as well as the creative force that is the team at the Carolyn Jenks Agency: Jonathan Hu, Siah Ruh Goh, AnneMarie Monzione, Michael Tucker, Rebecca Hartje, Phoenix Bunke, and Eric Wing. I have been fortunate to work with such an accomplished editor as Paula Wiseman with Paula Wiseman Books/Simon & Schuster Books for Young Readers. Her suggestions helped me to see this project with fresh eyes and make it more accessible to more readers out there. Many thanks, too, to Laurent Linn for his design skill and for getting the fabulous Amy June Bates on board for cover art. Heather McLeod did an amazing job of sleuthing for errors in the copyediting phase. Thank you, Heather, but please don't tell my students how many grammatical and usage errors I make.

Final thanks must go to Henry Morgan for living such a thrilling and ethically dubious life. Don't worry, H., I'll dwell on you plenty in the final installment of this tale.